Eraserheads 2:

The Decision

A Hood Misfits Novel

Eraserheads 2:
The Decision
A Hood Misfits Novel

Brick & Storm

www.urbanbooks.net

Urban Books, LLC
300 Farmingdale Road, N.Y.-Route 109
Farmingdale, NY 11735

Eraserheads 2: The Decision; A Hood Misfits Novel
Copyright © 2019 Brick & Storm

ISBN 13: 978-1-62286-117-0
ISBN 10: 1-62286-117-5

First Trade Paperback Printing September 2019
Printed in the United States of America

10 9 8 7 6 5 4 3 2 1

Distributed by Kensington Publishing Corp.
Submit Orders to:
Customer Service
400 Hahn Road
Westminster, MD 21157-4627
Phone: 1-800-733-3000
Fax: 1-800-659-2436

Chapter 1

Code

I left that cemetery with the weight of the world on my shoulders. For the last three days, I didn't know whether I was going or coming. Life as I knew it had been turned upside down all in the name of my papa, Caltrone Orlando. It was all good just a few months ago. Business was booming. My family was still intact. Lelo was still alive to argue with Stitch. Seymore was still rolling around in his wheelchair, laughing and watching Reagan with a look of wanting in his eyes. Auto was still my brother. My pseudo-family was none the wiser about who I really was. Our merchandise was being transported without a problem.

Then it all went to hell.

I'd been a part of an elusive group called the Eraserheads. We specialized in a lot of things. To the outside world, we were just a group of young'uns who owned an auto shop. That was what we did on the surface to wash our money. Behind the scenes, we stole cars, chopped them up, rebuilt them, and then sold them to the highest bidder. We erased identities and made fake credit cards, bank cards, government-issued IDs, passports, and the like. We could erase your whole life if we wanted to, wipe out your bank account so smoothly that before you realized what was happening, it was already too late.

That was before Papa, my grandfather, pulled a triple cross that even I didn't see coming. How he was able to reroute three shipments of our fleet of cars, then steal a shipment of unique bullets, which he'd already negotiated to buy from the dealer, and then make it seem like the dealer's crew had double-crossed my crew was a conundrum. Although it shouldn't have been. My old man was cold and calculating. It shouldn't have come as a surprise that he would be able to do something so crooked. Nothing should have surprised me when it came to my old man.

But like a sheep led blindly by a shepherd, I followed his lead no matter where it took me. I foolishly believed that because I was his favorite grandchild, he would never do anything that would cause me grief.

I couldn't really explain what it was like to be an Orlando. We were either feared, hated, respected, or all three. Nobody wanted to cross us, and no one dared to tell my old man no. That was until Auto, the man who'd become my brother by default, came into the picture. He took me in and didn't care that I had a sketchy background. He didn't care that I kept the true nature of my blood family hidden. At least, he didn't until it bit him in the ass. Auto told the old man no when he'd asked him to ship drugs across state lines for him, and it was an answer he'd come to regret.

Three of our friends had been killed in a hit orchestrated by Papa. Seymore, Dunkin, and Lelo had all been killed when Papa sent my cousins to spray the auto shop with bullets. I hadn't been able to go to Seymore's or Dunkin's funerals, but there would be no way I would miss Lelo's funeral. Lelo had been like a big brother to me, never letting anyone harm me but always quick to call me on my shit. I'd loved him like he was blood.

That still didn't negate the fact that my family saw me as responsible for the deaths that befell those they loved. So going to Lelo's funeral had been less than pleasant. Carmen, Lelo and Stitch's baby mother, had all but smacked me hard enough to cause delirium. Reagan wouldn't even spare me a glance, and Stitch, Stitch had gotten in my face. He'd yelled and cursed me to hell because he couldn't understand why I would put them in such peril.

"Did you really think they were going to welcome you with open arms?"

I looked to the left of me. There was a metallic blue Audi cruising beside me. Boots, a man who I originally thought had been the one to steal from me and my crew, was glancing back and forth from me to the road. There was barely any traffic on the side street leading away from the cemetery.

"Fuck off," I told him.

He chuckled. "We had a deal. You weren't supposed to leave my crib."

"You said I wasn't supposed to leave in the three days you allotted me. I didn't."

He stopped the car and looked at his watch. "Technically, you did, but we won't get into that right now. Get in the car."

I kept walking, ignoring him even when he stepped from the car.

"No. I have to go talk to Papa."

"Why? So he can kill you?"

"He won't kill me."

"Bullshit. You betrayed family, blood family. He's going to kill you. You even said so yourself," he yelled after me.

I stopped then turned to look at him. On his head was a black Stetson to match his all-black attire. Black snakeskin cowboy boots adorned his big feet. There was a piece of straw in the corner of his mouth that moved each time he chewed on it.

"I need to make sure Auto—"

"You need to get in the car. You think your old man doesn't have eyes out here right now? Think he's not watching so he can calculate his next move? You asked me to make sure your people were secure, right? So let me do my job. Get in the damn car, Code."

While his voice was calm, I could hear the sternness in his words. A few days ago, if he would have taken that tone with me, I probably would have tried to shoot him. I didn't take kindly to any man trying to control me or tell me what to do. That had been the very thing that caused me and my grandfather to clash all the time. But I knew Boots was right. He'd proven himself to be a smart businessman during this whole thing. And while I was willing to put on a front, deep down inside I was scared shitless that Papa was indeed going to kill me.

I didn't really care about the dying part. I knew that day would come sooner or later. It was the look of disappointment in Papa's eyes that would probably cut me to the core. It was a strange relationship my family and I had, but you had to know the ins and outs of my family to understand it.

I slowly walked back to Boots' car. Although he had the upper hand, his cocky disposition still annoyed me. I spit where he stood, then got in the car. I could hear him chuckling as he walked around to get in. I looked down at his feet as he did so.

"I know of a man who used to wear boots," I said as I stared out the windshield.

Boots stilled beside me. Out the corner of my eye, I could see the muscles coil in his arm as he gripped the steering wheel.

"They called him Bootsy. Very eclectic individual, I'm told. You know why they called him Bootsy?" I asked Boots.

"No. I've no idea what you're talking about."

"Legend has it, he had a collection of boots from all over the world. He was fascinated by the craftsmanship. Bootsy always had a thing for craftsmanship, which is what made him a legend in the realm of assassins. I'm told that if Bootsy came after you, you were as good as dead. Was no way around it."

Boots cut a glare at me that would have stilled Lucifer himself. I didn't waver though.

"How long do you think it's going to take Papa to figure it out, Boots?"

"Shut up."

"Did you really think he wouldn't notice?"

"Shut up."

"You walk around here in fucking cowboy boots, boots period, and you really think there won't be a connection made? You know, for as smart as you are, you really made a dumb decision. To wear boots, I mean. Bootsy used to be the only one to wear boots too—"

Before the words finished leaving my mouth, I had a gun to my head.

"I want you to shut up and I want you to shut up now. Another word from you and I pull my team from security detail on Auto and the Eraserheads," he spat out venomously. "Say another word about boots or Bootsy or whatever, I'll kill you dead before the old man has a chance to. Are we clear?"

When I didn't answer him quick enough, he cocked the gun to show he wasn't in the mood for games.

I made a show of turning to look at him. When I turned, the gun was aimed dead center between my eyes.

"We're clear," I answered.

"Good," he said. "I'm from Texas. We all wear boots in Texas. Is every nigga who come to the A wearing boots connected to whoever this Bootsy nigga is? Who the fuck is Bootsy? I think I'd like him if he was styling like that. Besides, I think I look damn good in my boots."

He laid his gun on his lap then cranked his car as he chuckled. I shook my head at his arrogance but said nothing in return. I didn't know if any of what I'd said had been the truth. I had no idea if Boots was connected to the legend of a man my grandfather sometimes spoke highly of. As far as I knew, Boots had come out of thin air. But it was the nature of my bloodline to fuck with people mentally. And since I felt as if Boots had too much control over me, to gain some of it back, I had to fuck with him the way I did.

We pulled off, and silence enveloped us while he drove through Jonesboro. Traffic on Tara Boulevard wasn't as bad as it could have been. Jonesboro reminded me of a town that was stuck between the past and the future. Actually the whole county of Clayton reminded me of such. In one part of Jonesboro, it would look as if you'd just walked into *Lifestyles of the Rich and Famous*. Then, on the other side, it looked as if they needed to catch up to the new millennium. Old storefronts and plantation-style houses still littered quite a few of the streets.

In the midst of the silence, my mind was rambling, thinking about nothing and everything so I could figure out just when my life took a left turn and ventured onto the road paved to hell. *The moment you were born an Orlando,* whispered in my mind.

"Oya is going to try to get your boy Freddie so we can make sure he's safe," Boots finally said, breaking me free of my mental prison.

"She should leave him where he is. He'll be fine. I shot him so it wouldn't look like he was going against Papa's wishes."

I felt when he glanced at me. "So you're just going to leave him up shit creek?"

"It's not about that. If she goes in—"

"She's already been on the inside."

"Then I can assure you, once she goes back, Papa won't let her out. She's everything he likes in his women. She's dark, built like an Amazon, and smart as a whip. Don't let her go back in."

"And what about Freddie?"

"He won't leave anyway. He can't."

"Why not?"

"Papa has his daughter. Freddie will never leave unless he can get her, too. The only way Oya convinces him to leave is if she can assure getting to Cuba to get his daughter. And that won't happen. If you even look at that man's grandchildren the wrong way, you're dead."

Boots sighed and shook his head. Papa was big on family, and from the time we came from the womb, he was in his grandchildren's lives. They loved the old man about as much as I did. He could do no wrong in their eyes. It wasn't until they came of age that they realized his unconditional love came with a steep price. "Blood in, blood out," was a part of the Orlando creed.

Boots drove toward 75 North, heading into downtown Atlanta. Traffic was light, but Georgia's highway patrol was on the hunt. Every three or four miles I saw they had someone pulled over.

"I need my merchandise back," he said to me.

"What?"

"My bullets, I need them back."

I chuckled. Through the whole melee it had totally slipped my mind that Auto still had the man's bullets. Shaking my head, I told him, "Good luck with that."

"This isn't a game."

"I'm sure it isn't, but I don't know why you're telling me. Auto just told me I was all but dead to him."

"That doesn't mean you don't know where my shit is."

I looked at Boots. Tried to look past the fact that he was good on the eyes and had just put a gun to my head.

"Sorry to tell you, I really have no idea where Auto put your shit."

"I knew you would say that."

"So why did you ask me?"

"I wanted to see where your loyalty lies."

I shrugged. "I don't get it."

"You'll always be an Orlando, but your loyalty is still split. You know where my shit is."

I rolled my eyes. "Okay, Boots, whatever you say."

"When you lie, you look at me. You look me right in the face and lie with ease. That's some weird shit. Most times, when people lie, they tend to look away from the eyes. You will look me right in the face, eyes never wavering, and lie to me."

I gave something of a cool smile, more of a smirk, while thinking about what he said. He was right. My poker face was strong, but that came from years of growing up in a family of men whose entire agenda was to break a woman down to her bare minimums.

"You're asking the wrong person about your bullets. You need to talk to Auto. That's all I can tell you."

"I figured as much," he responded.

For the rest of the drive, he was silent, and I was fine with that. I found the more Boots talked, the more I became mesmerized by the man he was. I didn't have time to be in my feelings about a nigga. In the end, they were all like Papa and all the men he warred with. I had yet to find a man who wasn't consumed by rage, revenge, money, or power.

I was content to be as silent as Boots until he ventured onto the exit for Moreland Avenue. I glanced at him as he drove casually with one hand. The muscles in his jaw ticked. His brown skin as smooth as mine. While his right hand gripped the steering wheel so tightly you could see the white of his knuckles, his left one stroked his beard as if he was in deep thought.

There was no need for me to pay attention to my surroundings since I knew the area very well.

"Where are we going?" I asked him once we passed the Starlight Drive-In movie theater. The bottom of my stomach started to rumble. I ran a hand through my hair. Chewed down on my bottom lip as my leg started to shake.

Boots didn't answer me. After a few more miles, he didn't have to. We turned down a side street whose name was hidden in the tall trees just above the street sign. All the houses seemed to be run-down and abandoned, but I knew that to be furthest from the truth. There were no children playing on this street. People who had been sitting out on their lawns and on their front porches started to go inside their homes. Frankie Beverly and Maze stopped singing about what would happen before they let go. The old folk went inside and the young ones started to file out. Wife beaters and Dickies were worn like it was a uniform requirement.

Mean mugs and grilled-out scowls adorned the faces of the males and females who let their eyes follow Boots' car.

"We shouldn't be here," I told him.

Boots cruised all the way down to the end of the street. Just beyond the dead end was a warehouse hidden behind barbed wire and a secured gate. Boots stopped his car right at the entrance of the gate. Before he could even put the car in park, red beams decorated the interior of his car and us.

"What the fuck are you doing?" I snapped at him.

"My bullets in there?" he asked me.

How he'd found this place was beyond me. It scared me, to be honest. If Boots had found this place, that meant he was more powerful and resourceful than I'd thought. Auto kept this place hidden, secured by the neighborhood he took care of. No one on this street ever had to worry about anything, all because they were family and kept his secrets safe here. Anytime we stole high-end cars and wanted to wait until the heat died down, we would hide cars in the secret warehouse. We always hid things here. It was where we'd placed Boots' bullets when we'd taken them.

"We need to leave—"

"We will. As soon as you tell me what I want to know."

I shook my head, then opened my car door. I made sure not to make any sudden movements. I stepped out one foot at a time, hands in the air as I did so. A line of red dots decorated my chest.

"It's just me," I said with a smile. "It's Code," I yelled into the camera sitting at the top of the light pole.

"What you doing here?" a soothing masculine voice rang out.

I turned to see Wolf holding a shotgun at his side. Behind him were six more of his henchmen. Wolf and all of his brothers looked, exotically, like wolves. Their eyes were cunning and hypnotizing. They drew you in with their intensity. Wolf and all six of his brothers stood well over six feet and were built like they lived in the gym. Wolf's ropy locs fell around his sculpted chocolate brown shoulders and gave him a mysterious appeal. His white wife beater clung to the muscles in his chest, and my pussy jumped in remembrance of what he looked like naked and felt like inside of me.

"Is Auto here?" I asked.

"Nah, but you knew that already," Wolf answered.

He held up two fingers and pointed at the Audi. His brothers fanned out then surrounded the car, guns drawn.

"Who's driving?" he asked me. "And what the fuck you doing here, Code?"

"I have to have a reason for being at my own warehouse?"

"You do when Auto says you've been erased."

"What?"

"You've been erased," he repeated, this time with a smirk on his face.

Wolf still had a bit of animosity toward me since I'd broken our arrangement off with him. He wanted more than I was willing to give, and that had never sat too well with him. But that wasn't important at the moment. What had my attention was that he'd said I'd been erased.

I didn't know if I was nervous or if anxiety was riding me, but my body felt as if it were shaking internally. My palms and every pressure point I owned started to feel warm. Sweat beaded my forehead as I snatched my phone from my hip. I dialed Auto's number at the shop.

"We're sorry, but the number you have reached is no longer in service," greeted me.

My eyes started to burn with anger as I blinked rapidly. I dialed his cell. All I got was a busy signal. I tried again with the same outcome. I called Reagan, Stitch, Jackknife, and even Lelo's cell for the hell of it, and I got the same thing. Wolf chuckled. Any other time his chuckle would have given me goose bumps. It was deep and melodic with the power to make a woman wet her panties. None of it had that effect on me at the moment.

I forgot about Boots in the car behind me. I didn't even see that the red dots decorating my body had started to do the same to Wolf and his brothers. I called

Wells Fargo, then Bank of America. I called Regions and Suntrust, only to find that all my accounts had been wiped clean. If I knew Auto, then I knew the wiping out of my accounts meant he'd also erased my existence. I could guarantee that my social security number along with my driver's license, and anything else that made me Maria Rosa Orlando, was nonexistent.

Erasing someone wasn't all that hard when you had all the right provisions set in place. The program we ran was a very intricate system. It took years to set everything in place. Training was always intense and thorough. We had people set up in several banks around the area to pull off such heists as stealing money from someone's bank account or shutting an account down altogether.

All Auto had to do was make a fake ID with my name on it, have someone pretend to be me, and walk inside any bank where I had an account set up. Since we had some-one working in high positions in all of the banks, it would be easy to shut down my accounts and no one would bat a lash, especially since it was "me" who decided to close out my accounts.

Erasing someone's identity was a bit harder. Technically you couldn't erase someone completely unless you killed them or made them a new identity. Still, you had to kill the "old them" to make the "new them" seem more legit. It was a tricky scheme, but it could be done. And since I wasn't dead, the idea of being erased frightened me.

"Fuck you, Auto!" I screamed. He'd obliterated me. Expunged my very identity and left me with nothing.

"Now that you know I'm telling the truth, tell the driver to exit the car and we won't have any problems," Wolf coolly ordered me.

"No need for her to tell me to do anything, my good men." Boots' smooth Texas drawl washed over me. I could hear his boots crunching against the gravel behind me.

"Nigga, are you wearing cowboy boots?" Wolf cracked. "And a cowboy hat? My nigga, what?"

Boots gave a lopsided grin that said he was used to catching people off guard with his attire. Even though it felt as if anger rumbled in my gut like the beginnings of a volcano about to erupt, I could tell that the smile on Boots' face wasn't a friendly one.

"You *niggas,* as you all like to call each other so much, need to pay more attention to your surroundings," he said, then pointed at Wolf's chest. "Call your boss and tell him the outside of his parameters have been penetrated. Now your boss and I have had some run-ins with one another over the last couple days. I'm sure you know it wasn't because we chose to. But since you six are only peons, ain't no need for this nigga in cowboy boots and a Stetson to get into the logistics of this shit. Once you call your boss, tell him we need to have a sit-down conversation to discuss something he still has that belongs to me. You got that?"

As Boots spoke, Wolf looked down at his chest to realize his heart had a target on it. He balled his lips, then looked over at Boots like something stunk.

Instead of Wolf addressing Boots, he looked at me with a scowl. "So you brought this nigga to our door?"

My chest was still on fire with the knowledge that I'd been erased. "I didn't bring him here."

"Then how the fuck did he know where to come?"

I yelled, "I don't know!"

"Sure, bitch."

Before Wolf's next breath, I'd punched him in the face. His neck snapped back and the shotgun in his hand fell to the ground with a loud thud before he got his balance and charged at me. To my left, his brother, Siberian, lunged at Boots, only to find the tip of Boots' boot in his nuts. Siberian groaned and fell over. Shots rang out, and another brother, Amoux, caught a bullet to his shoulder. His screams and yells halted the other brothers' fight. Amoux screamed so loudly I thought his soul was being ripped from his body.

I jumped over Wolf's leg sweep. I glanced to see Boots elbow Siberian as he tried to stand back up. Boots snatched his gun, then backhanded him so hard that Siberian flew back. Siberian was built like a defensive end. The fact that Boots had that much power in his hit surprised me.

Wolf wasn't letting up on me though, and I really wasn't in the mood to fight. So I pulled my Beretta from my waist and aimed it at his right eye. He stopped his fist just as it was coming for my face.

"Do it, nigga, and I'll end you," I snarled at him.

Amoux's cries and whimpers were getting to me. I looked down to see his shoulder was shredded. His long jet-black hair spilled around his face as his brown face was riddled with pain. His arm looked as if it was about to fall off, only hanging on by threads. That told me that one of the men Boots had surrounding the neighborhood had shot him. Only bullets manufactured by him could do that much damage. A sharp discomfort shot through my shoulder just imagining the pain he must have been in.

"Now like I said, tell Auto Boots stopped by, and if he'd like to discuss giving me my shit back, I won't have to take what's mine by force," Boots said then spat on the ground. "Motherfucker got me scuffing up my boots," he fussed.

"Get in the car," he told me. "Oh, and take li'l homie to Grady Hospital. Ask for Dr. Akil J. Heath and he'll be able to save your boy's shoulder," Boots told Wolf. "Better move quickly though."

Boots gave a lopsided grin, then shrugged as he backed up. Siberian mumbled something under his breath, and Boots caught him with another blow to the face.

"That's for trying to sneak me and scuffing up my boots. Brand new boots, too."

Any other time I would have been in the mood for a little gunplay, but my mind was all over the place. I got in the car without question. Boots tossed the gun in the back seat, then cranked the car. He put the car in reverse at high speed. We swerved and kicked up dust, then sped out of the quiet neighborhood. As we sped away, I could see people running toward Wolf and his brother.

"So I guess you're not going to watch over the Eraserheads anymore?" I asked him.

Boots was quiet for a while. Then he looked at me as he stopped at a red light. "Why do you care? You've been erased."

I swallowed back the bile that rose in my throat. I honestly didn't know if I was sad or angry. Probably a combination of both. I wanted to kill Auto just as much as I wanted to beg him to let me back into the Eraserheads.

Chapter 2

Boots

What an interesting way everything played out. Keeping my friends close and my enemies even closer was proving to work out in my favor. I learned a couple of things riding around with Code. She knew a little too much about my personal background, however wrong some of it may have been. First off, my pops didn't get his nickname for his love of boots. Nah, it came from his obsession with that musical playa, Bootsy Collins.

He had all of his records back in the day and would quote the man like water, so she was wrong in that aspect of things, but I wasn't going to tell her that. I figured by playing along and acting bristled it would only help with the game of things, although the rest of what she said was true. My father was a beast in the art and way of the assassin. However, I was the one with the boot obsession. Blame my life and upbringing in Texas.

Machiavelli said, in so many words, that the weak, the hungry, and the ones with mad aspirations will do all they can to get that seat on the throne of power. Those same people began scraping like starving animals to keep that power and to keep the throne secure. It's basic. You always want what you don't have, and once you got it, you make damn sure to keep that shit. Code was now in the position of living as a lost one.

It was cute seeing how she sat there dumbstruck, confused, lost in it all once finding out she was erased and finding out that I knew where my product was. To shake someone like her, someone who was strong in her foundation but torn in her loyalties, was satisfying to me, no lie. Why? Because I was now privy to seeing baby girl in all her raw form. It was sexy as fuck to me, yet it had me annoyed, because her kind, people of her royal Orlando lineage, could strike back and kill you like a snake when they were shaken down to their raw from. One such Orlando, star football player for the Atlanta Nightwings, Shawn "Enzo" Banks, was making news right now for it. He had the Feds after him.

So I knew what I was playing into with Code. Didn't give one shit if she came at me heavy. I was still enjoying watching her break at every level but the one that counted. The one that she was forgetting fueled her, her tenacity, and her survival skills. That was what let me know who this woman was about. She still had that fire in her eyes though she may not have even realized it. That's why I pulled her up in her crew's ground zero. I needed to have her understand who the fuck I really was and what I was really about.

Chuckling to myself, I kept my eyes on the road in silence, basking in her shock. Everything had a reason to it for me. The small fact that she had an inkling of knowledge about who I really was kept me fresh to def in all of this. My records had no link to anyone but my long-dead mother, but those were the things I knew and she didn't.

I was curious about how she even knew about my pops in the first place, although I shouldn't have been. If I knew all the shit I knew about her and her family, why wouldn't she know about mine? Especially since her old man used to be a part of my family, according to the stories my pops had told me. But again, the world was a stage and I was an actor in it. So I'd feed her whatever to keep her occupied and to learn what I needed for the next level of things.

Heading back to the highway, music thumped low, and I watched my guest from the side of my eye. "Ah, why so serious, baby girl? You and your friends seemed very surprised out there. I wonder, why?"

"Fuck you, *culo!* That's why I'm so serious," Code spat out like a hissing cat. "Because of you and the way you sit there trying to mind fuck me over. Trust me, I'm smarter than any game you have to play."

"I'm saying though, we can pull over right now and knock this shit out. I'll leave you with a good nut then leave you with a nice hole between the eyes. We can call it even-steven, but I'm not about to sit here with you pouting. I didn't think that was something you'd do, *mamacita.*"

I was being an asshole on purpose.

Code gave me that tilted head with the neck jerked to the side with a narrow eye. "Seriously? Are you for real?"

I didn't know why, but I started laughing. Clearly I was annoying her and she wasn't amused by my antics. *Mami* went off on me in the tongue of her people.

I caught it all, but still it was a jumble of, "You think you're cute. Think this is a game. My life is done and my loyalty questioned. Fuck you where you sit. Choke on a diseased dick," along with some other things about who she thought I was, ending with, "All you niggas are alike. Nothing but dick grabbing pussies in this game for revenge, greed, and sex. Nothing original!"

Her words didn't bother me one bit, and I decided not to make it a secret.

"My sista, I'm in this for honor, and I'm in this for the lotus—or pussy, if you didn't understand my meaning— weed, money, and international status. How can you ever go wrong with that combination, *mami?*"

Again, I was being an ass, though the international thing was truth. I enjoyed when she got a red face. It made Code's naturally beautiful looks screw up, and it gave her some edge. I watched Code ball up her fist and get ready to hit me. I gave her a stern look that stopped her before she could.

"Hit me all you want and disrespect me with your venomous words. As I have said, I could pull over right now and we can do this thing, but I really don't have the desire to do all of that. The both of us have business that we need to clear up, and you, mama, need to figure out just how you're going to get my product back for me since you're cut off from everything. Until then, sit there and think about how you're going to pull your weight as my guest. Because"—I reached up to adjust my hat on my head, then wrapped my hand around the stick of my car and worked the shift—"all trust is out the door with everyone but me, little killer. I never trusted you, as you know, but, my friend, you need to find allies quickly."

"I know how. I got this. I got me, pinja," she mumbled. "All my trust is in me."

Clicking my tongue, I kept laughing and took the highway to Decatur. I figured that I'd take her to my other warehouse, the one I didn't care a bit about. My crew knew the deal. We'd keep her away from any real business of mine while having her around what she thought I did, which was manufacture my bullets. In other words, I'd have her at my testing ground and see how she handled it.

Exiting the highway, I took a right past Scott Park. We rode in silence through the winding neighborhoods with overgrown property and vacant lots next to simple homes. I let the sound of Wale chill me out until it switched to some Fuse ODG talking about wanting a "Million Pound Girl."

"Where are we going now?" I heard Code ask in her usual upset tone. "I'm tired of being in this car with you."

Slowing down, we finally pulled up to my gated warehouse. To the average person it appeared to be a dump yard, and it was, but it was so much more than that to me.

Glancing at Code, I took off my hat as we rode through the opening gates. "Why does it matter? I know that you're trying to remember every turn I make, and every street name we pass. Outside of being tired, why does it matter?"

"Because it does, and you're right. I am. I don't trust you either, so don't get your head turned around thinking that I do," she said with a hard-edge stare. "And that's no lie."

"Yeah, I know. You blinked that time, scarecrow." Parking, I hopped out of my car, locking it before she could get out.

Good upbringing, manners, and just being a gentleman dictated that I open the door for a female passenger, and that was what I did. I gave a nod to the eyes that were watching us from my security detail from different vantage points, and then I moved around to open her door.

Pushing out of the car and not taking my hand, Code moved around me while clocking my spot. "Do you always have to do that? I'm capable."

Ignoring her, I moved to empty my ride out and nod at my right-hand man, Shango. He casually walked up in his typical way, wearing a purple button-down with rolled-up sleeves at the elbows and black jeans, his hand halfway in his pocket, his eyes filled with wisdom and slight intent. Dude was sporting a tan, so it made his typical light brown tone a richer color. Or how the sistas on the block called him, caramel brown sugar. He also sported a full beard like my own.

I pulled out a mint-flavored toothpick from my pocket, then slid it in my mouth. It was a good day, regardless of Code's drama trying to kill it. The wind was sweet today, cooling me off as I stood there having a conversation with my right without even saying a word.

"She's at the fort," Shango answered my silent question. By "her" we both meant Oya, and that calmed me down. After what Code said about her old man possibly taking her, it had me rethinking moving my knight piece to another side of the chessboard. What I needed was for Oya to seamlessly get her in where she could fit in without suspect or danger to self. None of us were afraid to die, understand that. None of us were afraid of torture, but what a brotha didn't like, or any man, was if someone touched what was mine. Oya was mine, like a sister, a down friend, and anyone who touched what was mine would end up falling into fair exchange. But yeah, Oya had always been able to handle herself, so there was no stress outside of pride and loyalty to my people.

"Little *mamacita,* walk straight ahead inside if you please," I casually threw out there to Code.

Every member of my team was a person I grew up or did lifelong business with. I specifically chose them to be a part of my world and team because each one had the mentality of a killer and because they could be trusted. Fuck, if we were tortured, every one of us would get off on that shit and chuck the deuces later. That's how functionally crazy we all were and we knew it. It's what helped us when targeting a man like Caltrone and what would always put us ahead of other mob bosses and street kings.

When Code didn't budge, I folded my arms across my chest and turned my attention to her. "Did I stutter? There's business to talk about, and since you want to play as if you can't get my product back, then I have no use for you today." Placing my hand against the small of her back, I gave a slick smile then dropped my voice while I leaned close to her. "I can tell you're tired, so make this easy for us both. You had a stressful day but a day you can use to your advantage. Think on that."

"First off, I don't know how to get your shit back, and second, don't touch me." With a flip of her hair, she yanked out of my touch and got ready to head into the warehouse until a car whipped in her way.

The sound of a door sliding up on its phantom hinge then heels hitting pavement had my vision focused on the fly black Lamborghini. Thickness and curves for days sashayed our way, confined in a form-fitting pair of purple overalls. Crinkled dark hair fell over ample melons that peeked from a black tank under it. Alize had been playing and playing well as she stood with pride, her hand on her hip.

"Washam! Fresh from the stage floor to replace the one we lost, boss," Alize bragged with a wide smile of her ruby red plump lips, causing her dimple piercings to flash in the sunlight.

"Hey, Coke, you made a friend, I see," Shango called while licking his lips. He'd always called Alize Coke, short for Coke bottle since she was shaped like one. He was referring to one of Alize's "gots," as she called the people she ran cons on, mostly men who were taken by her beauty.

Shango laughed, then murmured in Portuguese, "*Eu não sei como me sinto sobre isso. I don't know how I feel about that.*"

Sucking her teeth and running her tongue over her lips, she rolled her eyes then flipped her hand. "Ya nuts should feel itchy from all the pussy ya keep dipping in, li'l boy. That's what ya should worrying 'bout."

"Aw yeah? So you saying you have ratchet pussy? Or Oya does? I only really fuck with you two," Shango countered, then added, "Sometimes."

"Fall back. No one is talking 'bout Oya. That's my girl. But you, on the other hand, can spread my ass open and kiss it," Alize snapped, then stopped when Shango rubbed his hands together. "Ew. Shut up, Shango."

I just stood there holding Code's arm, since she was trying to dip in a different way, and I laughed. "Told you about your personal life, my friend," I said to Shango, then turned back to Alize. "Strip it, fade it to white, and then lace it up. After, it's yours to use. We'll need it for quick shipping of all of our things, so fix it up with secret compartments."

"Cool, I got ya, boss. Hey, fee, come talk with me for a moment. I'm about tired of listening and looking at Shango. Song should have been called 'These Niggas Ain't Loyal,'" Alize said, speaking to Code.

"Don't do me like that, Alize. Whenever you want it, you can have this dick be loyal all day long. I just also have to have it be loyal to Oya too. You know the situation," Shango quipped as he added safe distance between himself and Alize.

My boy knew better. I guess he just wanted to rile up Alize today for whatever reason.

"Gotdamn, nigga!" Alize yelled, ready to fight.

Code stared in confusion at Alize's thick accent, and I laughed again. Alize's accent only thickened when she was angry, and right now Shango was pissing her off.

"She said come holla at her for a moment, and I'd like you to before my right hand dies," I explained, letting go of Code's soft and supple arm. "She'll show you where you can relax and lay your head while we're here."

Code said nothing as she stomped away and moved to talk to Alize.

No lie, Alize was like family too, but the way her ass always bounced kept me from calling her little sister. So as both Shango and I watched two shapely, plump asses battle it out before us while Alize and Code walked around the car, we both gave a slight grunt, then turned back each other's way for business.

"What's that new info?" Tossing my toothpick around my mouth, I adjusted my hat again and waited.

"There hasn't been any new movement since you left the Eraserheads' ground zero," Shango explained.

"What about the old man?" I asked. "How are we doing there after everything?"

Crossing his arms, Shango shrugged. "From what Oya reported, it is the same deal. He wants what you're offering and the longer we hold back, the angrier he's getting."

"Pinja is still being slick, huh? Unsuccessfully tried to screw me over and he wants to play innocent. Okay. I see. Are the kids safe?" Both Shango and I moved to my car to hop in while we spoke.

Right before we found out Caltrone had screwed us over, we found that one of our shipping trucks had been stripped of my original merchandise and then loaded with kids. A few of the kids had explained to us that they had been kidnapped. We rescued them and set them up in safe houses until we could get each one back to where they belonged.

Shango nodded. "Yes. We've placed them in safe homes in Macon. For now, they are getting counseling, and family is being investigated before we call them to determine that they can safely return home and weren't sold."

"Good. Now we have to maintain my agenda. Let's get into the guns. Is the printer working?" I parked then sat back.

"Smiley is on to something. It's coming out perfectly, and once we're done with making a few additions to it, we can test the bullets out," Shango said with pride.

Disposable weapons were my new project now since dealing with the old man, along with getting my bullets back. Auto and I had lost a lot in our battle with Caltrone. Working with Smiley had become a short-term goal until Auto denied me my property. Once that occurred, shit became a major problem for me, and he had instantly started to gain an enemy in me the longer I did not have what was mine.

"Good. If we need to snatch her up, then we'll make moves to do so. Otherwise, she might be a threat," I said. At that same time, Code walked by and glanced at me. "So you know what to do?"

"Definitely. In the long run, it might be better that way. She's got an interesting mind to think of something like a disposable Glock, then also the other stuff she does? She's not good for the streets," Shango added as we exited the car.

"Exactly. We need to bounce in about three hours. I have a meeting with some cartel leaders," I said while heading to my offices. "It's good that Alize was able to get in with the sheik. I'm thinking that he and his crew will be able to help in this expansion of ours." Closing the door, I turned on my monitors, then glanced at my calls. "The Dragons are leaving crumbs."

"Oh, yeah? They want in with us?" Shango asked while finding a seat opposite of me.

"Yes, which not only helps us but adds to our backing if the old man wants to continue his games. I'm doing my best to keep his view of us positive in the midst of it all."

"Understood. I'll get a ride ready for you to head out then." He stood and smoothed down his shirt.

Reaching in my drawer, I unlocked a panel in the side of it and pulled out some dough, tossing it his way. "Give that to *mamacita*. Tell her that it fell off her grandpop's truck. It'll help her out. And have Oya dress her up sweetly. I want to test her by taking her with us, since Alize needs to stay here to keep things good with the rest of our crew. Oya and Shredder are back at the complex with PT. Want to see how much more I can gather from her. Code knows some of my past, man, and I aim to figure out how."

Shango stopped by the door and scowled. "How much, bro?"

"She said it was stupid of me to walk around in boots, boots like a man she heard about who had a love for these things and who had a son," I explained.

"Fuck! I can waste her," he quickly stated.

"Code isn't some weak woman you can just kill, bruh. And that wouldn't sit well with the overall agenda. Besides, now that she has this clean slate, I'm interested in seeing what she does and how she does it. She might tear down a kingdom or two, and I think I want to watch." I gave a grim smile, then tossed my hat to the side. "Besides, we all know that famous quote that was paraphrased from a passage of Machiavelli's: 'Never do any enemy a small injury, for they are like a snake which is half beaten and it will strike back the first chance it gets.'"

Stretching out at my desk, I folded my hands together and watched my friend. "Little *mamacita* is injured. She's injured real bad. Therefore, it is only a matter of time before she strikes out, and that's what we are waiting and watching for. For now, that's the next part to my overall agenda. So she may know a taste about me, but let's see if she reveals anything more. If she becomes a bigger threat than any of us ever see, then even my interest in seeing if she tastes sweet between the sheets won't keep my finger from getting trigger happy, you get me?"

"I understand. Always, brother, like usual I'll kick-start some shit then," Shango said as he left me in my office alone.

Fooling with my cell, I sat back and thought about everything. My father was making moves behind the scenes, meeting with the elders, and I had my role to play in all of this. High priority was my bullets. There were only a select few I wanted to play with them, but until then, I'd see how everything went, including how my own chess piece was positioned on the grand board. My agenda was simple: loyalty and honor, nothing more and nothing less.

Chapter 3

Auto

I want my bullets.

Boots' message was clear as I looked at the words riddled across all of the screens in my security room. I had to respect a man who was about his business and didn't let the faux display of friendship cloud his judgment. At the end of the day, both of us were businessmen trying to recoup a loss. However, I wasn't giving up shit until I got my money back for the loss to me and my team.

Besides, as a businessman, Boots should have thoroughly checked out who he was doing business with. I mean, the same could have been said for me, but I trusted a man who I'd always done my shipping through. Judging by Boots' reaction and from words spoken the night he killed Mouse at Joy Lake, he'd never done business with Mouse before.

Still, he'd found one of my main warehouses and had left one of my men with a damn near severed shoulder.

"Question," I started as I thumbed my nose and turned to study Wolf. "Tell me how he was able to get y'all surrounded like this? That means there have been some new faces around the way that y'all ain't been paying attention to, or we have a fox in the henhouse. Which is it?"

Wolf stood with his head high, shoulders squared. One of the reasons he ran this area was because he never cowered and never backed down from a fight. He, along with all six of his brothers, had all been in the group home with me. He was loyal, always on point, until now.

"To be honest, Auto, I don't know. That nigga is thorough is all I can say. You know I'm always on game. If there had been any new faces, I would have seen them or known about it."

"So you're saying there's a fox in the henhouse then?"

Wolf sighed. "I don't know, boss."

"You don't know?"

"I fucked up," he answered.

"No shit, Sherlock," I retorted, then turned back to look at the flat-screen monitors.

Boots had hacked into my security system. According to my tech heads, all he'd done was shut down the main gateway so he could code that message into the system. I grunted and turned to my left to ask Lelo if he could trace the breach in our security. I needed him to flex his muscle to see who had been paid to look the other way. Only I turned to find he wasn't there. Stitch wasn't even there. I half expected Seymore to roll up in that beat-up moving truck with that goofy smile on his face as he talked shit. My boys were no longer with me though, and they were never coming back. Although Stitch was alive, it was as if he were dead to me too. He'd made no mention of coming back to the Eraserheads.

I shook the demons off me, then looked at Wolf. "Call Reagan, tell her gas up the Cessna, and y'all move my shit out of here," I told him.

He nodded. "The bullets too?"

"Yeah. Everything. I want this whole warehouse cleaned out by the end of the night."

"Damn, Auto. By the end of the night? All this shit?" Wolf pointed out to the warehouse floor. Phantoms, Bugattis, Ferraris, Mercedes, Audis, and Porsches of all colors sat around like we were at some exotic car show. Car parts sat stacked neatly by make and model. In the safe against the back wall, Boots' bullets sat guarded by sentries.

"Yes, Wolf, all this shit needs to be gone by the end of the night."

"We're going to need—"

I cut him off, already annoyed by the fact that he'd let Boots catch him slipping. I didn't want to call him out in front of his men though. The last thing I needed was for them to start to lose respect for him because I was pissed at him.

I stepped closer to him so only he could hear what I was saying. "You really have no room for error right now, Wolf. So what I suggest you do is get this shit out of here and headed down to Savannah. I don't care how you do that, but my inventory better be intact when I check it. When Reagan gets here, she needs to have those bullets stored so she can get them to the Cessna and out of here. Understand? Don't fuck this up. You're on strike one. There won't be a strike two."

Wolf grimaced, but he nodded, shook my hand, and walked away. I passed all my people standing around. Not many knew where this warehouse was, so not many people worked the area. Still, I expected Wolf to use the resources in his grasp to make what I said happen.

I looked at my watch as I walked out of the warehouse. The sun glared down on me. Wind was blowing but didn't help with the stifling heat. Standing next to my Ford Shelby was Smiley.

Shorty didn't smile much, so I was still trying to figure out where that moniker came from. She'd changed her hairstyle again. When I'd left her that morning to go to Lelo's funeral, she had faux locs. Now she had a wild 'fro that blew whichever way the wind tossed it. Purple tights wrapped her toned legs. A thin white halter top did little to hide her nipples and areolas. For some reason that annoyed me.

"You should wear a thicker shirt," I spat as I walked toward the car.

She didn't look amused. "Did you really erase Code? She said you took her money."

I glanced at the phone in her hand, knowing she could still communicate with her cousin, then ignored her question. "Should I drop you back off at my place? I have a meeting I need to get to."

She studied me for a moment. "Thought she was like your sister. If so, why you do her like that?"

Running a hand through my shoulder-length hair, I sighed.

Smiley kept at it. "If you can do Code like that, how do I know you won't do the same to me?"

"Never cross me, and you won't ever have to find out."

She tilted her head to the side, then gave me a look I couldn't read. "Duly noted," was all she said.

I wasn't in the mood to discuss my decision with her. What had happened to me and my family over the last few weeks had changed me in a sense. I no longer saw things in black and white. There was a gray area I'd completely ignored, and because of that, I'd buried three of my team members. Code had been like a sister to me. I didn't have any real family. I made my own. I was an outcast, so I took other outcasts and bonded with them, took care of them, so they never had to worry. I'd let a fucking snake into our mix, and it had cost me dearly. Never again.

Keeping Smiley attached to my hip was more because I was trying to feel her out. So far, she had been a woman of her word. Smiley would be a far better asset if I could use her the right way. Even with all that being said, I didn't have time to wallow in self-pity. I had work to do.

I called in backup. I never thought I'd be making that phone call for this reason, but a man had to do what a man had to do.

Which was why, two hours later, I sat in a desolate house that I sometimes called home, anxiously awaiting the arrival of an old friend. In my hand was a glass of bourbon. Silence enveloped my place. Smiley sat next to me as I anxiously watched the front door. There wasn't much to the house. There was one sofa, a flat-screen TV, a few barstools, and cream sheer panels up to the windows.

"Why are we sitting in the dark, and who are we waiting for?" she asked me.

I ignored her questions and said, "If you're going to be rolling with me, you can't communicate with Code. She's dead to the Eraserheads from this day on."

I could tell she was studying me. I didn't have to look at her to know she was thinking about what I'd just told her, and she was thinking hard.

"On some real shit, I really don't know Code like that. I mean, I appreciate all she's done for me, but at the end of the day, I don't really know her. Same as I don't really know you. All I know is since I've been in this camp, shit has gone from crazy to crazier, and I don't know who to trust."

"I feel you. I do. But all I need to know is, do you want to be a part of this team? There is room here for someone with your skill set and talent. The rest, all that trust shit you talking, will come in time. Just tell me now if you want to be a part of this team."

I set the glass down on the end table beside my sofa, then looked at her. "I'll be a part of this team only if I can make stipulations."

"And what might those be?"

"I need my own place. I need a car, and I need to be able to have my own clients on the side as long as they never know I'm an Eraserhead and as long as it never interferes with our work."

"Other clients like who?"

"That's confidential."

I shook my head. "I'm not taking my chances on my team being burned again."

Just as she was about to say something, movement outside the patio door caught my attention. Smiley jumped up and grabbed her gun from underneath a pillow on the sofa she was sitting on. She cocked her hammer and aimed at the two shadows. The locks on the sliding doors clicked. A few seconds later, I could hear the smooth sound of the doors sliding open. Smiley quickly glanced from me to the door and back at me as the two shadowy figures walked in. One was in a hoodie that framed his entire face. By the look of it in the dark, it seemed as if a shadow had just walked in, cloaked by a hoodie. The man flanking him was built like a Mack truck: tall and solid, thick with muscle, which some would call fat. I knew better.

"You got chicks guarding you now, nigga?" asked the one with his face hidden.

Before I could answer, Smiley spoke up. "Wait. Trigga? Is that you?"

I cocked my head to the side and looked at Smiley, then back over at a young man who was the sole reason I could even own an auto shop. Trigga had also been in a group home with me when I was younger. He'd run away eventually, but we'd meet up on the street from time to time to hang out. He'd have rather slept on the street than suffer the abuse at the hands of those who were supposed to be protecting us. He'd always been a different breed than most of the other boys we'd been housed with. Because of this, we clicked.

He kept me from getting jumped many times on the street. Sometimes my race played a factor in whether niggas would pick on me from day to day back then. Trigga didn't care one way or the other, but because he was my friend, he made it his business to fight next to me. Sometimes we won the battle and lost the war. Sometimes we won the war and lost the battle. It didn't matter to us as long as we won in some way.

I flipped the light switch on just as Trigga slid his hoodie back.

"Oh, shit, it's Smiley." Big Jake cracked with a familiar grin.

"Well, I'll be damned," I muttered. "You know these two?" I asked Smiley.

She dropped the hand with the gun to her side, then nodded. "Yeah," she answered but didn't offer anything else to explain how she knew them.

I looked back at Trigga with a rare smile on my face, walked across the room, and greeted my old friend. Not too much had changed about him since last I saw him. He looked a bit taller and stockier. More muscle mass had broadened his shoulders. Red, black, and white Jordans adorned his feet. Dark denim baggy jeans and his signature skull hoody made up his attire. His locs had grown longer, and the nigga still looked like his eyes were lined in kohl with the reddish tint to his skin. Nope, not much had changed with him at all.

Since Smiley already knew the two, there was no need for introductions. I watched her hug both men like they were family.

"How in hell do you know Smiley?" I asked.

"Shorty did some work for me back in the day when I had beef with a few of the cartel heads after Dame died. She also made these tracker things. They looked and functioned like stickers, but they weren't. She's low-key on my team when I need certain things done."

"What in hell you two doing together?" Big Jake asked.

"Long story," I answered.

"We got time," Trigga chimed in as he watched Smiley then looked at me.

Although he was my friend and I knew without a doubt he trusted me, he had always been a stickler for detail. There was no way he would talk business until he knew all the facts. After all the greetings, the four of us made our way down to the basement, where the home office was. There wasn't much to look at with the naked eye. A big glass desk with a metal frame sat in the far-right corner. On top sat a twenty-four-inch flat-screen computer monitor. There were red blackout panels up to the windows, and other than the stained concrete flooring, that was the gist of the setting in the basement.

Once drinks had been poured, drinks which Trigga declined, I filled them in on how Smiley and I met. But in order to do that, I had to start from the beginning. I had to tell him how all this shit started. I told him about the two shipments that had been stolen from us before the third one alerted us to the grand scheme of things. Told him about the bullets we'd found that were in the shell of one of the cars. Told him about Boots, the bullet manufacturer. I gave details on how we busted Smiley out of prison thanks to help from Code's cousin, Fuego, who was a police officer. I explained to him how Code's old man had pretty much fucked me up the ass with no lube.

Once I was done, Big Jake grunted, and Trigga stood. "Have you been watching the news?" he asked me.

I shook my head. "Ah, I haven't really had to time to be watching TV, man. Did you hear anything I just said? I got a crime boss or whatever the fuck he is on my ass. TV isn't on a nigga's agenda right now."

"Sometimes, Auto, you have to look at the full picture to get all the details. The man who you're at war with, don't underestimate him. That could mean your death."

I studied Trigga closely. Out of all the years we'd known each other, I'd never known him to speak out of turn. Word around the hood was that he'd even taken down Damien Orlando and his brother. No one would ever say that shit out loud for fear of retaliation, but the stories were legendary. "This man's last name is Orlando—"

"Yeah, he's related to Dame," he answered, picking up on where I was going without my having to ask him outright. "His grandpops to be exact. Only thing is, according to my people, this nigga is nothing to play with. Dame was a saint compared to this nigga. Caltrone ain't survived this long by being stupid. You can't fight a nigga like him with weapons and shit, my nigga. You gotta use your thinker," Trigga said, pointing to his right temple. "You can't go at this man with guns and violence. Not unless it calls for it."

I stood, poured myself another drink, then asked, "If not guns and violence, then what? He sent a fucking hit squad after me, Trigga. Took out three of my closest friends, and you're telling me to what? Turn the other cheek?"

Jake spoke up. "No, what he's saying is you need to hit a man like Caltrone where it hurts."

"Exactly," Trigga chimed in. "A man like Caltrone only has respect for few things: loyalty, money, respect, and power. You have to hit him where he can feel it. You've already hit him with the loyalty aspect, because you've gotten his blood to turn against him, or so he sees it in his eyes. You told this nigga no, which no one has done and lived to tell about it. You're still alive. Now all you need to do is hit him in his pockets and find a way to take his power."

I heard Trigga. I respected everything he was saying, but there was something that was bothering me. "You've been checking up on this dude. It's like you've been studying him. Why?" I asked.

"I killed two of this nigga's grandchildren. I like to know my enemy as well as I know myself. Nigga, you never did read that Sun Tzu book, *The Art of War,* I gave you, did you? If you know yourself and not the enemy, for every win you will also suffer a loss. You've suffered four losses, Auto."

"Appear weak when you're strong. The supreme art of war is to subdue the enemy without fighting," Smiley spoke up.

Trigga looked at Smiley, winked, then smiled. I got the feeling that something was or had gone on between the two of them, something more than just friendship and work as Trigga had stated. That shit made my eye twitch, and I couldn't figure out why at the moment.

"Niggaa, Ray-Ray will fillet your ass," Big Jake quipped.

"That was my way of telling her good job for remembering, nigga."

Big Jake cast Trigga a look that said, "Yeah, right, nigga."

Smiley giggled. I looked between the two trying to figure out what was going on between them. Trigga nodded at Smiley. The fact that she was paraphrasing Sun Tzu told me she had known him longer than I'd thought. While they continued to talk, I let Trigga's words sink into my skull. That old man owed me. He owed me for coming after me and mine.

"Use everything you have in your arsenal, Auto. Don't hold shit back. You've been disrespected to the nth degree. It's time to fight back. Caltrone is an old-world cat. You're new school. Just like he had to take someone down to get to where he is, so do you. I don't know who this nigga Boots is, but my guess is he wants his shit back, right?"

I nodded. "Yeah."

"You don't give shit back until you get something out of the deal. The way I see it is this: it was his men who intercepted your shipment, correct?"

I nodded again.

"There're levels to this street war shit, my nigga. As a show of respect, he should have been offering you something before he even asked for his shit back, if you even have his shit. On principle alone, if he's a man of honor like you say he seems to be, he should have offered something for his mistake."

"As I would have," I spoke up.

"Exactly. You got the world at your feet, my nigga. As far as this nigga Caltrone, you got something this old-ass nigga don't have, and that's tech savvy. All an old nigga like Caltrone knows is murder, death, kill, and mind games when he's trying to get his point across. You're smarter than this nigga, and you have something not many can say. As this nigga's opponent, you've seen his face and lived to tell about it. Use that shit to your advantage."

Big Jake chimed in, "Not to mention, Smiley over there is on the same level as the Eraserheads when it comes to this hacking shit. Your whole team could probably shut down the A in no time flat."

"I steal money," Smiley chimed in.

Trigga gave her a lopsided grin. "So go steal some money, li'l shawty. You're one of the only shorties I know who can walk right up to an ATM and jackpot it."

"What the fuck that mean?" Jake asked.

I answered, "It means she got skills to reprogram an ATM using the built-in keypad. She has the ability to make an ATM think it's spitting out ones instead of twenties."

Trigga tilted his head and gave a nod in Smiley's direction. "Shawty bad with it."

Jake nodded. "Yup, Ray-Ray's going to kill you. And then I'm going to have to fight with Gina based on that alone. Not cool, nigga. Not cool."

I listened intently to these two men I had great respect for, as they'd survived some tough times, even as they joked about Trigga's impending doom with whoever Ray-Ray was. They were two of ATL's most wanted at one point in time, and then like magic, their entire existence had been wiped away. Trigga had given me a lot of information. Caltrone and Boots wanted to play tug-of-war? Well, now it was game time.

Chapter 4

Smiley

Okay, confession. I had an old-school crush. Like that Alicia Keys "Teenage Love Affair" type of deal, kinda. But it felt so long ago that it was crazy that I was literally sitting there feeling all hot and shit in memories about us when Trigga and Jake came through. Yeah, there was a slight "us." We were friends who clicked, and I would have let him hit, but the day we were supposed to go there was the day he got called up to do some business for his boss. Pick up some girl.

The streets wouldn't allow us to be anything deep or crazy, and we both were cool about it. Above everything we were friends, and there was nothing that I wouldn't do for the homie. He had schooled me in so much stuff. He helped my mom out when she was in the hospital, too, so my loyalty would always be to him in some way.

I guessed that's why I was still blushing and feeling all loopy in the heart. It was also why I was happy when I heard about him and Ray-Ray. I had seen her and thought she was cool, so when I did some background work to help her and the rest of the crew out, I was able to learn that she and Trig were something more than friends.

Street love wasn't always guaranteed. With Trigga, his heart was his own or belonged to the ghost in the walls, and I was fine with it. I wasn't about to be in some stupid "stuck on a nigga" type shit, not when I had my mom to worry about, so I was the silent voice whenever he needed to call. We were cool and close friends. We were almost lovers, and while I didn't know what it felt like to be his girl, I could say his mouth game was on point. He ate pussy like a pro.

Listening to Trig and Jake joke made me feel good again. I missed the jokes, but it also made me anxious. Dudes who were lethal and who had trouble following them at every chance surrounded me, while little old me was just scratching and grabbing for a safety net of my own.

We all sat and talked for hours. I learned what went down with Trigga and Jake, and they both helped school Auto on Caltrone. Through it all, I spoke up here and there, laughing and joking.

After all of that, they disappeared as they came, like ghosts before the sun was ready to rise. I felt a whole lot sad about it. A large part of me wanted to go with them, but through the night, it was Trigga who had me trusting Auto more. Even after we went through the rough patch of both Jake and Trigga learning about Code being my cousin—which meant that I was, like it or not, an Orlando too—and I could tell that bit of info gave Trigga pause, he didn't stress it.

Stretching, I plopped back down on the couch as Auto locked up. I braided my hair into two fishtails and then pulled out a tech kit.

"Is that the sticker thing?" Auto asked, coughing through the weed smoke that saturated the room still. He walked up slowly, then sat in front of me on the table, watching me intently.

Digging in the pack, I pulled out an iPhone, a flat, coaster-sized rubber mat, and a thick phone case. "Yeah, and I have this heatwave detector, too. I use it to snatch up PINs."

Auto glanced over what I had spread out on the table. "Wait, snatch up PINs? Show me."

I rubbed at my eyes, feeling damn high, and I felt a little warm at Auto's closeness. He was chilling, wide legged with his forearms on his thighs, silky black hair spilling over his shoulders, while being nosy in my bag. Dude smelled good, too. Brushing it off, I got up, fixed my black leggings, and then walked barefoot to his front door.

"Come check it out." I clicked the phone case over my iPhone and turned it on, waving Auto over. "See this? All I do when I want to snatch a PIN, I work it like this. I flip on the heat sensor, use the camera option, put that shutter sound on silent, and then take multiple pictures back-to-back."

Flipping the phone to show him, I continued explaining what I do. "See, you have a steel door, so it's easy to check out the heat signatures. Each color represents how recent each finger was on the surface. From that, I'm able to guess, because the last digit is turning blue at this point, that it was the first to touch the keypad. Then I work it backward to collect the PIN."

"And you can use this on any type of keypad?" Auto asked, now standing over me to get a better view.

My arms wrapped around me while I still held the phone out, and I nodded. "Kinda. The problem comes when a person wipes their heat signature by pressing their whole hand on it while they're punching in a code."

"Damn, but if you think about it, how typical is that?" Auto added.

I laughed and shrugged. "And that's why this shit works. People just don't know."

Auto watched me for a long time before stepping back and stretching. Dude's eyes were bloodshot from the weed and liquor he consumed. I could tell that he had let his guard down a lot because Trigga and Jake were here. I also could tell that he had drunk so much because he was missing his homies, and I couldn't judge him for that.

"I'm going to bed, but before I do, think about this. You should get close to the family if you can and see if you can steal some of their codes. We need your skills for this, Smiley. And now that Trigga can vouch for me, I think you should take the position and be an Eraserhead."

Yeah, I trusted him a little bit more, but tying myself to an actual group of people bothered me. It wasn't like how I was with the Misfits. I got called to help whenever. I knew the inner circle, but I didn't know the inner workings. It kept me safe, and I appreciated Trigga and Jake for that. But now, with thinking about becoming an Eraserhead, that meant some of that safety was going to go out the window. I just wasn't sure right now, but I was thinking about it.

"I need that answer, mama," Auto chimed in, interrupting my thoughts.

Squeezing my arm as it lay relaxed against me, I thought about one of Sun Tzu's nine situations, then moved to walk past Auto like I wasn't tripping off of him. "You have to grow your army again because he hit you hard at your core. You fought bravely but ran out of options as you lost your people. In the art of war, you learn that many calculations can work for you or break you."

Turning around with my hand on my hip, I continued, "He attacked you when you were unprepared. Number one rule is to always stay prepared, so if I can bring what I learned from Trig and what I learned on my own, I mean . . . Trig and Jake have you as their number one backup crew. I can't leave them or you hanging, so a'ight. I'm in. But I want my own contracts. Trust me, it ain't no games with it, but I have deals with people who I was down with before joining y'all, so I want that freedom."

He thought about it for a moment, then said, "A'ight, I can do that. Tomorrow you work on that tracker and that heating sensory gear." Auto walked past me, then stopped. "I appreciate your help."

When I turned to say, "You're welcome," he had walked off and closed the door to his bedroom. I stood there realizing that I had just committed to something huge, something that could end my life, and it freaked me out. But in the middle of it, I had gotten him to agree that I could have my own clients, which meant Code could officially be my client. He told me to treat her like a pariah. Well, now that was going to change. Tomorrow I would do what he said, and then go back to my mom's house while thinking of a second pad I could use in case of emergency.

I laughed to myself, bopped on into one of the empty bedrooms in the place, and called it a night.

Chapter 5

Code

The next day, back at Copper Hills where Boots housed up when he wanted to see what was going on in his hood, I started to see what a day in the life of Boots was like. As usual, the apartment complex was alive. Half-naked women and girls walked around advertising to the highest bidder. The smell of barbeque was in the air, same as it always was. Music blasted with Schoolboy Q rapping about collard greens. People gave peace signs and nods as Boots cruised through until we made it to the apartment building that belonged to him.

Boots would never let me open my own door, and I'd gotten tired of fighting him about it. So I just let him do it. Once he opened my door and I stepped out of the car, I walked ahead of him as little kids ran up to greet him.

"Hey, Mr. Boots, I got my progress report. I brought the C up like you said, but only to a B minus," a cute little boy said. "Can I still get that bill like you promised?" The little boy had the smoothest chocolate skin I'd ever seen, and his eyes shone bright with enthusiasm.

"I told you to get an A," Boots told him with a slight frown on his face.

"No. Nah, you said bring the C up to a better grade, Mr. Boots. You didn't say it had to be an A. I did the exact thing you asked me to. Followed your words to a T."

I chuckled at how comprehensive yet innocent the little boy was. Boots tried to counter his argument again only to have the little boy pull out his cell and show Boots the recording of their last conversation. Boots had no choice but to pay up. I stood there watching the exchange. I watched all of the kids as they talked to Boots, and I found myself wishing I knew what it was to be a kid again.

I stopped being a kid at age 7. By the age of 9, I'd killed my first person. By 12, I was in Canada, living like an everyday schoolgirl in a private Catholic girls' academy, only I was there to kill a high-ranking official who'd wronged my *familia*. By 15, I was a full-blown assassin.

I walked into the walkway of the building, then up the five money green stairs. Oya was waiting at the top. Her crinkled hair was held back by a headband that represented Brazil in colors. Six-inch heels adorned her feet, while dark denim skinny jeans seemed to be painted on her thick, toned thighs and hips. The purple button-down top she had on fanned out over her hips, while the thick belt she wore contoured to her shapely waist. Mama was a baddie, and it was easy to see why Freddie had become enamored with her. Her dark skin was mesmerizing.

"You didn't try to go back to that house, did you?" I asked her.

She shook her head. "Not yet, but I'm going back in."

"No, you're not."

She frowned. "I am. Freddie is hurt badly, and while I was there, Caltrone questioned him excessively before allowing him to even get help. Something's wrong with that old man," she fumed.

"You only see what's on the outside, Oya. There is more to him than this monster he's made out to be," I defended Papa.

Oya gave a look akin to pity before catching herself. "I've never heard one good word about that man, and based on what I've seen in this short time, I can say that everything I've heard is true."

"You shouldn't believe everything you hear, Oya. Papa has many layers." I felt my pressure points getting heated. People only knew the legend of the man who many people likened to Lucifer himself. Only, the papa I'd grown up with wasn't that man.

"You're delusional, Code. Stockholm syndrome is what it's called. You have to quit looking at the trees to see the forest."

"No, I'm not delusional," I shot back. "Do you know what Papa has done for our people back in Cuba? To even hear you speak this way of him would get you killed. This man, this monster that he's been made out to be, isn't the core of the man I know. He's built neighborhoods, schools, hospitals—"

"With blood money."

"No, with money he built his empire with. Papa ain't ever bit a snake that didn't bite him first."

"You're brainwashed."

"Don't patronize me."

"You're brainwashed, Code. Whether you want to believe that or not is on you. Your papa is an evil man."

I narrowed my eyes at her and stepped to her because I was all set to knock her on her ass. She squared up with me. She didn't back down like I knew many women, and men for that matter, would have. She was taller than I was, but height had never stopped me from kicking ass before and it wouldn't now. I think I was more angry because nobody knew Papa the way the family knew Papa. They only knew what they had heard from people who had no doubt only told half the story—the half that favored them, I'd bet.

"You've got one more time to say something about Papa and we're going to have a disagreement. And it's going to end with my foot in your sternum," I spat at her.

"You don't scare me, Code. You never will. Sure, we can fight, and you might win, but I promise you I'll leave you with a scar that will make you remember me for the rest of life. And in the end, you'll still be a brainwashed little girl running around blinded by the rose-colored glasses she likes to wear. If Papa never bit a snake that didn't bite him first, ask yourself, what did Auto do to him? What did the other three members of your team do to him?"

I swallowed hard. My emotions and anger blinded me. If I'd had the wherewithal to think logically, I wouldn't have lunged at Oya. I would have been able to discern what she was trying to say to me. But fury caused me to see red. Thoughts of my team turning their backs on me saddened me. Lelo, Seymore, and Dunkin, all dead. I didn't blame Papa for that. I blamed myself.

Seething anger made me forget all the teachings I'd been schooled in. I shoved her hard into the apartment door behind her. I went to give her one of those Spartan 300 kicks. She grabbed my ankle, then kicked my other leg from underneath me. I fell to the floor in a split. That didn't hurt as bad as when her knee connected to my face though.

Oya was calm as she grabbed two handfuls of my hair and tossed me down the stairs. I rolled over my head as I tumbled down and hit the wall hard. The knee to the face and then the throw down the stairs had dizzied me. My world was spinning, and before I could react, Oya was over me. A punch to the face kept me down on the floor. My head hit the wall again, and I blindly kicked out. From somewhere beneath my hooded lids, I could see I'd kicked her in the stomach. She stumbled back, but she was quicker on her feet than I was. I could taste the copper flavor of blood in my mouth. I knew my nose was bleeding by the drip falling down my lip.

Oya grunted as she straddled me and sent a rapid succession of fists to my face. I'd never met a woman who could go toe-to-toe with me. I'd even fought men in my family and won, and somehow Oya was whupping my ass. I didn't like it. It felt like I was back in sparring sessions with Papa. He'd shown me no mercy and kicked my ass as he'd done to all the males I'd had to train with. Oya pulled me to my feet by my hair, and in that small entryway, we rumbled like two wild banshees. She wouldn't let up and neither would I. If I got in a few good punches, Oya got in even better kicks. Then it reversed. If she threw a few good punches, I got in even better kicks.

Oya swung at me. I ducked, rushed behind her, then kicked her in the back of her left knee. When she went down to her knees, I put her in a sleeper hold. Heavy breathing, scratching, kicking, and clawing could be heard in the small entryway. Oya was fighting for her life. I wasn't trying to kill her. I just wanted to send a message. I smiled as my arm tightened around her neck.

My cockiness was showing, and that had been a mistake. I'd underestimated her, and in the end, it had cost me.

It happened so quick that I never saw it coming. By some kind of way, Oya managed to lean forward, only by a few inches. The back of her head went flying back into my face so hard that it blinded me. Searing pain tore through my head. I struggled as Oya flipped behind me. Around my neck was a piece of her belt that had come off during our fight. I fought against her hold. One hand clawed her face while the other tried to keep the belt from choking me to death. I hissed and wheezed as she grunted and squeezed tighter.

"I told you I would make you remember me," Oya spat. I could tell she was speaking through clenched teeth by the intensity of her words and the vibration against my ear.

"You have no one left but us," she kept going. "Me and my family. The old man you're attacking me for has all but banished you. I was on the inside of your domain for hours. The walls have ears, Code, and the old man wants your head on a platter."

Tears rushed down my face. I tried to scream out, but all I could do was whizz and grunt. Her words did way more damage to me than the fight had.

"Let . . . me . . . go," I choked out.

"Nah. I want you to feel what it's like to have death tapping at your door. I want you to feel what it is to have the walls of life closing in on you. You think you're invincible, but you're not. You're a mere human, same as me. You ain't the only one who had to survive in a family of men," she growled. "I grew up part of my life in São Paulo and Salvador. You know how hard it was for a girl like me? Want to know what it was to be violently raped and left for dead? Want to know what it is to see the gates of hell then welcome entry because it looked better than home? Bitch, you're not special. You walk around here like the world owes you something and it doesn't. Your papa wants to kill you, and yet you defend him, Code. You would give your life for a man who wants to take yours all because you chose to go your own way, play by your own rules and not his."

I yelled out as my eyes burned. I hadn't cried since I was 7 years old, locked in a room full of snakes. I had never fought emotionally because I had no emotions. I hadn't been taught to love or to feel. I'd been taught to kill.

Oya loosened her hold and shoved me forward. I staggered forward, then turned with my back to the wall. Oya was bleeding just as I was. I'd gotten in more hits than I'd thought. My breathing was ragged. Clothes torn. Chest hurt and heart heavy. Oya was sweating. I couldn't tell what blood was hers or what was mine. In her right hand was the piece of the belt she'd choked me with.

The door swung open and in walked Shango and Boots. Shango was busy talking about fucking Alize up when he saw us. He stopped abruptly and asked, "What in hell happened in here?"

Boots frowned and stepped around Shango. He looked from me to Oya then from Oya to me. "You okay?" he asked her.

I knew if she told Boots I'd attacked her first, I'd be out on my ass. With no money and no identity, I didn't want to run that risk. Especially with Papa out for my blood.

She sniffed and used the back of her hand with the belt in it to wipe the blood from her nose. "I'm fine. This bitch thought she saw a snake and went ape shit. We handled it though. Right, Code?" Oya answered Boots, but her eyes never left mine.

I wiped my nose and face quickly, then nodded once. "Right. It's nothing."

"Nothing at all," Oya said tersely. "We need to go clean up since we're meeting with the Asian Dragons. Come on, Code. Alize will be here shortly."

With that, Oya turned and walked back up the second flight of stairs. I glanced at Boots and Shango, embarrassed and feeling pity for myself.

Oya looked down. "Come on, Code. If you're going to be living here, you have to pull your weight."

With the burden of the world on my shoulders, I made my way up the stairs and followed Oya into apartment A.

It took me an hour and a half to shower and patch up my wounds. I had cuts, scrapes, and bruises all over my body. My face wasn't as bad as I thought though. A small cut was above my lip, and my nose was swollen a bit. The hot water felt good, but the homemade salve Oya had left for me felt even better. I stepped out of the shower to find her in the bathroom, setting clothes out for me.

"Your grandfather questioned Freddie because he wanted to know how you managed to kill four of your cousins with direct aim and precision but only managed to shoot him in the arm and leg. Your grandfather knows you don't miss unless you want to. He thinks Freddie may have been working with you, but he managed to say that he just moved quicker than your bullets and pointed out that you hadn't shot Mark at all. That calmed the old man for a while. Enough time to get Freddie seen about."

I didn't care about her seeing my nudity if she didn't care. I grabbed a white bath sheet hanging on the silver towel rack and wrapped it around myself. I sniffed and wiped the mirror free enough of steam to see myself. Oya was dressed in a full body white cat suit that sat out in stark comparison to her skin tone. She wore minimal makeup, which only enhanced her beauty and hid the bruises from our fight. Her hair was done in goddess braids and brought her cheekbones out.

"I still don't think you should go back in there," I told her.

"I appreciate your concern, but don't worry yourself about my safety. I'll be fine."

After the way we'd fought in the entryway, I had no doubt she could handle her own. I still knew Papa though. If he decided he wanted her, nothing she could do would stop him from taking her.

She continued, "I'll be gone by the time you're dressed. Just so you know, I wouldn't have hit you if you hadn't have come for me first. I don't hold any ill feelings, but the next time you come at me, one of us will be going to jail and the other to hell. Alize is across the hall if you need anything. I have work to do," she told me, then walked out of the bathroom.

Being around Alize and Oya was different. Yeah, they could fight and kill with the best of them, but they had a comradery that I wasn't used to. The women in my family wouldn't know how to be sisterly. The only women who had even a taste of motherly love were a few of the many wives Papa had. That wasn't saying much, because even with that knowledge, it was Papa who taught me about female hygiene when they fell short.

It was Papa who bought me birth control and condoms. Papa was the one who told me that if I got pregnant, he would take me to the first private abortion clinic he could find. He said I wasn't meant to carry children as of yet because I had work to do and a child would only hold me back. Papa read bedtime stories to me, and Papa tucked me in most nights. I remembered a time when I would kill and come back home to find Papa throwing a celebration in my honor. Just as much as he'd turned me into a cold-blooded killer, he'd also spoiled me.

I picked up the salve Oya had left me, and I started to rub it on my cuts and scratches after walking to the front room. It tingled and burned a bit, but for the most part, it eased the aches. I looked around at the place. There were vast differences between this one and the one Boots lived in across the hall. Red and purple made up the color scheme. The purple sofa and the love seat were made of a microfiber fabric. Red microfiber throw pillows sat nice and neat on them. African artwork adorned the walls, while the hardwood floor had been polished to a mirrored shine. There was a burnt orange accent wall, which housed a silver-framed photo of black couples in various stages of sex. It wasn't pornographic, but the erotic edginess of the photo stood out to me.

I took my time rubbing the salve on myself, and after I was done, I spread the towel out on the sofa and lay down. I just needed to rest for a few.

"Code," a hardened male voice called out to me.

I shook and stirred but didn't answer. Someone shook me. I jumped up and awkwardly fell off the couch. My hand reached under the sofa, and I aimed the gun I pulled out at the man in front of me. I'd been asleep and didn't even know it. My head was a bit foggy, but my aim was still dead-on.

Boots tilted his head to the side and studied me.

"What?" I asked. My throat was dry, and my eyes watered a bit.

Both his brows rose. "You're naked," he said.

"What?" I asked again because my mind was still trying to wake up.

"You're naked."

I looked down at myself and remembered I didn't have any clothes on. I dropped my hand and shook my head. I'd been so out of it over the last few days that I could just add this to the list of things that had gone wrong since Papa had sent a hit squad to kill my team. I picked up the towel and held it in front of me.

"So," I snapped, "what do you want?"

"To be honest, I came over here to see what was taking you so long to get dressed, but since you're naked with a gun aimed at me—"

I cut him off. "Don't even go there, Boots. Don't."

"Don't go where?" he asked, then chuckled. "Because I can assure you if I was going, you'd want to go too."

I ignored him and shook off the heated way he made me feel as he stood there dressed like he was going to a business meeting. The purple dress shirt he had on hugged the muscles in his chest and arms just enough to make me forget that men like him were only good for breeding, as my mother had taught me. He didn't have on a hat, so I could see all of his unique features clearly. The beard he sported made me want to touch it. The way his black dress pants sat grown-man low on his hips made me want to know what he looked like naked. He'd always worn his clothes well and today had been no different.

I plopped down on the sofa.

"Mama, you need to get up and get dressed," he ordered.

"I'm not going," I answered.

"You don't get to make that decision."

"I'm not fucking going," I yelled. "I'm sick of you trying to order me around because you feel as if I owe you something. Are you even still protecting the Eraserheads? Or are you just keeping me here to make my life a living hell? I'm not fucking going!"

Boots pulled his hands from his pockets, then slowly stalked over to me. The easy way he walked reminded me of a panther. The muscles in his arms and shoulders flexed and rolled as he closed the gap between us. I leaned back on the sofa as he stood over me. I didn't like that I felt trapped when he caged me between his arms. My chest swelled as my heart started to beat harder. I reached for my gun, but he snatched it up, then let the muzzle graze between my breasts as he spoke. He was face-to-face with me as he spoke in a low tone. His baritone mixed with that Texas drawl had always piqued my curiosity. The smell coming from him, I couldn't place. It reminded me of a spicy earthiness. I'd never had a man this close me that made my body react the way Boots was doing.

"I'm only going to say this once, so pay attention, *mami*. You're going to get up, get dressed, and leave when I do, understood? We both know the only reason you're here is because you know nowhere but here will be safe since Caltrone wants you dead. We both know I'm not holding you here against your will and that you're free to go anytime you want, right?" he asked, then let the gun trail down my stomach and back up to let the muzzle circle my left nipple then the right one. My lotus had all but blossomed.

I gazed up into his light brown eyes.

I didn't answer him, because he was right. I stayed under his lock and key because I hadn't figured out how to keep death away long enough for me to put a few things in order. It wasn't that I was afraid of dying, because I wasn't. I knew the Reaper would come for me sooner or later. I just didn't ever think it would be at the hands of my family.

Chapter 6

Boots

Yes, indeed, there was beauty in the killer under me, and yes, indeed, little mama's badass, alluring body had a brother aching, but on some business and street shit, the pussy could wait another day. Though she had nipples so pretty that I wondered if they tasted like toffee or cinnamon, I wanted to see if I even had an effect on her. The challenge that was Code made a brother interested. I was amped to see her in another new element as well. That's why Shango and I just watched on the sly as she and Oya scrapped it out. Each hit that went into each other's face or body had me thinking.

Was Code able to adapt? Was she going to twist the game and work through those walls of hers that her old man strategically placed in her mind to groom her into the woman whose loyalty to him was breaking her down? I didn't know. I just knew that it was showtime and money called.

Code stood in front me, decked out in a contour-hugging black bandage dress. When she turned, I could see the curve of her bare back, the opening stopping right on top of her apple bottom. If I were some dirty, rude ninja, I would have said fuck it all and dug right into the kush. But again, I was a gentleman, and I always liked fucking when a woman is willing.

"Oya picked well," I said, adjusting my black vest then placing my black Ascot cap on my head.

Taking a seat on the edge of the bed, I watched Code slip her red bottoms on, her hair loose and falling over her breast while watching me at the same time.

"Why do we have to look so *Ocean's Eleven?*"

"Good name," I said, laughing. "Because we are running some *Ocean's Eleven* deal on the Dragons. They have money I want, and I plan upon taking it while enticing them with my new toys. Anyway, let's go. You don't need any perfume. You smell good already."

I offered my arm, but Code walked past me. I laughed, following. We exited the complex. We started in one car because I hated being that type of guy in the hood flashing money in the form of a ride. When heading to meetings, we always switched rides out.

Once that happened, we chilled in my blacked-out Mercedes. Shango drove, and Alize was in the passenger seat. Oya and Shredder were back at the compound handling business and production with the rest of the extended team. There were only two right hands for me, and Oya and Shredder had the capability to keep the rest of the team on their business with the production.

Riding out of the neighborhood, we took the highway toward Chamblee and Doraville. Dragons business typically hit many different hoods in the Atlanta area, but when it came down to cartel meetings and business, it always happened in Chamblee or Doraville. Both areas were called the international corridor or international district in the A. Oftentimes I'd send one of the crew to hit up Buford Market to grab specific food and spices that I liked in reference to my Eritrean culture or the crew's varied cultures.

Music played lightly in the truck as the city turned dark. I watched various cars ride by on the highway, traffic becoming congested on the opposite side as Jay-Z spat some shit. Alize kept slick talking to Shango about his habit for stringing females along, as he laughed and turned up "Give It to Me," speaking to her through the music. Code sat beside me, not saying a thing through the deal. I felt like messing with her mental a little bit, but the quiet was actually soothing me and allowing me to run down in my mind everything that I was going to say when presenting my new line.

"We have a call," I heard Shango say, knocking me from my trance.

Habit had me checking my cell to see who it was. Once I did, an amused smile spread across my face. "Handle it. I'll listen."

With the partition rising to keep the conversation private from Code, I popped my earpiece in, hit it on mute, and waited.

"So you don't trust me enough to handle a phone call, but you have me going to a meeting about your product?" Code said bitterly.

When she narrowed her indigo-lined eyes, I chuckled with my response. "Why ask something that you know the answer to, *mami?* Just relax and enjoy the peaceful ride. I like that indigo you have on. I find it interesting that you'd choose that color. For now, you have no worries."

She shifted where she sat, then crossed her arms over her chest. "I like it, and I doubt that, Boots."

"Yeah," was all I said, watching her from the corner of my eye.

Shango's conversation came through, and I listened as he spoke. "Who are you?"

The voice gave his name, then began spitting out questions about loyalty to Shango.

"Hold up. Questioning whether we are capable of delivering you a solid product is like wiping your ass with your bare hand, my man. You have toilet paper in front of you, yet you feel the need to feel shit on your hands. Who are you again?"

The sound of the caller got quiet, and I laughed to myself as Shango continued, "You called us about hearing the streets talking about a new line coming out, and you wanted to see if it had to do with us? I find it funny that you decide to call us about it yet threaten us about what we guarantee we would ship to your boss, amigo. You can't run hot and cold with us and think that you can control us. Either you trust us and how we handle business or you don't."

Shango was speaking with the handler of one of the Italian cartel leaders. The quick word of mouth about the production of a biodegradable gun had the streets buzzing. Everyone wanted to find out how to cop the gun and be the first to test it out. That was when I put the word out that I was the man everyone needed to see. Cartel leaders had been falling all over themselves trying to get to me.

I lit up a cigar and saw that we passed a strip mall with various ethnic restaurants, shops, grocery stores, and other outlets catering to the international community. It didn't take long for us to ride down the street and land outside of the Dragons' meeting spot, which was a small, family-owned Korean sauna and restaurant. Shango continued talking, and I listened to the agitation in his voice.

"Amuse me again. Explain to me what it is your boss is asking?" my man said in mock curiosity.

A voice responded, asking if we knew anything about biodegradable weapons being sold in the streets.

Shango allowed silence to do his talking before saying, "No."

The voice then insisted that Shango was lying.

Calling Shango a liar was never a good thing. Many men who dared to say so to his face always left with a missing part of their body. Fortunately for the caller, he was on the phone and Shango knew the importance of getting an in with highbrow businessmen.

"I'll stop you there. It's funny how questions are formulated. Getting a response to a question is important, especially if we ask it the right way. Which you didn't," he said, voice dripping in malice.

The caller immediately spat threats in Italian about what they would do to us.

Shango cleared his throat. "We would be open to arranging a meeting with you to discuss any extension to our business arrangement," he said. "However, until then, we must put this conversation on hold. Money is to be made and business to be had. Next time, I expect to speak with someone who is familiar with doing business with us. We either speak with the boss, or we don't speak at all." Shango then hung up.

My man. I laughed aloud with how Shango goaded the handler on the other end. More than likely, the fool was going to get his ass kicked for not securing a proper deal with us. However, I didn't give a damn. Shango thought like me sometimes, and he knew what to do to snag a person. Tease him with the best and the exclusive, and then you'll gain his attention.

Hitting the partition, I leaned forward. "Set that meeting as soon as he calls back. I'm positive that he'll hit redial."

Shango laughed, then gave a nod. "You know he is."

Then, like that, the cell started going off. I took it upon myself to exit the ride, open Alize's door, then walk to Code's door to do the same. All actions were done in a way that had me keeping my face shielded by my hat.

"Keep your face low at all times," I said to Code. I smoothed the bangs that swooped low over her eye, then offered her my arm. "The area is clear, but I still don't trust my surroundings wherever I am."

"You shouldn't. You never know who's running game on you," Code said with a shrug while walking at my side.

Her words were funny to me because it was damn true. However, wasn't that why she was now by my side anyway? Walking on, I had nothing to say but, "You know that well, don't you?"

"Fuck you," was the reply from her.

The grimy in me wanted to counter with something nasty and slick, but I chose not to only because we were here to handle business and I didn't want a fight on my hands.

Flanking us, Alize handled business and made sure it was safe for us to walk into the side of the family restaurant. An all-black crisscross jumper pantsuit with ankle boots was Alize's choice of style. She sported a cropped purple blazer that hid half of the weapons she was concealing on her shapely body. Behind us was Shango, finishing his conversation while watching our backs. He matched Alize in her choice of all black, and the purple he sported was his tie. They both carried briefcases with our product within.

Once we stepped into the small restaurant, we all stood in a line, staring at a large mural wall that parted to reveal a huge kitchen. Both Alize and Shango briefly glanced at each other, then moved to stand in front of us, waiting to be greeted by an elderly man. We all studied the man who came our way. He too wore a tailored suit, accents of his culture reflected in the lapel of his suit and cufflinks.

"Greetings," was all he said.

Both Shango and Alize stepped to the side to allow me to speak to the gentleman. I responded by returning his greeting in Korean, then said, "'An empty cart rattles loudly.'"

No expression came from the man until he bowed and said, "'Even if you know the way, ask one more time.'"

I gave a respectful bow and held out a small box, showing a tattoo on the inside of my wrist. I said, "'In a place where there is will, there is a road.'"

"Ah, welcome. Follow me." A warm smile came from the elderly man as he took the box.

Several intimidating men appeared by our sides, and we fell into the routine of being checked for weapons. We all were strapped down, but in keeping our good weapons close to us, it revolved excellent positioning. As the goons before us searched us, we allowed them to find trivial weapons, such as an ankle gun or gun against our back. Once they felt that we were no threat and there were no more weapons to be found, the older man motioned for us to follow him through the back way.

For a moment, I assumed that we were going to head through the kitchens, but that was not the case. Instead, we took a back way that led us to a private dining room. Doors opened, and we were escorted into the room where several men and women moved around waiting to greet us. We followed the cultural rules dictated, then sat at a long table. All around us was money. Either the walls, statues, and light figures were dipped in all gold, or they were inlaid by all gold. Incredibly detailed paints were nested within the gold framings on the wall and other pieces of artwork, reflecting the culture around us.

Once we were settled, I noticed that on every side of us were sliding doors. Shadows appeared behind them, and a large flat screen rose up from the table in front of us. Accepting the tea I was offered, I noticed that Code wasn't drinking.

"Drink and eat. They won't kill us through food, trust me on that. One of them had personal experience with that," I muttered to her.

"You never know," she answered. "But you're correct."

She then lifted her cup to her lips and took a sip. As soon as she did that, each one of the screens opened, and several figures appeared on the screen to present various factions and cultures of the Dragons' clan street leaders. I had felt their eyes on us, but it took Code sipping from her cup to kick things off, huh?

To the right of me were the younger members of the Dragons, which was how I knew that they were the street leaders, and in front of me on the screen were the men I really wanted an in with: the older leaders. They were the corporate Dragons who handled things at a level I intended to take my team. Each man on the screen wore a crisp suit and a stoic expression that would cut a lesser soul.

They were waiting for me, so I put on my business face and motioned behind me. "The house of Dragons, I received your welcome message, and I am honored to be requested to do business with your clan."

Both Alize and Shango moved around the room with one of the briefcases open. Inside were small gifts, and since I was a man who always did his homework, at the same time on the screen, several attendants appeared with similar gifts for the overseas Dragons. Having stood, I gave a bow in respect, then returned to my seat.

"It is our pleasure to do business with a man we have heard so much about. Let us begin then, shall we, Mr. Sunjeta," one of the elders addressed me.

Standing again, I bowed, then moved to Shango, who held up a case. Alize reached over to open it where they sat on their knees while playing the role of the body-guards. She let her fingers lovingly brush over the surface of the object within. She pulled it out to present it to me. Laying it in my hands, I gripped it, secured its barrel, and outstretched my arm to point it at a clear spot at the wall.

Young and old watched me curiously as I turned the Glock in my hand sideways, showing the pristine detail of it. The material of it was shined so meticulously that it seemed like it was silver, which was the point. Several days was all it took for me craft this baby's hand base and removable barrel from Smiley's design. Usually, for those creating such guns, it could take longer, months or years, depending on experience, the type of printer used, and finding components that worked to keep the gun stable. With me, I was a weapons man, and I had a large team. To make bullets, you had to know the guns they would be used for, and that I did. I had the majority of the parts around me, so there was no issue there. Besides, this was really a show about my bullets. Using this prototype was just to garner extra attention.

In the cases of 3-D guns, it wasn't nothing to create the initial shell if you knew what you were doing. My team and I specialized in creating weapons, so a plastic shell was nothing for us. It was small, and Shango built a top-of-the-line 3-D printer from the equipment we already had. Testing a material that was both biodegradable and sturdy was the next thing.

Alize called our people overseas and my other right hand who handled that business, Sweetness, in Paris to get them started on the production of that. She also asked them what we could quickly gather in the States. Check off the list. Then the next was creating the inner components, the chambers. Usually, a printed gun could shoot only one bullet. However, using a 3-D printer such the well-known Liberator helped change that years ago. Now, people had perfected it and were still testing ways to make shooting more efficient.

My team and I sat around and thought about this prototype, using gun parts and adding them inside of the 3-D gun, while testing and constructed inner components that would remain sturdy and shoot off multiple rounds for later models. This was why, in the case of the gun I held in my hand, it was the only one. The rest that I gave out as tests were mere copies that we used for research purposes only. Smiley had given us a blueprint, and it was on us to make that shit better than the rest.

This was another test of mine, and I enjoyed being a show-off. An amused smile spread across my lips, then I quickly flipped it, pointed, and pulled. Quicker than a blink of an eye, red splattered on the back of a wall in one of the rooms watching us, and I studied the body of a street Dragon as he fell to the side. For a minute, shock silenced the room. Once the shock wore off, younger Dragons stood ready to rush me.

Both Alize and Shango dropped their cases, pulled out guns from their sleeves, and started pumping iron, more like my special-grade bullets, right with me. Code slid to the side for cover in confusion. I thought this all shocked her, which was cool. I enjoyed a good show from time to time.

"Code," was all I said, holding a gun out to her. "Clear 'em out."

Like that, no question came from her. She just grabbed my gun and started shooting. Any time Code started busting her guns, I could see the years of training. Caltrone had literally created a monster, a killing machine.

While they all handled business, I walked around the table and turned the monitor to show the damage my guns caused. In the midst of it all, two large beasts burst into the room and tried to rush us, but they, too, easily went down, except for one. The man had found a way to move past me to snatch Alize up by her neck and slam her against a wall.

"Fuck!" was all I heard her say.

Rubbing my hands together, I took off my hat, then glanced her way. "You know how to handle it, mama, so do that."

Light laughter came from her, and she gave me a salute.

Code made ready to point her gun at him, but I stopped her. "Let her work her magic, *mamacita*."

Stepping over bodies, I saw Shango stop his shooting to move to my side as we watched Alize work. Baby girl kicked, then dug her nails into the dude's arms. Her eyes were bucking from her pretty face, and we all knew that she had to move quickly and just right or he'd break her neck.

"This is disrespect to the Clans!" was all the guard said.

Alize laughed and then crossed her arms against her and him. "No, it's not."

With a whip of a hand, the sound of a pistol going off and slamming into the man drew our attention. We watched as Alize contorted her body, moved her leg to wrap it on his shoulder, and squeeze. She also at that moment took a knife from her body to run it across her attacker's thick neck. Blood colored the floor like paint. Sweat and spit slid down Alize's face, but it was as the goon let go while dropping her gun that we panicked.

Alize had been hit as she took that wide receiver down. Her neck was bruised, and she stumbled forward holding her side with a smile. Rushing forward, I snatched her up and put my hand to her stomach, trying to stop the blood. "Fucking presentation is over. You do business with us or not. We took care of the weak links in your street team. Now ante up!" I shouted in a fury. "Grab our guest. We need to go."

"Mr. Sunjeta. Money has been transferred to your account. It is our pleasure to secure a contract with you. Take the young lady to the kitchens. She will be tended to there." Then, like that, the screen blacked out.

Worry had me picking up Alize. "Hold on, baby girl, we got you."

Alize gave a laugh. "Don't stress. Once this is done, I'll cover it with a cute tat, ya heard?"

I tried to laugh at her words, but stress had me rushing to the kitchens and pushing anyone and everyone out of my way. I could hear Code shouting, and it started grating my nerves in the process.

"What?" I shouted while I held my partner in my arms.

"What part of the game is that?" she shouted out while trailing me. "Us dying was a fucking presentation?"

"Chill. They are still deciphering our trust," was all I rushed out once we made it to a small room by the kitchens, where a woman waited for us. Laying Alize down, I stood by her side, holding her hand, as Shango appeared and started shouting about how fast they had better work on her. Certain business transactions required a sacrifice, but this was not one I was willing to make. Luckily, today was not Alize's time. The bullet missed vital organs. Damn bulletproof shaper she had on had no chance against one of my bullets.

I was straight pissed that that nigga had pulled her Glock away and used it on her. As they patched her up, we were told that she'd heal fast

Because of one of my people being hurt, the older Dragons felt that we should be introduced to the new Dragons street lords—six members, three females and three males. Each one wanted our bullets, and each one was interested in our Glocks.

The point of this game was to draw out Caltrone. After the streets got wind of this, he would be. Business was good, and business was done for the day.

Chapter 7

Auto

Two Days Later

"I'm sorry, Auto. I'm just not ready to come back right now. Carmen is still crying every day. The kids don't understand why Daddy isn't coming back home. I got a lot on my plate right now."

I looked at Stitch as we sat in the front room of his modest townhome. He lived in a working-class neighborhood. It was a newly built area, and for as long as I could remember, he and Lelo had always lived below their means. It had always been a smart decision on their end. The less attention we brought to ourselves, the better. On the white walls were family portraits framed in black and silver of Lelo, Stitch, Carmen, and their four children: two boys and two girls.

To them, they'd had the perfect family. No TV was in the front room, as Stitch and Lelo didn't believe in letting their children watch more than a few hours of what they called the idiot box. Mocha-colored carpeting was wall-to-wall throughout the home. It smelled of cinnamon and apples mixed with the wafting aroma of fried chicken.

He sat in the leather armchair across from the matching sofa I sat on. Dressed in loose-fitting slacks and a white wife beater, his eyes watered as he continued to talk. "It's only been two weeks, bruh. My family needs time to heal. I'm all they have now. And with Carmen depressed, I have to look out for my kids."

I dropped my head, then quickly looked back up to him. "I feel lost, man. I feel lost without my family intact. Every day I wake up hoping that this is some kind of sick joke or a nightmare. I pray that I'll walk into the shop to hear the noise of my machines and the laughter and jokes from friends. I want to hear you and Lelo arguing about the stupid shit you two argue about. I want Seymore to be rolling around in that wheelchair, pushing up his glasses, watching Reagan like he wants to eat her alive. I want Dunkin and Jackknife to be in their own world, signing one another jokes. I want to watch Code rush in at the last minute because she knows she's late."

Stitch chuckled solemnly. "I know what you mean. How is Code anyway?"

I shrugged. "I don't know. Haven't had any contact with her since I erased her."

"Still can't believe you erased her, but I understand why. I hate it had to be this way."

I nodded, then stood so I could discreetly hide the water in my eyes. I walked to the bay window in his home and looked out at the flower garden Stitch and Lelo had made for Carmen. The woman loved flowers but couldn't keep a plant alive to save her life. So the men in her life did it for her. The sun was shining, wind blowing. There were little kids of all races out on bikes and scooters. A few little girls stood off to the side, jumping rope.

"I do too, but it is what it is. I got some major shit about to go down in the next few days. I get why you can't roll with me on this, but I wish you could. However, it's family before everything," I said, then turned to look at him. "If anything happens to me, I've left everything to you, Reagan, and Jackknife. Y'all take care of the rest of the crew."

He nodded and stood. "How dangerous is this coup you're about to pull, Auto?"

I shrugged and answered truthfully. "It's quite possible that I will lose my life, but I have to make this move. Armando and Nicola are asking me what I'm going to do about it. All my business has basically halted because word around town is that Caltrone Orlando has tried to snuff me out. Even the two I've done business with since I opened the shop are hesitant to continue doing business with me. I have to do something. This is my livelihood, bruh."

He took a deep breath, then nodded. "I'll come back."

"No, you won't," I said, going over to the black duffle bag I'd brought in with me.

"You need me."

"Your family needs you more."

"You came over here to specifically ask me to come back and now—"

"Now you've made me see things clearer. You put your family first, and I respect that. After hearing the passion in your voice, there is no way I can ask you to step into this fire with me."

"Auto—"

"No," I told Stitch, then tossed him the black duffle bag.

"What's this?" he asked me.

"That's Lelo's cut of the profits for the year."

Stitch opened the bag and looked in. His eyes widened, and then his brows furrowed. "Where in hell did you get this?"

"I saw Trigga a couple weeks ago. Told him about my plan. He dropped some dough on me. Told me he wanted his cut if I pulled it off."

Stitch smiled. "That nigga's in the A?"

I nodded.

"Never thought we see him and Jake again."

"Said he was here to deal with something concerning that Nightwings player who's been in the news."

Stitch shook his head. "Trigga is always around. The boy in the hoodie. He's going to have to retire that damn hoodie soon," he said and chuckled.

I chuckled as well. Nobody ever knew his name, but when you mentioned the boy in the hoodie, everybody scattered. I stayed there and spoke to Stitch about a few more things, most of it for shits and giggles so the burden of what I was about to do wouldn't weigh on me.

Before I left, I broke bread with him and the kids. Carmen didn't want to eat. She looked as if she hadn't eaten in days, and it was starting to show in her eyes and face. If she didn't come out of her depression soon, she would start to look gaunt. I spoke to her, told her their children needed her more than ever now. She agreed but said she just couldn't believe Lelo was gone.

While Lelo was alive, he and Stitch allowed Carmen to live life while they took care of the children. Carmen was well loved and protected by the two men she loved. She was the only woman I knew who was okay with Lelo and Stitch having a relationship while at the same time having a relationship with her.

After dinner was done, I bid my goodbyes and headed off to see what the future held for me.

Later on that night, as I sat in my apartment, I thought about the plan I'd set in motion. I'd already spoken to Jackknife and Reagan. They knew what they were supposed to do. Now all I had to do was wait for Smiley to come out of the shower so I could give her the rundown. She had been back at her old crib for a few days. That was the deal I'd made with her, but since I asked her to come right over after she finished her runs for the day, she was back at my place.

I didn't know what I was expecting, but it wasn't for Smiley to walk out of the bathroom in fuchsia cheerleader shorts and a matching sports bra. For a minute, I just stopped and looked at her. Shorty made me remember how long it had been since I'd had female intimacy. The Zen music I had playing for relaxation did nothing to relax the primal male energy resonating within me.

"You don't have any clothes to put on?" I asked her.

The question came out way harsher than I intended it to. Her skin was shimmering and glowing with whatever female products she had put on. Her hair was still wet from the shower, and the way her clothes—or lack thereof—were fitting her made me roll my shoulders. Shit, how long had it been since I'd fallen between a pair of soft, plush golden thighs?

"I do have on clothes," she told me, a frown on her face because of the way I'd come at her.

"How are we supposed to talk business if you're half naked?"

"The same way we talk business when I'm fully clothed. Look, you asked me to come over here as soon as I was done jackpotting my ATMs for the day. I did. This was the only clean thing I had in my bag. Deal with it."

I stared her down for a few minutes. My eyes roamed from her head down to her full, perky breasts, then settled on the gap between her thighs. I tried not to look at how plump her pussy was, but it was sitting out there so I couldn't help it. I grunted, then tossed the magazine I'd been reading on the table.

"Whatever. I was wondering if you'd had time to do what I asked."

She huffed and nodded. She walked to her bag and dumped several iPhones onto the kitchen table. They clacked and clanged as they hit the wood and scattered across the circular, flat space.

"As much shit as I know how to do when it comes to hacking and cybercrimes, this was new for me," she said. "But I figured it out."

I took a seat at the table and listened intently while she demonstrated.

"With the way all these newer-model cars are set up with remote entry, alarm systems, GPS, rear-facing cameras, or whatever, it was easier to do this than I thought. All of this shit is mostly connected to the cellular phone networks. Each car that comes equipped with such things also has their own phone numbers. This means they can receive commands through text messages. With a few quick text messages, I can unlock a car, shut it off, start it up, or whatever. All I have to do is use a sniffing tool to listen for cellular traffic around the car. Once I figure out it's a secret phone number, I'm all in. Basically, I can steal any car I want with an iPhone."

. She walked around to where I was to show me a video on her phone of the few she'd tried her method on throughout the day. I looked at the videos where she had Jackknife holding the camera while she unlocked and started several cars in a parking deck. I wondered if people knew how easy it was to steal their car with an iPhone.

I cracked a smile. Although I knew what I'd set out to do would be dangerous, I'd done what Trigga suggested I do. I had to stop treating Caltrone like he was a regular, low-level thug on the street. He was a businessman. He was cutthroat and ruthless, but he was about his business nonetheless. He didn't do things the way your everyday hood would. He was cold and calculating. Not too many would agree with me, but just hearing Trigga give me the rundown on the man had made me realize that respect, honor, and loyalty were big in Caltrone's eyes. If he didn't respect you, you were as good as dead to him.

That was why he came after me and my people. He didn't see us as formidable. He saw me, as the Eraserheads leader, as nothing more than a pawn on the bigger game of chess. That old man owed me, and I intended to make him pay what he owed.

After Smiley finished showing me how she was going to carry out what I'd asked her to do, I fixed her something to eat since she said she was hungry. She was going to leave, but I didn't want to be alone.

I told her I would feed her. I wasn't all that hungry. I'd eaten a big meal with Stitch and his family. And since she said she didn't want to eat too heavy, I made us chicken wraps in spinach flat bread.

"Are you sure you're going to be okay with outing yourself to Caltrone?" I asked her as I washed the dishes. I handed her a plate to dry.

Smiley nodded. "I am. I'm tired of running and hiding. I want to live life, Auto. I've never lived life. My mama would want me to without having to hide and look over my shoulder."

"And you think allowing Caltrone to see you will allow you this freedom?"

She shrugged. "To be honest, I don't know."

"Trigga killed his grandsons, and as far as I know, the man hasn't batted a lash. What makes you think he'll protect you or let you go to roam free? Why be so impetuous?"

She dried the last plate, walked past me, and placed it in the dish rack, then stood directly in front of me. She wasn't close, but close enough for me to smell the body soap she'd used to bathe with. She looked up at me with no fear in her eyes. I saw bravado there, one that even I didn't have at the moment. I found myself wanting to reach out and touch her. But I didn't know her like that, so I kept my hands to myself.

"I'm not being impetuous, Auto. I'm being a part of the team. I'm an Eraserhead now. Wherever they go, I go."

Two Days Later

I was late. Behind schedule for an impromptu meeting. I headed down the opposite direction toward Centennial Park and waited. Traffic wasn't too bad as of yet. Families were rushing about, either going to the park or to Philips Arena for whatever was going on there that day. Coca-Cola memorabilia could be seen, and citizens milled about.

"Auto, the man has just left his post," Reagan said in my earpiece.

She and Jackknife had been watching Caltrone's money man, Bryan Clark. For the last two weeks, he'd met with Caltrone at the same time each day. That man kept a tight leash on his money. He was thorough, and Bryan had to account for every dollar spent. Thanks to the tracker Smiley had put on Bryan's car, we knew where they were and where they were headed. I glanced at Smiley. She had been quiet the whole time.

"You're ready?" I asked her.

"I am."

I nodded. "Let's do this then."

We sat quietly for another good twenty minutes until a white late-model Lincoln Town Car came cruising down the street. Smiley pulled out a red iPhone, and in a matter of seconds the car slowed down and then completely shut off. It was good that Smiley and I decided to sit back and watch before we got out of the truck I was in. There were two men in the front of the car in addition to the driver who exited the car, and another in the back, where I knew Caltrone and Bryan were seated.

We pulled the ski masks over our faces and nodded to one another. I stepped out of the car at the same time as Smiley. With silencers on our guns, we aimed at the two men who'd been in the front seats. Kill shots to the heart dropped them quickly. Smiley took aim and shot down the other one as soon as he tried to go for his gun. There was no need for me to try to shoot through the window since I knew they were bulletproof.

"Unlock the doors," I told Smiley.

She tapped the touch screen on her phone, and in seconds the locks on the car could be heard clicking. I ducked down after pulling the door open. Smiley had told me Bryan was always strapped, based on her observation over the last two weeks. Just as she said, bullets whizzed by as soon as I snatched the door open. While Bryan was busy shooting at me, Smiley opened the other side. She took her ski mask off and climbed in. I snatched Bryan from the car, twisting his arm until the gun fell out. His yells when I stepped on his elbow and broke his arm soothed me. I gave him a swift, hard kick to the head to keep him out while I handled business.

I slid in the back seat of the car and waited for Reagan and Jackknife to get into the driver and passenger seats. Once they did, we pulled off and blended into traffic. I sat face-to-face with Caltrone Orlando.

His eyes were on Smiley when he spoke. "I'd know the eyes of an Orlando anywhere. And being that you look like Lorenzo, it's safe to assume you're his daughter who was lost to me once he left Atlanta."

Smiley said nothing as she stared glumly at the man in front of her.

Caltrone chuckled, then turned his attention to me. I slowly pulled the ski mask from my face. For a moment, and only a quick moment, surprise registered across his features.

"Didn't expect to see me, I assume," I said to him. "Surprise. I'm not dead."

"It's not that you're alive that surprises me. It is that you, of all people, have all but kidnapped me in broad daylight in the middle of downtown Atlanta. I see fear of what I can do to you isn't on your mind."

"Fear doesn't need conquering. Fear tells you where the edge is. We all need fear. For if we don't fear, we lose our grip on reality. Tell me, old man, have you lost your grip on reality?"

Caltrone chuckled. He was dressed impeccably in a tailor-made gray suit that fit his still-athletic frame perfectly. The wing tip red bottom shoes on his feet went without a scratch. The watch on his left wrist was too expensive to name, but the golden crest ring on his finger left no doubt that he was the king of the Orlando creed.

"I fear nothing, young man, because I've seen my death and it isn't you who will take me from this earth," he answered smugly.

Only God knew how much I wanted to empty my gun in his chest to prove him wrong. My hand shook so badly that if I even blinked the wrong way, the gun would go off inside the small confines of the vehicle we were in. But I wasn't there to kill the man. I was there to rob him. The suitcases that lay on the seat beside him had everything in them that I wanted. But just for the hell of it, I shot him in his hand. Put a bullet through his palm and watched him bleed like his name was Jesus.

Caltrone snarled, gritted his teeth, then balled his lips as he held his bloody hand close to his chest. I watched as the man before me turned into a demon in the flesh. His face scowled, and his eyes darkened to the point where it looked as if a storm was brewing behind his pupils.

"Grab the suitcase, Smiley."

She did so quickly. One was already open, which was a plus. I was glad we didn't have to worry about trying to crack it open. She rummaged through the case, taking pictures of documents. I watched as she tapped on her phone quickly. She was working like a madwoman because time was not on our side.

"So you think robbing me will bring back your friends?" Caltrone growled out at me.

I shook my head. "No, not all. You took them away from me because you're a piece of shit who thinks lesser of the man who chooses to play by a different set of rules. But I intended to get some kind of payback, old man. I can't let you walk into my home and stick your hand into my refrigerator without asking."

"You really want to play this game then?"

"This isn't a game. This is my life. I do this shit because if I let you disrespect me once, you're going to do it again and again and again."

"I can't unlock this laptop while in here," Smiley interrupted me.

"Fine. Take it with us."

"You take my favorite grandchild away from me, and now you get another of my blood to do your dirty work as well? You will pay for this."

"There is nothing more you can do to me."

Caltrone grunted as blood pooled around his suit jacket and pants. "But there is. I can take the rest of your family away in an instant. I know boys like you, Auto, because I used to be that boy. I used to be that boy with no family. So I latched on to anyone I could so I wouldn't feel alone. And then finally, finally one day I found a family who accepted me as their own. But in the end, boy, in the end, I still wasn't blood. Blood will always be thicker than water. And the family I thought I belonged to, in the end, they turned on me to protect their own."

I chuckled. "What the fuck does any of that have to do with the price of tea in China, old man?"

Caltrone was silent for a second, and then he smiled. "Because I know where you belong, Auto. I know who your mother was. I knew your father very well. He used to be the leader of the Asian Dragons."

Smiley snapped the silver suitcase closed and tossed it back on the seat beside Caltrone. She kept the black one and the laptop. "We need to go now," she said.

Reagan had stopped the car. I kept my eyes on Caltrone. Did that nigga really know my mother? And my father? Or was this a mind game? The Asian Dragons, I knew of them. Knew how they got down. Jackknife had opened the right-side door for me to get out. I wanted to think it was all a part of Caltrone's way of trying to manipulate me mentally. How in hell could this nigga know who my parents were just by looking at me? Or had he been checking up on me?

"We need to go, Auto," Reagan said from outside the car.

Caltrone smiled coolly as his hand dripped blood. "Your father was a good man, Auto. Fearless leader. But you can never be him, because you align yourself with the wrong people. It is what got him killed in the end," Caltrone said.

I was deep into my own thoughts, letting his words replay over and over in my head. I had a pops? I mean, of course I knew I had to have a daddy somewhere, but did Caltrone really know who he was, or was the old bastard simply fucking with me? I didn't have time to find out.

Caltrone launched at me. The old fucker was stronger than most young men I knew. His hands were around my throat as he tried to choke the life out of me. I swung my fist and connected with his jaw. To be honest, I thought it hurt me more than it hurt him. There was a madness in that man's eyes that was unmatched by any-thing I had ever seen before.

I saw Smiley race around the car. Then I heard a zap and a buzz. Caltrone's body jerked and then spazzed as he fell to the floor. Smiley had Tasered the old man. It was high voltage, judging by the way his eyes widened and he started to slobber out of the mouth.

I took that as my cue to jet. I'd let him rattle me, and it had almost cost me. I crawled out of the car and grabbed Smiley's hand. Me and my team raced down the street to the Greyhound station, where we had parked our getaway car.

"You okay?" Smiley asked me as we hopped into the back of the Suburban.

I coughed hard. My throat burned and my eyes wa-tered, but I nodded. "Thank you," I told her, winded from the fight with the old man and the run.

She took my face in her hands and urged my neck upward so she could take a look at me. "You're bruised badly."

I may have been bruised, but something told me I was lucky to be alive, again. Still, I couldn't shake the demons I'd seen in that man's eyes.

Chapter 8

Smiley

"I'd know the eyes of an Orlando anywhere," played on rewind in the voice of a man I wanted nothing to do with. It was a new day after our hijacking. All of the Eraserheads were busy in their warehouse, preparing for the next move. After staring at my own reflection in the bathroom, I fixed my piercings: the hook in my nose, the ones around my ears, the one under my lip.

Then I glanced over my tattoos: the image of a skull mask on my ring fingers and hand that stopped at my forearm, the ones paying homage to the African Queens and my mom in Egyptian script under my breast that etched down my side, disappearing in my low-riding black leggings, and the one down my spine. I stared at my burgundy-painted lips, the dark lining of kohl around my eyes, and I looked at how my fluffy, thick, crinkled hair fell to the side over my shoulder, showing off my shaved hair.

To me, I never saw an Orlando. I didn't really know who they were until New York and meeting Code. It sickened me. It pissed me off because that meant that, no matter what I did, I'd always be linked to the bipolar-ass, alcoholic, drug-addicted killer who got kicks out of hurting me and my mom. I didn't want a thing to do with that. I looked like my mama. Fuck what anyone else had to say.

My hands began to feel foreign to me as I held them up. Same with my body. I ran my hand over the tattooed side of my hip where an O surrounded by a crown was seared into my flesh. I could feel it even though I couldn't see it, and it bothered me. I really had no intention of outing myself to that man. Family was my everything, which was why I felt alone once my mom died. When I met Code, I hadn't expected to like her so much, or to easily trust her, but I did. I guessed because I too missed family.

Sighing, I held the side of the porcelain sink in front of me. I had family, but I'd be damned if I let them change me or make me into something I wasn't meant to be. I remembered my father saying that I wasn't going to be worth nothing to the old man because I was a female, but once I turned sixteen, that lingo died away. With him, there was a sudden pride because I had learned all the things he schooled me on military-wise. There was a deep pride because I had become some pretty fixture, and that's why years later, when I learned that he wanted to take me with him to be a breeder for the Orlandos, I crept into a dark place in my mind.

I thanked my mama for saving me from him, and I thanked my mama for putting that fire in me to go after him and kill him as I did. Pills and potions.

I slid my hands in the overalls I wore with my typical sports bra top, then headed to where I had set up my computer and building station.

"I'd know the eyes of an Orlando anywhere."

Stepping over the walkway that led to the floor of the shop, I took a moment to breathe and get that voice out of my mind, then ran right into Jackknife. Old dude watched me with a frown on his face. How he stared at me had me backing up in confusion.

"Stop looking at me like Huck from *Scandal*. I'm going to start calling your ass that, just watch," I griped.

Jackknife raised an eyebrow, then gave me a smile.

"What's up?" I asked, remembering how to sign it.

That was when his whistling started, and he snatched my hand to drop my iPad on it. The screen was on, and all I saw was a note saying, We told you we would help you if you helped us, remember?

I nodded.

He typed away on the iPad again and then showed it to me. We kept our end of the bargain.

He swiped his hand, and I stared at a news article showing mug shots of Keisha and her boo, Ramon. Excitement coursed through me, had my heart beating a mile a minute, as I read about how they were charged with fraud, identity theft, and other criminal activities involving pension theft and insurance scams. I grinned. Good. That cunt funky bitch had snitched on me. We worked at a steakhouse and ran scams by skimming customer's credit cards. When the shit had hit the fan, Keisha had snitched on me to cover her own ass, and in the end, it had backfired.

I reached up and hugged Jackknife, then laughed when he put me down and started whistling and signing. My photographic memory was kicking in as I slowly understood some of what he said, which included, "Thank Auto."

Jackknife gave the thumbs-up, then used it to motion to the large truck being serviced. Black boots and jeans-clad legs peeked out from under the truck, with tools next to them. Since our hijacking, Auto had been chilling to himself. I knew that he was in his mind with the knowledge Caltrone spit out about knowing his father. I really couldn't blame him for being shook up about it. I knew from what I was learning about Caltrone that the man always spoke truth as a means to mentally fuck with you and break you down. At that time, I truly felt that was what it was, and I tried to explain it to Auto, but he wasn't hearing it.

Seeing him slightly spaced out was bothering me. It had me worried for him, because if he was weakened, then the team was too, and we couldn't afford to lose anyone else. That's why I reached out to hug Jackknife again, lost my brief moment of a smile, then went down to talk to Auto. I had other thoughts about the information we had about the warehouses, and I wanted to share that with him.

Tapping his leg with my black boot, I dropped down in a squat, waited for him to unroll from under the truck, which he didn't.

"What do you want?" he said between loud clanking.

Dudes can be the most extra sometimes. "I'm trying to say thank you for helping me out, Auto."

A long pause then the loud sound of a drill had me annoyed before he replied, "Told you that we'd hold you down, especially with you coming into the family, so you're welcome."

I figured that by saying nothing he'd come out from under the truck, but I was wrong on that. Having dealt with dudes all my life and being called a tomboy at one point, I didn't think nothing about it when I reached out and tugged at the waist of his pants.

"Auto, I'm trying to talk to you. Damn."

On some funny shit to me, I never saw a dude move as fast as Auto did at that moment. He slid out from under the truck, then pushed my hand away. "The fuck are you doing? Trying to touch my dick and shit?" he asked, more like snapped.

Tears lined my eyes as I laughed hard. His slanted eyes and golden-tinted face were a twisted-up red shade of pissed off. He kept looking me up and down and adjusting his pants, all while I held a hand to my chest, trying to catch my breath.

"I said that I wanted to talk. Stop tripping."

"If you want it, then . . ." His words cut off the moment I stared at him. "What's with you and no clothes, mama?" he added, and I punched him in the shoulder.

Crossing my arms, I stood up and stared down at him. "Look, I wanted to talk about yesterday. Don't let what he said twist your mind. He gave you a kernel, so if you feel like you need to go deeper in it, then do it on your own. Don't seek him out for anything, because that's part of the play. He'll weaken you and try to use it against you. I know this from how my own father was. So like, you have all this capability around you, use that instead. Use your team, I mean."

Auto sat laid-back, oil on his face, hands, and overalls. From how he was watching me, I figured I might have stepped over my boundaries with him, but I wasn't sure.

"It's not that deep," he said quickly.

I didn't know why I was trying, but I was. "It is that deep. After hijacking him, he's going to come for us. You know it. We all do. We need you thinking right and . . . and that put me on the warehouses. I don't think that we should look into them. I mean, if we do, send some people you don't care about, because I doubt that he hasn't ordered his people to secure it or move everything. We have to think steps ahead of him."

Wiping his hands, Auto stood, towering over me. "So you have all the answers now?"

"No. I'm just saying . . ." I trailed off.

Something was off about Auto. Not in a bad way. He was just off. It had me nervous. Had me feeling like I was being challenged. Had me feeling like if I didn't back up, this nigga was going to try to get the pussy, and I wasn't sure where that was coming from between us. But I wasn't mad about it, I realized. Since being around him and learning him some more, there was a strong quality to him that had me digging how he ran things around him. Everything Caltrone had said about Auto being about his family, I actually liked. It reminded me somewhat of Trigga, and I could see why they were close friends. I had a sense that Auto's aura was about family, and how it was put out in the world was why everyone gravitated to him, forming that family that he and they needed. It was kind of nice.

"What are you saying, Nia?" He used my real name, and that drew my attention.

"Nigga, I'm saying that you need to get your mind right and get what you're owed from that dude, but make sure it's done right and in order," I rushed out. "I'm done. You can get back to you."

As I turned away, Auto grabbed my arm and held it tight. He was so close that my shoulder touched his chest, and I could feel his heat as he shifted to speak low in my ear. He smelled like oil, sweat, and a hit of cologne.

"You need to do the same: get what you're owed. I see it like this: since your father was an Orlando, you have a stake in whatever share he had in the family," he simply stated.

Nerves played in my belly at his closeness, but what he said had me annoyed. "I don't want shit to do with that dude."

"I understand that, but you're not hearing me. I spoke to our boy last night and was privy to something that might benefit you and benefit us in what we're owed. If you go through this person, you'll be protected," he explained to me.

Turning, locking eyes on him as I looked up, I raised an eyebrow. "What are you talking about?"

Auto explained to me that I had extended family in the exact same situation and it might be smart of me to seek that line out and have a talk. After that, he let me go and went back to fixing his ride.

Staring down at Auto, I suddenly felt confused. I felt like he'd just given me a royal mind fuck, and I felt the start of a connection I didn't think I wanted. Family. Family with a dude who was feeling just like me? I didn't know where I could go with it, or if I even wanted to pursue it for real, but the thought was in my mind. If I could use it to help the Erasherheads out, and essentially erase every grimy thing my father tried to put in me, then I'd try it. But for now, I had that in my mind, and now I needed to go somewhere and think.

I was my own person. I didn't want to play chess, but curiosity had me looking into my extended family on my iPad while transferring money from Bryan Clark and Aliyah Michael's clients' business accounts. Everything seemed fine, nothing out of the ordinary, until I stared at a face that looked like mine. Piercings, tats, he had an edge that I felt in my spirit. I knew then that I shouldn't have looked him up. Why? Because now I wanted to seek him out. Fuck.

Later in the day, I sat a block away from Bryan Clark and Aliyah Michael's condo. Reagan sat next to me in the driver's seat, popping her spearmint gum, while I sat with a pack of trackers on my lap, working them. No corner was being left unturned, and since Reagan and I seemed to work well together, I was with her as we watched these people.

Several WWE-looking men exited the condo complex with Bryan and Aliyah in tow. From my view, while I clipped wires and twisted them together, I could see that they had a bounty of suitcases with them. We watched them drive off. Then we followed.

"So since we're cool and all, and now that you're part of the family—I'm calling you little sister—I have something to confess," Reagan started.

Over the weeks, I'd learned that Reagan had a big heart and a dark sense of humor. She could be very serious as well, which I connected to. Which was why when she told me that she had to confess to something, I listened.

"It's not some creepy shit, is it?" I said, trying to make her laugh.

"No, girl. It's something I can't tell Auto, and since you're the only female around now, I feel that I can rely on you" she explained.

"For what?" I interrupted.

Reagan maneuvered her car as if it were a lover. She drove that baby so well through the Atlanta traffic that it had me impressed.

"To watch my back, dang. Like, I'm going to need some help, see? I'm pregnant, and I don't want Auto to know. Not yet," she finally said with a sadness and deep seriousness in her pretty dark irises.

The fact that she had just said that she was pregnant tripped me out. I didn't know how to handle it, and I didn't know what she wanted me to do about it. It had me nervous for real.

"Like how? You want me to take you to the clinic? Who's the dad?" I asked, rambling.

When I stopped my tinkering with my bag, I looked at Reagan as we sat a stop sign, and I saw tears in her eyes.

Embarrassed, I quickly tried to correct myself. "I'm sorry. I mean, I don't know how to deal with emotions and stuff like this. Only time I dealt with this type of stuff is from hearing the girls on the block talk about how they were pregnant and wanted to go to a clinic or something. I'm sorry, Reagan."

Reagan quickly gave a shrug then drove on, not looking my way. "Nah, it's cool, no judgment from me. I don't need to go to a clinic, and I don't want to. The baby is Seymore's, and it's all I have from him now."

"Seymore's? You and he were together? I didn't even know," I said, astonished as I studied Reagan in a different light.

"Yeah, we were low-key with it. Just didn't want to pull the family in it or have them feeling funny about it since he was in a wheelchair and stuff," she explained. "I loved him . . . still love him so much, girl. I have to do what I have to do for this family, but I need to protect our baby, too, get it?"

Relationships were complicated, and when you added sex in it, shit, that's when things could go crazy, so I understood in my own way. She wanted to honor what she had with Seymore, and I couldn't blame her. If it were me, I'd have done the same. This game was wicked, and a person's life could be snuffed out quicker than a blink of an eye.

"I have your back, Reagan. I'll put in double time just to keep you covered, I mean it. I think your family will be geeked over you and Seymore though, so like, you should tell Auto."

"I can't. I need to keep working and keep busy. I just can't, not right now, girl," she said with slight panic in her voice. "Thank you though."

"You're welcome." I shifted back in my seat then put my trackers in my sling bag. "I used to like this nigga so much that I thought I was in love. Would do anything for him. Still would, though I don't love him like that anymore. So I know how it is to want to protect but feel scared about it at the same time."

Blocks of houses passed us by. Cars faded out, and we found ourselves near one of the warehouses on the list we found.

"Yeah, that's true, sometimes it was hard being in a crew with a whole bunch of dudes. I had Code, and we shared some things, but with her, it was always a wall.

You, you seem like a mad cool chick, and I appreciate you for holding us all down. I mean, yeah, everything turned up when you got in, but how your mind works . . . it's crazy," she said, quieting then pointing. "Check that out."

Ahead of us, Bryan and Aliyah were exiting their ride. Several dudes of various hues and tattoos surrounded them as they talked. I clocked every small detail that I could in my mind, holding it there for later and noting large silver packets being shown to Bryan and Aliyah.

"I know them," Reagan said at my side. "I danced for some of them back at Dame's spot. They're Los Lo. They handle some of the drug shipments for Dame. Well, Caltrone now, I see."

We both sat low in her SUV with hoodies on.

"Los Lo?" That name triggered a memory from back in NYC. I recalled everyone on the block calling my father Lo. Everywhere he went it was Lo this and Lo that, handing him packages, money, gifts, and sometimes women. I remember being so deep in stalking that nigga and learning his patterns that I watched him nut off in some big-booty Latina chick with curly hair, and now I sat here looking at a group named after him. It baffled me and pissed me off.

"They are grimy and about that dough. We need to go hit up Auto ASAP." Reagan pulled off slowly, still watching.

Turning in my seat, I took pictures in awe. "Yeah, because they just pulled out with a shipping truck and four vans. I'm dialing Auto now. We might need to check those other warehouses."

Hitting these goons up might work very well in our business, which was why I hit speed dial and got to telling Auto what we just came across. It might be a goldmine, but it might serve a bigger purpose as well.

Chapter 9

Code

The rain was falling hard outside. Just earlier today it had been sunny. I guessed Mother Nature was feeling the way I was: unpredictable. Auto and the team constantly stayed on my mind. The only one who even remotely reached out to me was Smiley, and even she had been silent over the last few days.

It had almost been three weeks since Boots had introduced his new biodegradable gun to the Asian Dragons. The Italians had been calling nonstop. Apologies and offers of monies were in abundance.

Oya and I hadn't gotten into any more fist fights, and I'd chosen to stay with her instead of across the hall in Alize's apartment. Besides, I didn't want to run into Boots, and since her apartment was connected to Boots, it would have been quite possible that I'd have to see him. Don't get me wrong, I liked the guy. I just thought I liked him a little too much. It annoyed me more than anything.

"Why are you standing there watching the rain, *chica?*" Alize asked me.

She'd decided to stay with Oya to get away from Shango since he had come to her apartment earlier. They'd had an argument that ended with her threatening his life. She walked to the kitchen—more like limped, since she was still healing from the wound to her side—scratching her plush back side. She had on boy shorts that had ridden way up her heart-shaped ass. Her full breasts were on display, but she didn't seem to mind.

I was only wearing a thin white night dress because it was kind of hot. I looked at the clock to see it read midnight. I'd tried to go to sleep, but word on the street was that Auto had robbed Papa a few days back. I didn't see this ending well for the Eraserheads, and that had me worried.

"I've always liked the rain. It soothes me," I told her.

She drank a glass of milk then nodded. She was about to say something else until someone knocked on the apartment door.

She snatched up a gun from the kitchen drawer. Oya peeked out her room door, then walked out, gun in hand. I'd armed myself as well, grabbing the gun that I'd laid on the windowsill.

"Who?" Alize barked out, then winced in pain as she'd moved too fast and her injury reminded her of it.

"It just me," Shango called out.

Oya rolled her eyes and stalked back to her room. The door slammed shortly thereafter. Alize yanked the front door open.

"What?" she spat at him.

I had to do a double take. Shango stood in only drawstring linen pants that hung low on his hips. Caramel toned abs rippled under the dim lighting coming in from the hall. His beard had been shaped up, face cleanly shaven. His eyes drooped a bit, which told me he was either sleepy or high.

"Can I talk to you for a minute?" he asked Alize.

"About what, li'l boy?"

"Is Oya in here?"

Alize frowned then huffed. "Yeah. Want me to get her?"

He shook his head. "No, I came for you."

"Now you know you can't have me without Oya."

"Ali, come on, shawty," he goaded, seeming a bit irritated that she wasn't as willing to talk as he wanted her to be.

"Your words, not mine," she snapped.

Normally Shango would be playful. He would have something snide or rudely suggestive to say, but tonight he seemed calm and genuinely looked as if he wanted to say something of meaning to Alize. Even though his eyes couldn't help the way they roamed over her body.

"Damn, woman! Can a nigga ever talk to you without you being slick at the mouth?"

Alize didn't seem to want to be bothered one way or the other, so she moved and tried to slam the door in his face. Shango wasn't having it though. He slapped a big hand against the door and shoved it back open, making Alize stumble back. The door stubbed her toe, causing her gun to fall to the floor with a loud thud. Not only that, I could tell she'd hurt her side again. She let out a flurry of cuss words before catching her balance and slapping Shango so hard I was sure that nigga was blinded.

My eyes widened, and I felt as if I were watching a movie. To be honest, I was so enthralled because I'd never seen a woman wear the emotion Alize had on her face. For a while, I thought she hated the man. I thought the same for Oya, but something about the way Alize's eyes held a fury of emotions stood out to me. Could it be possible to hate a man so much that you loved him?

Shango grabbed her wrist after she went to slap him again, lifted her from the floor as gently as he could, and laid a kiss on her that caught even me off guard. Alize was still fighting mad. She was kicking her legs, trying to free her wrists of his hold, but the longer he kissed her, the more her fight faded.

I frowned. See, that was what my mother was talking about. If you gave a man any emotion, he took away the very essence of you, the fight that made you the warrior you were. I grunted and decided to make myself disappear. I took my gun, grabbed the covers from the couch, and headed across the hall. No man was ever going to make me lose myself like that.

I was going to knock on the door but figured, to fuck with Boots, I'd just walk right in if the door was unlocked. It was. I walked in and got a contact high immediately. The smell of weed was so strong and potent that, for a minute, I didn't even see Boots looking at me from the couch.

I coughed and waved a hand in front of my face. "What in the hell is going on in here?" I asked, although I already knew.

"Close my door, lock it, and have a seat. Don't bother me. I'm working," Boots grumbled, then looked back at his laptop. In front of him lay shipping receipts, drawings of bullets and guns, and beside those lay a joint smoking in the ashtray.

"Can I sleep here? Alize and Shango having some kind of couple's moment I guess."

"You can sleep where you want. Your original sleeping area is still where it was before," he told me without looking up at me.

He was only in black boxer briefs and a wife beater. I felt out of place, so I trekked on down the hall and made my way to the hidden entrance of Alize's place and where my sleeping quarters had been designated. As I lay in bed, I wondered how soon it would be before I tried my luck with fate and got the hell on. There was only so long I could stay cooped up without saying fuck it and moving on.

When I couldn't sleep, I decided to get up and head to the kitchen. My stomach was talking to me. All the lights were out, and I didn't expect anyone to be in Alize's place but me. I walked to the fridge and opened the door. I took out a bottle of Moscato and poured a glass. I grabbed some leftover Chinese food I'd had and closed the door.

"Why are you sitting in the dark watching me, Boots? I'm not going to run away," I said while I poured the food from the Styrofoam plate onto a glass one. I knew someone was there without even having to look. I could feel his presence.

"I don't know that, but I do know that I've read you pretty well since I've known you these last few weeks. I can tell that you're antsy, and sometimes I can see what you're thinking because your eyes give you away."

I placed the plate in the microwave, set the timer, then took a sip of the wine without turning around.

Boots continued his assessment. "You're a fighter, Code. However, all this staying locked away in hiding is starting to bother you. You come from a family who prides themselves on not giving a fuck about dying. They're people who enjoy fighting to the death of them. You see, you get that look in your eyes every now and again that says you want to go face your old man, see if you can dance with the devil, and still come out alive. Am I right?"

I didn't answer him. I didn't want to. I didn't think he would understand the dynamics that made up the genealogical DNA code of being an Orlando. We didn't hide. It was disgusting and shameful to hide from a fight. Men in my family had been killed for bringing such shame to our family name. I figured that since I had already shamed the family anyway, I may as well get it over with.

I took the rest of the wine to the head, then reached to pour myself another glass. I turned and stared at Boots' outline in the dark. Even though I couldn't see him, his silhouette was a magnificent sight.

"Why do you want to protect me so much, Boots? You don't know me. What's in this for you?" I asked.

For as long as I'd known the man, he'd always shot straight from the hip. This time was no different. He leaned forward with his elbows on his muscled thighs. The moonlight showed just enough of his face for me to see his eyes.

"I want you to say fuck this loyalty shit that has been beaten into your mind and do something that won't be a suicide mission because that's the only option you feel you have left. I want you to tell me what I want to know about Caltrone Orlando's enterprises here in the A. That's the only way you're going to protect Auto, Smiley, Reagan, Stitch, and his family, Jackknife, and everyone else you hold dear to you, including your cousin Freddie."

I frowned because I was irritated. He kept asking me to betray my family, my blood family, like it was so easy to do. Like he would do the same if he were in my shoes.

I slammed the wineglass on the granite countertop, then stormed over to where he was. He knew I was a hothead, which was probably why he stood up from the sofa before I made it any closer to him. I hadn't expected him to be shirtless. That kind of threw me off a bit. He'd put jeans on, too, so the sight of them sitting on his hips, bringing my attention to the silky trail of hair leading to where his privates were held, helped in throwing me off-balance.

"If you put your hands on me, I'm going to break your arm," he threatened. "I don't like to hit women, but I'll back you the fuck up off me. Therefore, I'd advise you to rethink whatever it is you're about to do."

Images flashed in my eyes of the last time he and I had fought, and I ended up speared through a table in the end. That wasn't what stopped me, because I was afraid of no man. He could do no more to me than I allowed him to do. What stopped me from smacking the spit from him was the roaring attraction I had to the man. Something about that unnerved me.

I yelled, "You keep asking me to go against everything I know, like you would do the same if you were in the same boat, Boots. We both know you wouldn't do that."

"Listen," he belted out as he stared down at me, "you have no idea what I would do if I were in the same boat as you. But I tell you what, I'm not so loyal to anybody that I would be willing to get myself killed because I'm so fucked up in the head that I think it's the only way to go."

"I may be fucked up in the head, but so are you. You've had the unmitigated gall to show your face to Papa, Caltrone Orlando, knowing that sooner or later he's going to figure shit out. You think he's not going to look into you? Try to figure out where this kid with so much pull came from? You're just as fucked up in the head as I am," I shouted.

I was enraged. My blood was boiling to the point that I wanted to claw this nigga's eyes from his skull, because while he was calling me out for being blindly loyal, I could say the same about him. We both came from families who had lived and died in this blood feud between the two, and yet here he was in Atlanta. If what I was thinking was true, and there was indeed a connection between him and the man Papa had called Bootsy, I was sure Papa would figure it out in time.

I didn't realize I'd said all that I had been thinking until Boots' guttural command for me to shut up stopped my tirade.

"You shut up," I screamed back at him.

I didn't know what I expected to happen next, but Boots's mouth on mine wasn't it. I was so startled and taken aback that it took me a minute to realize I was enjoying the kiss. It was aggressive and primal. Something about it made me forget that I wasn't supposed to enjoy intimacy with a man, especially not one like him. I wasn't supposed to moan or tilt my head so I could get a better taste of his bourbon-laced tongue. The aftertaste of the Moscato on my tongue blended well with the aftertaste of the burnt molasses and smoky taste of the liquor on his.

My chest swelled, nipples hardened, as he yanked a handful of my hair and brought my body closer to his. Was this what Alize was feeling when Shango had kissed her? If so, then I started to think I could understand how a woman could lose herself in such a kiss. It seemed as if all the energy that made me female settled in the pit of my stomach, then trickled down to swell my vagina. I didn't even realize my hands were on Boots' arm. Didn't know when they had started to explore his chest, his abs.

Probably about the same time his right hand snaked around and gripped my ass. The grip was forceful. Made me growl then purr out, showing me a side of my femininity that I didn't know I owned. Women like me shouldn't have enjoyed what was happening this much. I wasn't a breeder, not like the other overly feminine, pretty women in my family. Only they should have been carrying on as I was. And while I was thoroughly enjoying every sexual minute of it, it scared me. Scared me so badly I broke the kiss. Heavy breathing serenaded us, probably more so me than him. I ran a hand through my wild, thick, and nappy hair, then looked up him. My hands went to my lips as they were swollen from the kiss.

I didn't like—or so I told myself—what had just transpired. The look in Boots' eyes made me squirm around. Those light brown eyes were heady with lust and told me he would do some major damage to me if I'd let him. He had control of me and the situation. That wasn't right, was it? *"Stupid girl,"* I heard my mother in my head, admonishing me.

I bolted from the front room and back into the bedroom I'd come from. Left Boots standing there aroused, because I could clearly feel it, and shut myself away from a feeling I wasn't all that familiar with. Yes, I'd had sex plenty, but none of the sex I had had come with any of what I was feeling at the moment.

I crawled into the bed and sat with my knees pulled up to my chest. I didn't move until I heard Alize's front door closing. Only then did I lie down. For the life of me, I couldn't get comfortable enough to fall asleep. I couldn't get my pussy to behave. My body was talking to me, and she was speaking loud and clear. Still, I fought the feeling. Many women had lost their lives because they couldn't control themselves. I wasn't one of those women.

Two hours later, as I looked at the red blocked digits on the clock beside the bed, I realized I was wrong. Fuck it. I'd be wrong. At four o'clock in the morning, I pushed the secret door in the closet open, trekked through Boots' office, and sought out his bedroom. Lucky me, I found it without much fuss. The light sound of his snoring led me right to him. I pushed his room door open to find his gun aimed at me. He was lying on his back, one arm placed calmly beside him while the other held a .48 Magnum aimed at my heart. I didn't think it was possible for that man to get any sexier, but with the beard and droopy eyes, low-cut Caesar with deep waves, I found that everything about Boots was sexy.

Just like the front room in his place, the room he slept in had the bare minimums as well. A king-sized bed and a TV. Black suede curtains were on the window. The floor was carpeted. The wall was lined with boots. His jeans lay tossed on a box in the corner with his shirt. On a shelf built into the wall, I saw all style of hats including the Stetsons he was known for wearing.

"You can get killed walking in on me like that, Code," he told me.

"Thought you were sleeping."

"You thought wrong. What do you want?" he snarled out.

I pulled the night dress I had on over my head and stood there as naked as the day I'd been born. "You," I told him. I walked over to the foot of the bed and stood there. He still had that damn gun aimed at me.

He quirked a brow as he watched me. "You're not going to run off this time?"

I shook my head. "No. Put the gun down."

"Nah, this is for if you decide to play with my dick again without finishing the job. I'm going to shoot you in the pussy."

I couldn't help but smile. "Put the gun down, Boots."

He shook his head. "Nah. Don't trust you."

"But you trust me enough to fuck me."

"My dick and my mind, two separate entities."

I watched the way his eyes roamed over my body. My eyes were on the bulge the black sheets did little to hide. I crawled onto the bed and all the way up his legs until I straddled his hips.

I took his free hand and placed it on my breast. "Either you're going to fuck me or I'm going to fuck you. Either way, we're fucking."

Boots grunted, then moved his hand from my breast to grab the back of my hair. When he brought my head down so I could kiss him, I welcomed it. I could feel when all the blood rushed from his head to his dick. It was like hard steel pressing between my legs.

"Reach in the drawer, grab a condom," he told me.

I did what he asked. Grabbed the golden-wrapped protection, then slid down to remove the sheet from what I wanted. I grinned wide when I saw what he was handling. I thought it was the smooth brown coloring and the way the thick veins rolled around underneath his skin that made me take him into my mouth. He had the perfect mushroomed head, and it only seemed to expand as I stroked it. I loved the way his abs clenched when I wrapped my mouth around it.

I'd watched the way Boots ate. Knew he only put raw fruits and vegetables on his plate most times. And if he decided to eat meat, it was only grass-fed beef, no pork, and minimal chicken. I was sure, as I worked my lips and tongue in tandem to swallow his dick down my throat with no hands, that if I chose to swallow his kids that the taste of his semen wouldn't be acidic and repulsive.

I found that Boots didn't care that I knew my head game felt good to him. He grabbed a handful of my hair and lifted his hips to meet my head movement. My mother had always told me I had a big mouth. I wondered how she would feel if she saw exactly what I was using it for at the moment. It would probably kill her if she knew it was someone from his bloodline I was using it on, too.

I was so into my own head as my saliva coated his dick that when he moved my head and flipped me around so that we'd be in a position to please one another in sixty-nine ways, I yelped out. But that no longer mattered when his lips sucked my clitoris into his mouth. My eyes rolled into the back of my head as they fluttered.

"Ooh, shit," I whispered.

That wasn't what I was expecting. Not the way his tongue parted my lips or the way his fingers felt as two slid inside me from behind. I couldn't even remember that I was supposed to be sucking his dick at that moment. I reached back to grab his wrist. He had my thighs cased in the crease of his arms, which had me locked to his face.

I was trying to make him let me go to no avail. I was about to come, and for the life of me, I didn't want it to be that quickly.

"Fuck, nigga. Shit. Boots, let me go," I pleaded through bated breaths.

I kept begging and moaning, he kept his face buried in my pussy, and after a few short seconds, I said fuck it. I came so hard, I thought one of my eyes were permanently stuck rolled into the back of my head. Boots flipped me back around. He grabbed the condom from my hand, tore it open, and quickly rolled it on.

He held his dick in his hand, then looked up at me. "Get on," he demanded.

There was something eerily attractive and mind-numbing about the way he said those words to me. I placed my hands on his solid chest and gently eased myself down on his dick. My breathing hitched. I chuckled low, licked my lips, then leaned down to run my tongue slowly across his lips. Me tasting my own satisfaction brought a slow smirk to his face. He bucked his hips just enough to make ride him harder and faster.

His big hand gripped and palmed my ass and spread my cheeks farther apart so he could go deeper. I watched as his eyes darted to the window then back to me.

"Tell me something, baby girl," he said.

"What?" I asked through bated breaths.

"Can you shoot a gun and ride dick at the same time?"

I titled my head, befuddled but not confused enough to stop riding his dick. "Say what?"

He put a finger to his lips to tell me to be quiet. It was only then that I realized he still had his gun in his other hand.

"There is a gun underneath my pillow," he whispered. "Grab it. I don't have to tell you what to do with it, because you already know," he told me.

I didn't really have time to think about it. Seconds later, the door to Boots' room flew open. With one arm wrapped around my waist, he sat up. I couldn't see what was going on as I grabbed the gun from underneath his pillow. All I heard were gunshots. I screamed out as Boots held me close to him. He jumped from the bed. My legs wrapped around his waist tightly as he moved.

There were four gunmen, and two were now dead on the floor with gaping holes in their chests over their hearts. Ski masks covered their faces, and being that they were dressed in all-black suits with the Orlando crest on the lapels, it was safe to assume that Papa had sent another hit squad.

Boots swung me around, then started shooting through the window. I aimed over his shoulders and took out another of the four gunmen in the house coming down the hall. The other ducked just in time as I sent a bullet chasing after him. Gunfire could be heard from outside. Boots' gunfire sounded like cannons in my ears as he rushed to his closet. As he backed inside, I tilted my body, and we both shot the man dead who ran into his room.

Boots closed the closet door behind us and tapped on the back wall of the closet. The wall slid aside, and we stepped through. Shango, Oya, and Alize were all rushing toward us, guns drawn.

"You good, boss?" Shango yelled out.

Boots nodded. "I'm good."

"What the fuck was that?" Oya asked. "Was that a hit squad?"

"Yes," Boots answered as we moved through the apartment. His strides were powerful as he rushed through the front room. Each step he took had purpose.

"What the—" Alize started to ask before Boots stopped her.

I thought it was only then that they realized we were both naked and joined at the hip. I was too far gone to be embarrassed.

"We should, ah, talk about what just happened," Shango said as Boots passed him by.

"Not right now," Boots said.

"What? Why not?" Oya asked.

Boots didn't stop moving until we made it to the bathroom by the kitchen.

He told Shango, "Call in backup. We need to move out." Then he slammed the door.

By then my orgasm was already on a hundred, and as he sat my ass on the countertop, my head fell back, smoking gun dropped to the floor. Boots' hand clamped around my neck once he laid his gun down, and I held on for dear life as he fucked me long, hard, and deeper than any man had ever done before.

For the next few days, ATL was on lock. Papa was on a rampage. He wanted Auto's head on a spike, but with the way Boots was keeping his end of the deal, Auto and the team were protected around the clock even if they didn't know it. Boots had a team on every corner. If someone even looked like they didn't belong, his people were on it. I was grateful. I was also shocked by the people in Copper Hills. There was always more than met the eye when dealing with Boots.

Those people I'd assumed were just regular, everyday hood urchins were actually all a part of his team. The gunfire I'd heard outside had all come from them, taking down the enemy who dared come into their community and cause a ruckus. Papa may have underestimated Boots. I was starting to think that he had.

It wasn't until Oya showed up with Freddie that I also realized how badly Papa wanted me found and brought to him.

I jumped up when Oya ushered him into Boots' new hideout. His right arm was in a sling, and he used a crutch because of the bullet I'd put in his right knee, but he smiled when he saw me. I did the same, and as we hugged I realized that it would probably be the last time I'd see him again.

"You good?" he asked me once he pulled back from the one-armed hug. He stumbled and hopped until he was balanced, then looked down at me.

I nodded. "They've been treating me well."

As we talked, I noticed the way he watched Oya. He was smitten. It made me smile, but not for long.

"Papa is scouring the hood for you, Maria Rosa. He's dead set on eliminating you for violation of the Orlando blood creed. Blood in, blood out. He wants you out," Freddie reminded me.

I nodded then shrugged. "I know."

"You can't hide from him. Sooner or later he's going to look everywhere, even those places he didn't think to look before. You have to get out of here. Somewhere far away."

I heard Boots before I saw him. The thud of his boot-clad feet on the carpeted floor announced his arrival. My body came alive remembering him inside of me.

"I got Code covered. You bring me that info I asked for?" Boots asked Freddie.

I looked between the two, confused. "Info? What info?"

"Yeah, what info?" Oya asked.

Freddie sighed, then reached into his inner jacket pocket. He pulled out pink and yellow slips and a folder with our family crest on the cover. "It's all there," Freddie said.

"Freddie, what is that?" I asked him.

Freddie ignored me and kept talking to Boots. "Everything you asked me for is there. Security codes to get into the buildings and keys codes to the safes."

"Freddie," I called out to him. "What are you doing?"

"My part to balance all the evil shit I've done in the name of Papa," he told me when he finally looked at me.

"He's going to kill you," I shouted.

Freddie shrugged. "I've been dead for a long time anyway."

I understood that, more than he thought I did, but Freddie still had a daughter to think about.

"What about Acindina, Freddie? You have to think about your daughter."

Freddie looked at Boots. "I kept up my end of the deal. You keep yours. And please understand the people in that village in Cuba see Papa a whole lot differently than you do. They will try to kill you because, to them, he's God. He feeds them, clothes them, provides free housing and medical care. He sends their children to schools, good schools. You don't hurt those people. Their hearts are in the right place."

Boots looked inside of the folder and then up at Freddie. "I won't have to hurt them," he said. "They won't see me as the enemy."

"They will."

Boots shook his head, then nodded at Shango. "Nah, they won't. Because I'm not going in."

Freddie frowned. "What?"

"You are."

Shango hit Freddie in the back of the head, causing him to drop to the floor like a sack of potatoes.

Oya yelled out what I was thinking before I could. "What the fuck, Boots?"

"Calm down," he said to her and me as I was about to flip my lid. "I did it for his own protection. He has a child to think about and for him to throw caution to the wind and go back to your papa's mansion would be suicide. By this time tomorrow, he will be on a private plane to

Miami then on a boat to Cuba with one of my extraction teams. He will get his daughter, and they will be moved to a safe environment for the time being."

I looked at Oya while she knelt beside Freddie, and although I'd been pissed that Boots would ask Freddie to sign his own death warrant just a few moments earlier, I appreciated the method to his madness more so now than ever before.

Chapter 10

Boots

Standing in the office of the new place I'd moved to, I held Machiavelli's *The Prince* in my hand. The man was an insane genius. He said, "One has to remark that men ought either to be well treated or crushed, because they can avenge themselves of lighter injuries, of more serious ones they cannot; therefore the injury that is to be done to a man ought to be of such a kind that one does not stand in fear of revenge." What I took him to mean was that a man has to understand that he can be treated right or wrong to the point of being destroyed.

I mean, in life that's a given, because if a man can brush off the little things and can't drop the big things, then the way to handle it is to get revenge. My family life was founded on this principle alone. The idea is not some weak shit. It takes a powerful mind to take in the knife wounds from being stabbed in the back then turn around to make that shit even. A man who can do that is a true leader and a true king and has that real type of power.

That lesson was why I was here in Atlanta, and why I was working for my pops, Bootsy, also known as Raheem King-Kweli. There was, and still is, a lot of history that went down between the Kulu Kings and the Orlandos, shit that I have to honestly say can only be scrubbed out through bloodshed and war. There were wrongs and evils committed on both sides. There was shit no one knew about until years later of hunting that could have stopped the war, stopped the two families from breaking up, and stopped the death of my brother and his wife, but that's a story for another time.

Until then, my role here was always simple. I was the protector of the protector until I could deliver the peace for my pops, not on some kumbaya shit but on some real street honor truths. That was my agenda and always would be. Until then, I'd break down the foundation of a man who made it his own mission to wipe out my people. Why? Because fair exchange was no robbery, and sometimes a king could be so blinded by power that he forgot the truth and forgot the dogma of the streets. Thanks to the inside man my pops had at the Orlando compound, I knew the hit squad was coming. I'd been waiting for them. Glancing at Code, thinking of the way she felt around my waist as I let those rounds off into people I had been waiting to come erase me, I smiled.

My crew and I supplied bullets to bad people. Okay, so I was not a nice dude. I created weapons and supplied that contraband to bad people and sometimes government people.

I was a bad dude.

However, how I ran my supply and demand, and how I made sure to build my profit on a corporate level, showed that I was also a neutral dude. That made me a businessman above everything else.

This part of how I ran things contributed to the overall arch of my agenda. I caused wars, then I caused dialogue, which then caused some people to awaken. Was it good? Fuck no, but neither were my people in the streets dying due to the big, bad man bringing drugs and contraband in the streets. Same went with my people in Africa, London, Jamaica's Kingston, Paris, and more. This was some global shit, and I aimed to step into that role and wake up the devil himself. Check it and stay woke.

Looking around at my people, then settling my eyes on Code and a still-knocked-out Freddie, I closed my book and set it on my desk.

I told Oya, "I want to give you my apologies for not keeping you in the know. If you chop the limb off the body of a spider, sometimes another one grows in its place. The same for the head. You and Shango are my heads, along with Sweetness in Paris. If anything goes down with me, you all are the people to take my place. So I'm sorry, Oya. In this, I had to keep only Shango in the mix, because in connection with Freddie the less you knew, the safer you and Freddie would be while you were mixing with Caltrone."

Oya's big gray eyes were a mixture of sadness and hurt. I knew she felt hurt by my choice, but the trust was still there.

"*Não tô nem aí!* I don't give a damn about what would have happened to me," she said, swiping her hand through the air with passion in her voice. "You trained me well. However I don't like it, I get it."

"We would never accept anything happening to you, Oya," Shango added, watching her intently before glancing back at Alize.

When Alize was shot, Shango was by her side until she woke up. I knew my boy well. Even though he sometimes couldn't control his dick, his loyalty always was for two women only: Alize and Oya. Would he call it love? No. I would, but he would never admit that shit, so I wouldn't throw it in his face.

Oya glanced between me and Shango, then gave a warm smile while placing a hand on Freddie's shoulder. "I know, and I feel the exact same way, Shango."

"All right then, family, this is what we'll be doing. Freddy just reiterated that Caltrone is not going to stop until he finds Code. As you all just saw, he gives not one fuck about any of us. We're just rooks to be taken out, but not before he gets Code. Now is that how business should be done?" I asked while watching my crew with my arms over my chest.

Everyone broke out into knowing smiles except for Code and Freddie, who only shook their heads.

"I agree, so I guess it's that time to call a meeting between me and Senor Caltrone. Knowledge is power, and he has done bad business with me by trying to steal what was not meant to be his yet. Ink was not even placed on the contract." I tsked and shook my head. "Yes. It's time to handle some business."

Code slid up in her chair. She wore a pair of jeans from Oya and a top from Alize. Nestled behind her back was one of my pistols I officially started letting her rock around us.

"Papa is definitely going to be going after every place he may have trailed you. The fact that you have us in a neighborhood he wouldn't even think you'd be in was smart," she explained.

"Exactly, which gives us time to get our shipments together and prepare for a one-on-one. What I need from the two of you is a verbal agreement. I need to know that you two are down for us securing your safety. We don't have time for any changing of the mind shit and having you two back out on us. Are you two really down for this? Because once the smoke clears, Freddie is going to Cuba and I'm sending Oya with him."

Oya stood with a warrior's pride in her eyes. "I'll protect him and his little girl with my life."

"I know you will. I'll need you to also set up a satellite location down there to continue business. Since you won't be able to make contact with me, I'm trusting you to be in touch with Sweetness. I'll get any information you have from him and the few people we have down there," I explained.

"*Sim*. I'll do us proud," she said.

Sim meant yes in Portuguese so I nodded my understanding to Oya. Glancing back to Code, I saw the conflict in her eyes. I understood it. She was right, if it were me in their shoes, it would be difficult to drop family, but I'd learned in these years of doing what I was doing that not everything was as it seemed, and not everything got tied up in a pretty bow. That's why you had to step out on faith, and that's all I was asking them to do.

"This ain't easy by far. We'd die for family in a minute, but with Papa . . ." Code looked conflicted before continuing, "Right now, all I got is Freddie, and he's following my lead. He's my blood. I know his loyalty is with me and always has been. As long as I'm rocking with you guys, he will too. He just wants to make sure his daughter is safe," Code said. "You've been protecting my people. So if for no other reason, for that I'm down. You have my word."

I watched Oya rest a hand on the back of Freddy's head where Shango had hit him. There was something in how she handled him, and there was something in how he'd been receptive to all the help she gave, that let me know they'd be fine together.

"Then you will be working with my people to get operations going. I know how you Orlandos don't dig sitting in wait, so I won't have you do that anymore, but stay low while you work, okay?" I added, moving around the desk.

Code nodded. Then we moved on to discussing setting up a meeting with Caltrone.

It took two days before I called Caltrone's people and set up a meeting. I chose midtown as the location. I figured being surrounded by money would keep the lion tamed, meaning me. When Caltrone suggested a location of his choice, I declined it. He was doing bad business.

That didn't mean that I had to. I picked a hipster restaurant, known to the area for their brewery and delicious food at ridiculous prices.

Ascot hat cocked low, dark jeans with my black boots as well as a silver button-down shirt with a black vest, I sat in a reserved room with Shango and Oya as I usually did. All pretenses were the same. We knew nothing as far as they knew, and we'd make it look that way as well. After the meeting, both Freddie and Oya would officially be ghost. I had to put that on pause though because I needed her here with me and so we could fit him for the 3-D FlexiPRINT casting for his left arm and right leg. Once he got to Florida, it would be done and waiting for him so he could swap it out, heal faster, and have better movement despite his injuries.

Scents from the kitchen would've had my stomach growling, but I wasn't here for food. I did order a premium beer, and that's what I was casually sipping when the Orlandos finally made their way into the room.

In my ear, the sensual voice of Code came through my earbud. "Papa has two cars casing the restaurant: one out front, and one close to the back entryway. But that's not it. From what I saw by Oya's camera angle, in the restaurant he has two of my cousins blended into the regular customers, as well as two walking back and forth acting like casual people in front of the restaurant."

"Not even shocked about it. We're covered as well. Just keep being those eyes, *mamacita*," I said in a low rumble.

"Stop it," she curtly said.

It made me chuckle as I thumbed my nose and watched Caltrone being led in by his bodyguard, Mark, and a newcomer, a female.

"Shredder, what's your zone look like?" I muttered.

His usual stuttering started, then went away, and it gave me a sense of normalcy. "We . . . we . . . got it clear, boss. No worries or problems."

We were all back to doing what we do best, being con men and women, and it felt good. Shredder and Code were in my noon and evening positions. That meant Code was in the front, hidden outside in a building across from the restaurant, and Shredder was in the back. I had other crewmembers positioned as well. Alize was with Freddy back at our other hideaway to get him healed up.

"Good. Check back on this channel shortly," I said while standing.

Taking my hat off, I gave a nod to the men in front of me and smiled. "Well, look who's all bowed up and a sight for sore eyes? I think it's me, and it's good that you all have trusted me enough to try to kill me in your face. Let's have a sit-down, shall we?"

Waving a hand near some empty chairs, I watched Mark look me up and down with a scowl on his face as he passed me. Caltrone took a seat with a smug look on his face, and then his female bodyguard moved to stand behind him. In front of him, Mark positioned himself in a wide-legged stance with his hands in front of him.

"Say what you need to say, homie. We don't have time for some fuck-boy shit," Mark said and laughed.

Fuck-boy shit, huh? I sat down with cool ease.

"Mr. Sunjeta," the female before me interrupted, "Caltrone believes that you were not up to par in the nego-tiations of your bullets. Because you reached the deadline on delivering what you had promised—"

"Let me stop you right there. Key words were just spoken: negotiations and deadline. As of a few days ago, it came to my attention that a shipment of mine was intercepted by a group of individuals paid to steal what was mine," I said, then reached for my beer and took a slow sip. Seemed like this motherfucker wanted to be disrespectful and speak through his guards. That was cool. I could play that game.

I watched Caltrone make a hand gesture, and Mark stepped back to listen. He watched me as he leaned over, then smirked, standing. "That is not our problem. You just admitted you don't have the merchandise you promised. We don't do business with people like you who can't do anything simple such as keep his eye on his own product. Where they do that at, nigga?"

Out the corner of my eye, I could see Oya and Shango doing everything in their power not to respond. Me, I didn't care what this hating-ass bitch had to call me. I held the cards, so bitches who were held by leashes could continue yapping. I gave not one fuck.

"Let me be frank here, since all respect seems to be out of the window at this point." Setting my bottle down, I gave a sigh, then adjusted my cap. "You motherfuckers think that the only eyes in the A belong to you. I'm a businessman. Just as you check my background, I do the same, and the city has been talking. The city says Caltrone Orlando fucked around and tried to steal what did not belong to him. In the midst of that, he allowed what was mine, what was only in talks of being contracted to be his, to be taken due to some fuck-boy greed." Shifting back in my chair, I rested my elbow on the arm of my chair and laid a finger against my temple. "Did I make that up? Or nah?"

Mark's jaw clenched in fury, his fist balled up. "You don't disrespect us with this bullshit, nigga. You hit the deadline. You owed us that shipment, and you failed."

"I failed? I can't fail with something you all tried to take. Not only that, but you tried to double-cross me in the middle of it and caused some battle in the streets to go down that had you losing your precious Maria Rosa. Damn, if only you had been professional, everything would have turned up roses, my nigga." Narrowing my eye into thin slits, I thumbed my nose and sarcastically laughed.

"You owe me, and I deserve nothing but respect in being an ally as a businessman," I said, leaning forward. "And if that makes you want to kill me, then let me remind you that you don't have my bullets and I'm the one who makes them. I have the capabilities to make more. Don't think that's my only supply or that I don't have a set of them pointing on you right now."

Like that, lines of red flickered then focused on Caltrone's chest, his head, then the bodyguards. It looked like Christmas up in that bitch, that's how many red scopes were on that nigga. Satisfaction had me smiling. I knew it was just a futile attempt to show him that I was serious, but I knew if he wanted to, those same scopes could turn on me.

"I don't take kindly to being double-crossed or people attempting to kill me, so do we talk business or do we go after each other like two enemies? Either way, I'm more then capable of holding my own," I added for good measure.

Silence filled the room. Caltrone was red-faced, but he wouldn't be who he was if he didn't have to keep the upper hand. Mark moved across the room like lightning, and my hand moved up to hold off any shooting. I kicked back my chair to avoid his blows, then jumped out of the chair. This fool came at me on some super hulk shit. I dodged and then allowed my knee to land in his stomach as he landed a blow to my face. Boxing this cat had my juices boiling. I laughed at his shock, then hit him with another punch to the face.

"Pussy. I enjoy playing with pussy. Keep on and I'll make you my fuck boy, nigga," I taunted.

This fool seemed like the type who'd spiral with any threat to his masculinity. That's why I said what I did, and I enjoyed the results. We went slamming into a wall. I blocked what I could and took each hit like a pro. But his next blow was so intense that it had me spitting and turning to return the blow, causing him to fly backward near Caltrone.

"Marco!" Caltrone shouted, which had his boy pausing in attacking me.

I watched Caltrone stand and snap his fingers, motioning for Mark and his female guard to follow him.

"I am a man of honor, and I know this. Word on the streets says you have my granddaughter and have had her for quite some time. As a businessman, I believe that you have an obligation to return what is mine."

"That is true, senor," I said, rubbing my jaw and smiling. "However, there's just that pesky little issue of you attempting to steal my bullets and getting them lost, as well as you coming into my territory unannounced. You took from me, so I take from you. Guess that means that I'm not open to any negations. Ooh wee, this is better than a poke in the eye with a sharp stick. Good day, sir." Grabbing my beer, I walked to the opposite end of the room, and then I headed out to my ride where Shredder sat.

I heard Shango say, "That concludes our business. You have our number."

Closing the door to my Escalade, I waited for word.

"They've left, and everything is clear on his front," Shango said in my ear. "Oya is coming to your ride. I'll be on the side of the business, ready for you all to trail me."

As he said that, Oya hopped in. She slammed the door and looked at me, upset. "Thanks, Shango. Code, what do you see?"

"Nothing yet. No one has stopped their patrolling, so don't leave yet. They are watching and will trail," she let me know.

I held my hand out to give Oya dap. I mouthed, "Thank you," then spoke to Code, "We all figured that. What I need to know is, can you exit safely without being seen?"

"Yeah, I can. You lost your temper, didn't you? Let him goad you?" she asked.

Laughter came out, and I relaxed back, rubbing my jaw. "Yeah. He knows you're with me. He just doesn't know where I have you, so it's going to be some problems kicking off, but I'm good with it."

"It's always problems with Papa. All eyes have left," Code said as I listened to her move from her spot.

"See you at the base. Shredder is waiting on you," I let her know, since he had dipped to let Oya drive me out.

I wasn't sure how Caltrone would come at me next, but I didn't care. I had a good amount of information on him. The money wasn't what was important to me. Having his locations mapped out was. With Code and Freddy helping, breaking Caltrone's foundation was already underway. I was good with that.

Chapter 11

Auto

Everybody in my old neighborhood—elder folk, women, children—I'd made arrangements for them to move on. We had to be sure that everyone around us was safe. I couldn't afford to lose another life. Couldn't afford to have Caltrone take anything or anyone else from me. All I wanted was to get back the money I'd lost and make his life as much hell as I could. I'd told Stitch to take his family and disappear. I'd made sure they all got on a plane and got the hell out of the country.

Since we had robbed Caltrone, I'd moved the rest of the team to a new compound, per se. We lived underneath a mansion in Stockbridge. On the outside, it looked like a simple mansion for sale in the upscale neighborhood of Lake Spivey. Since I'd purchased the house from an auction for bank foreclosures, I'd had a team build a bunker underneath the place. I couldn't have anyone just build it for me, as people talked a hell of a lot. That meant I only used the team of builders Armando had recommended courtesy of his network.

I'd never thought I'd have to use the compound so soon, but I was glad I had it built. Most people would call it a bunker or a bomb shelter. With the way I'd had things set up, it looked more like an upscale hotel on the inside. We had enough water and nonperishable food stocked to feed us for an extended period of time: canned goods, dry cereal, rice, flour, and potatoes. Thanks to Trigga's connections in the U.S. military, we also had MREs: meals ready to eat. I was taking no chances and wanted to leave no bases uncovered. From this point on, every move I made counted.

It was late at night. The cameras we'd set up in the trees across from Caltrone's warehouse showed us how his team moved. I would have thought that the biggest warehouses, where most of the guards were, would be where Caltrone hid his most prized merchandise. That wasn't the case. After Smiley and Reagan had done some more research, we found that each of the warehouses we had found the layouts for in the suitcase were just decoys.

They were only there for show. Yeah, they housed merchandise, but the merchandise could be easily replaced. If Smiley and Reagan hadn't put trackers on some of the Los Lo's trucks, we would have never found the main distribution warehouse. It was nestled away on a hidden street in Lovejoy. I would have never thought to look to Lovejoy, of all places, for a hideaway location of drugs and guns. For one thing, Lovejoy was considered the city of peace. I guessed that made it a perfect hiding spot for a man as smart as Caltrone. It was a small neighborhood community whose politicians could be bought just like any other town's politicians.

"It's twelve thirty now, Auto. In another thirty minutes, the four at the door will switch out for two. The inside of the warehouse will switch rotations as well. It will go from ten men manning the stations to twenty. While it may seem like you would have to worry about the men on the inside, the men you should worry about are on the outside. No way you're getting past those two. They're locked and loaded and have on full body armor," Smiley informed me.

I held a case of Boots' bullets in my hand and knew full body armor would be the least of our worries. The white steel walls of the building were illuminated under the glare of yellow lighting. Gray and black trucks moved in and out. Men and women moved merchandise from the back of trucks. Others stood around shouting orders as armed men stood stoic, more than likely itching to kill somebody if need be.

"The two men who will be at the door, are they there all the time?" I asked.

"Nah. From what me and Reagan gathered, they each take thirty-minute breaks, but one is never far away from the other."

"Where does the first one go when he leaves?"

"He usually goes around the other building with one of the chicks who work in the building. Spends most of his time trying to have anal sex with her. She never likes it, so he gives in and—"

I cut her off. "I don't need that many details, baby girl."

She chuckled softly, and it made me roll my shoulders.

"Auto, listen, I . . . I have an idea," Smiley said.

I turned to look at her as she walked from the kitchen of the compound. She had on clothes today. That made me happy. I didn't have to deal with my dick wanting to sample what she showed off. It wasn't her fault she was born with that body, nor was it her fault that I couldn't control the chemical reactions my body had around her. Still, I was very happy with the full-body overalls she had on.

I sat up from the slouching position I'd been in on the couch, then nodded in her direction. "What's on your mind?"

"I know you told me that I had to let Code go, but—"

"If this involves anything Code has suggested, I don't want to hear it," I told her, cutting her off.

"No, Auto, just hear me out."

"If this has anything to do with Code, I don't want to hear it," I repeated myself, this time with a deeper baritone in my voice.

Smiley's eyes narrowed. Her face frowned a bit, and then she licked her lips and sat beside me. "You're so bent on erasing her from your life that you won't even listen to what I have to say?"

"Why would I listen to anything about a woman who betrayed me?"

"Did she really betray you, Auto? Or did she make a mistake? We don't get the method to Code's madness, but I don't want to act like I understand what it is to grow up in a family like the Orlandos, either. It's hard to undo something that you've been used to your whole life. She couldn't just walk away and turn on her family—"

I stood up in the middle of her Code defense and walked to my office. I slammed the door behind me. I had no desire to hear how hard it was for Code to do what she'd chosen to do. Who knows, maybe I didn't understand what it was like to grow up with blood relatives, but I knew that I would never do anything to jeopardize the one I'd built from the ground up, either. Code didn't give a damn enough to protect us before, so there would be no way in hell I'd trust her judgment now.

I opened the top drawer of my cherry-oakwood desk and pulled out a black picture book. Inside were photos of the people I held close to my heart, both alive and dead. I opened it to the very first page and looked into the face of a smiling woman. Her skin had the perfect lightly golden glow. Long, silky ink black hair fell down her back and around her shoulders. Full bangs covered her forehead, and almond-shaped black eyes stared up at me. The name on the back of the picture was Amina. She was dressed in skimpy black shorts, tall heels, and a simple white bustier. She was my mother, and the photo was all I had of her.

There were times when I wondered how my life would have been different if she had been alive. Would I have still grown up in the hood? Would I have known who my father was? Would he have wanted to know who I was? How might my life have been different if fate hadn't stolen her away from me?

I stayed locked away in my office for the next couple of hours. I studied delivery times and routes. Made little notes on the maps we would be following. I didn't know Lovejoy that well, so I made sure everything—time, location, people—was all ready to go.

My private phone rang out, jarring me from my thoughts. "Speak," I answered.

"Ah, Auto, me friend. Is our deal still intact?" Nicola asked me, his Russian accent thick. I could hear traffic in his background.

"It is. As long as your men are in their location when I need them."

"They will be."

"Then there is no need to question the deal."

"You know, Armando and I spoke before, and we've determined that you either are crazy or have a death wish. Which is it, me friend?"

"Probably both. Either way, I'm not backing down. Have your men at the location tomorrow night at the agreed-upon time. I'll get my money, and you get the drugs and guns you want."

"Have you heard from that asshat Armando since our last meeting?" Nicola asked me.

"I have."

"Has he come on board with this also?"

"He has."

"You know, Auto, I have a good mind to try to talk you out of this. Since I have known you, you have shown

great character and restraint on lots of things. I do have
a gut feeling you won't make it out of this alive," he said
solemnly.

For as much as a tyrant as Nicola was in the underworld,
he had always respected me and treated me fairly. He gave
me a chance when not many would. That was why he was
one of my top clients. I got a bit nostalgic thinking about
how just a few weeks ago life had been simple. Chopping
up cars, rebuilding them, and selling them was the hobby.
Erasing identities and bank accounts was where most
money came in. Life had been good for the Eraserheads.

"Nobody is going to miss me anyway, Nicola. I've got
no blood family, and the family I have made has been
shaken up so fucking bad that I doubt we'll ever be the
same."

"If ever you want to escape and disappear to Russia,
my friend, let me know how I can be of service. Any fool
brave enough to go after Caltrone Orlando deserves to
hide in peace and solitude for the rest of his life."

I had to chuckle. "Thank you, Nicola."

"All thanks to you, me friend. See you tomorrow night."

A loud banging at my office door alarmed me as I
pressed the end call button on the touch screen. I yelled
out, "What?"

"Wolf and his brothers are here," Reagan yelled back.

"Okay, I'll be out in a minute."

"Armando has sent the armored trucks as well."

"Okay, good."

"What do you want us to do about that other thing?"

I sighed and then got up. There was no need for me to
keep speaking to her through the door. I walked around
the desk, then pulled the steel door open. Reagan stood
there with a half-smile on her face. I'd noticed that no
matter how she smiled, she couldn't hide the sadness in
her eyes. I knew that feeling all too well.

"What other thing?" I asked her.

"You were supposed to meet Boots today about a trade."

I shook my head and waved my hand as I walked. Boots had to be out of his damned mind if he thought I was just going to hand them over. "I need him to offer me something since he's the reason shit is fucked up."

"Thought Caltrone was that reason."

"No. If Boots was as astute a businessman as he proclaimed, he would have never switched his shippers out like that without a detailed background check into their tawdry history," I said.

Smiley looked at me and rolled her eyes. Clearly, she was mad at me about earlier. I made a note to speak to her later.

"So I changed my mind about meeting him today. Maybe tomorrow."

Reagan laughed. "You're never going to give that man his bullets back, are you?"

Before I answered, I watched Smiley pull a phone apart. She studied the back of it, then removed the battery. She placed one of her sticker-trackers inside and snapped the covering back on. Her face was set in a frown of determination as she worked. Since the day I'd met her, it was easy to see she took her work seriously.

"Why don't you tell her you like her?" Reagan asked, catching me completely off guard.

I stopped walking to look at her. "What?"

"Smiley. Why don't you tell her you like her?"

I gave a quick nonchalant shrug. "Because I don't like her, not like you're thinking."

"You're lying. You watch her all the time."

I frowned a bit and decided to evade her question and ignore her useless observation. "Where're Wolf and his brothers?"

"In the back room waiting on you. You know we all

made bets about how soon it takes before the two of you get together."

I frowned before responding. "You and all the rest of them can kiss my ass."

Reagan didn't take my words to heart as her laughter followed me all the way down the hall.

For the rest of the night, I kept the team abreast of how everything was going to go down tomorrow night. I didn't have room for error, and I made sure they knew that. After dinner was done and everyone was off doing whatever it was they did, I grabbed a set of car keys and headed out.

"Smiley, I need you to ride with me somewhere," I told her.

She cast a quick glance at me as I stood on the third step leading to the outside. "Nah, I'm good," she said.

I sighed heavily. "Come on. I need to have someone ride with me."

"Take Reagan."

"I didn't ask Reagan. I asked you."

She twisted her lips and cocked her head to the side. "Why do you need to take me? My opinion don't matter obviously."

"It does matter."

"But not unless you agree with it, right?" she asked sarcastically.

"Look, I'm sorry, a'ight? I'm just not in the mood to hear shit about Code . . ." I stopped midsentence when Smiley stalked up to me.

"You do realize that half your people won't even come to you and talk to you because you're such a dick as of late. You run around snapping at everybody, and it has everyone on edge. You need to chill or some shit. All the tension won't be good for what we have to carry out tomorrow."

I knew I'd been a dick. That was because I knew I was walking into a lion's den with my team in tow. But before I let them be consumed by my rage, I would do everything in my power to make sure they all walked out alive.

"Are you going to take this ride with me or not?"

"You're a dickhead, Auto."

"Yeah, so?"

She put her backpack on her shoulder, placed a cap on her head to hide her eyes, then brushed past me to head up the stairs. I watched her ass the entire time we climbed the steps. Once we reached the top, she pushed on the wall in front of her, and we stepped out into another dark room. I bumped around the room until I found my way to the left wall, then pressed my hand against the flat-screen panel until heat burned my fingertips. The ground above us opened up. I let Smiley climb the ladder above first, and then I followed. We both looked back as the ground moved to cover the empty pool again. It looked as if the yard were moving, but it wasn't. The architectural design of the place would always amaze me.

"Where are we going?" Smiley asked me after we got in a van disguised as a painter's truck.

"To see a man about some guns."

The meeting didn't take long. We met in the back of an old red and black motel in Marietta. The signs were hanging off the building, and the only way I knew it was functional was by the dim lighting coming from a few rooms in the two-level building. It was the kind of place where seedy transactions and drug deals gone wrong took place. The back was mostly dark, only illuminated by a lone-standing streetlight. The road behind us had been blocked off some time ago, which was why I had to take the long way around and come in through a back road. Loud porn could be heard through the thin walls, or it could have been someone having sex. Either way, by the woman's loud, shrill moans, I would have said she was enjoying it.

Three masked women exited the truck. They all had on purple leggings that showed every curve they owned. Black leather jackets contoured to their breasts and waists, and combat boots adorned their feet.

"You have a package for me?" one asked, her voice like silk.

I nodded at Smiley, and she reached inside of her backpack to pull out a shoebox. She walked over and handed it to the Amazon in front of us.

"It's all there," Smiley said.

"Good. Follow me."

I made a move to follow the woman, and the other two women cocked their guns and aimed them at me. The leader turned back to me and said, "I only do business with women, which is why my connect told you to bring a woman with you. The young woman can follow me."

"But I'm the one who needs to see the merchandise," I countered, a bit pissed off at being played.

"She'll show you once she returns. I'm sure she's smart enough to tell you if all the guns are there."

I was about to say something else, but Smiley stopped me. "I got it, Auto. I know guns like I know my gadgets. I got it," she assured me.

I frowned and looked up when rain started to pour down on us. I nodded, and she rushed off with the black Xena. I sat in the van for a good twenty minutes before Smiley emerged again. I watched the woman escort Smiley to the van as she spoke on a cell phone. Once they got to the van, Smiley snatched the back door of the van open, and the women started loading the guns. While they worked in the rain, the leader walked around to me and placed the phone to my ear.

"Speak," she demanded.

"Who's this?" I barked into the phone.

"Bruh, you know you don't have to do this. You don't have to dive off this cliff headfirst. Put a parachute on," Trigga said as soon as I asked the question.

I kept my eyes on the woman as I spoke. "I know I don't, man. But I can't let it go and I won't. Not until I make this nigga respect me."

"He may never respect you though."

I sat in silence. I watched Smiley direct the two other women on how to place the guns in the truck while Trigga tried to get me to think about what I was doing. He never tried to talk me out of it, but he wanted me to think. He wanted me to make sure I had all my ducks aligned before I started shooting. I appreciated the sentiment.

I flexed my hands as the muscles coiled in my arms. Anger lived in me, took up residence like it was a part of my five senses. I watched Smiley hop into the van. She was dripping wet, and I thought about what Trigga had said to me. There was only one conclusion I could come up with.

"Then he's going to have to kill me."

Chapter 12

Smiley

After I finished loading the truck, I passed a folder to Auto with additional content inside that he needed. I sat there with him as he thumbed through the folder and watched how cut off he was. I knew from his lingo that he was speaking to Trigga, and it bothered me. Resting my cheek on the back of my hand, I played with the ends of my Marley braids, then covered my mouth with my hand in thought. My reflection was that of a hooded person with a skull mask on due to the tattoo on the back of my hand. It jarred something in me and had me deep in thought about Auto.

I was digging Auto. It was something that I wasn't expecting, and it was due to his loyalty to family. I had thought he had touches of Trig in him, but right now—right now—I was thinking this dude was mad nutters and not in a good way, man. I wasn't feeling how off he was lately. How he was reacting in his emotions but not in a smart way, in my opinion. Sun Tzu basically says that when a leader doesn't seek our counsel or listen to it, it can end in failure. Auto had done some of that with Trigga. But when I went to him about Code, all shit went ice.

Dude cut me off with no respect. I mean I got it, and I was salty, but he needed to listen. Ever since Code betrayed him, he had been off his game. He hadn't been thinking clearly, and it bothered me. I couldn't really say all that to him because I just joined the crew. All I knew about running a crew and doing all this street business shit was everything my father taught me in relation to military and hunting.

So it bothered me. I kind of felt out of place because I was new but also because I knew, hell we all knew, that Code was his ace boon and they needed each other. She was his go-to for a reason, a second leader for a reason, and now Auto was broken. It was frightening. He was a mastermind who was making incredible choices but also being faulty. That shit could get us all killed, something I didn't sign up for, and I believe he knew that, which was why he sent Stitch and his family away.

Now he was talking about Caltrone was going to have to kill him? Part of me wanted to call bullshit. The more I was able to learn about him, the more I knew that what he said had to be some punk shit someone who was still lost would say. But I wouldn't tell him that. I now trusted in him too much to do so, and I was still new.

I just didn't know what to do, so I chose to say it instead once he got off his cell. "'The proximity of an army causes prices to go up; and high prices cause the people's substance to be drained away.'"

Trees rolled past us as we sped away with our contraband. Music, Drake, was droning on, and Auto had a serious look on his face before he gave me a side look twice.

"What? What does that mean?" he incredulously asked.

Shifting in my seat, I looked at him for a moment, then reached down between my legs to dig in my backpack. I had various trackers, many that blended in with phone batteries, some that were crafted to look like wires for the phone, and my usual stickers.

"I mean that we are messing with a well-oiled machine, Auto, that requires going after it with bigger means than what we have."

Auto gave me a look. "Okay, and? You've been doing your homework."

"Yeah, man!" I said, taking a puff from my electric hookah. The scent of cherry filled the truck, and I glared at him. "I had to, because if you go against someone like him, you need to know all your angles. What you have us doing, it's dangerous."

I could tell that he was ready to go off just by how tense his body was and how his large hands gripped the wheel, but I quickly interrupted that and turned in my seat to look at him head-on.

"You need your focus. You need Code. I know you don't want to listen to me about it but—"

"Then why are you pressing, Nia?" Auto barked at me.

How he used my real name grated my nerves, only because how he said it all had so much bass in it that it had me silent. I wasn't trying to fight him, because he was bruised, but fuck it. I wasn't about to die for a cause that our leader wasn't working out right. So I shifted in my seat, crossed my arms, and went back to smoking my electric hookah as we drove down the now-wet streets.

Rain kissed our ride, leaving beads of water droplets over the van. The occasional car would shine its beams of lights on us while passing by, and I could swear the tension in the truck was thick. I wasn't about to be bullied by him not wanting to listen, so I stopped smoking and put my hookah pen away.

Sliding my hands between my thighs, I gave a sigh. "Look, you do need her, and you know it. It's not a bad thing. From what I heard from your crew, you two were like one brain sometimes. You need her. You need to bring her back, Auto. She can help us do this on an additional level of where you got it. I think it's crazy that—"

Auto cut in, then swerved the truck to park it at the entryway of his mansion. "It's crazy that you just can't let this shit be what it is, Smiley. You find out she's your cousin and now you're all gung-ho about doing whatever you can to be by her side? The Orlando she is doesn't give a fuck about you. She used you like she used us, Smiley, and the Orlando she is would have taken you to be bent over to breed the next generation of killers. So the fuck do I look like bringing her back? She aided in wiping us out and had no loyalty to us in the end. Back up off this shit when you don't really know everything."

"Why can't you just accept that people make mistakes?" I asked, using my hands to plead with him. I stared at him intently.

What he had said did cross my mind at one time, but I had dealt with so much that I had opted not to believe any of that. I trusted that she had never said a thing about me to the Orlandos, and that was verified when I revealed myself to him. So, though he tried to twist my dedication to Code, I refused to even accept that bullshit. I was trying to get the Eraserheads back to a level that could stand proudly against Caltrone and hold their own. He and I grew up with a mastermind, learned a lot from a mastermind, and Code did too. If we could just get the teachings together, then we could hold our own!

But he wasn't hearing it or believing it right now. He needed Code.

"Devin, just listen to me," I started, then backed up when Auto turned my way so fast that I thought I might get whiplash from it.

"What did you just call me?" he asked coolly.

A part of me felt a little smug that I had surprised him. Now he knew how it felt to have his name used like a weapon. "I did my homework on you too since being here and after what Caltrone said."

Auto gave me a cold stare and started the van up, pulling off to head to the back of the mansion. Frustration kept me quiet after that. Once we got back, I snatched up my book bag and angrily pushed open my door to climb out of the van. Rain pelted me hard and had me slamming the door behind me in annoyance.

"Niggas act the fucking worst sometimes but have the nerve to talk about us females and call us bitches for it. That's what I get for trying to help the team," I mumbled to myself in a rant while looking down at my feet at the water there and holding my book bag.

As I rounded the van, I ran right in to Auto. Dude was breathing so hard that I thought he might have asthma. I knew he was hurting over Code, but I didn't mean nothing about it on the level of hurting him. I just wanted to try to calm him and help the team out, but that wasn't working out as it should have.

Refusing to be intimidated, I stared up at him and noticed how the rain ran down his angular face. He had that slight tan tone to his yellow skin, which gave it an almond shade. His usually plump lips were now a thin line as his eyes had that hooded, angry look. I really wasn't trying to get into some fight with him, so I moved past him. He reached up and grabbed my arm.

My gaze locked on his large hand. I'd fight a nigga in a blink if he came at me wrong and tried to put his hands on me. I was in no way my mama when it came to that. I had a fight in me, and a motherfucker better kill me before putting his hands on me. So it took me a second to get my thoughts right when I stared at Auto's hand on my arm.

I guessed he could tell my mind-set, because he let go, then slid his hands in his pockets while giving me a bored but angry look.

"I'm not trying to fight you, Auto. I'm just trying to help the team, period, okay?" I angled.

Auto stepped up, and it had me stepping back because my nose was center in his chest. "Smiley, only the closest to me get to use my name like that."

"Yeah, well, you used my name, and I feel the same way," I countered only because he was annoying the fuck out of me.

"You're pissing me the hell off for real. Why do you have to be extra?" he asked with a slap of his hand to his face to wipe the rain away.

It was getting cold, and I was tired of fooling with him, so I tried to step away, but he grabbed me again. His brown eyes seemed to shift in depth of color, turning a darker cocoa than their usual walnut tone. He yanked me in front of him again, then held the back of my neck.

"I'm going to say this again: there is no way in hell that Code is coming back in here. She's gone. She's erased, and if you're not okay with that then . . ." he started, searching my eyes.

"Then leave?" I asked, feeling stupid all of a sudden due to the nervousness that had my stomach flipping. I hated confrontations, though I started them with the best of them.

"If that's what you want to do. If not, let that shit go, because I'm not changing my mind."

Rolling my eyes, I moved past him and headed into the garage. I was going to help him with the unloading, but I didn't give a fuck at the moment. I was annoyed, wet, and really wishing that Auto wasn't so blinded by his anger. I had a habit of trying to control things because, for a long time, all I had was me, so I knew then and there to let it go.

I was still talking to Code. I had called her earlier that day, so that's all I could do. There was some hacking that I had to do, specifically an untraceable virus that I had to upload into Caltrone's financial attorney's offices, but as I heard the garage close while I moved into the main house, I felt like I needed to press Auto again.

As the door closed, I could hear my kicks squeaking on the wooden floors. Maybe I could convince the other Eraserheads to talk it out with him. I knew they missed Code too. I could see the sadness mixed in with their anger toward her. Family sometimes messed up. It was always about coming into the fold and fixing it that could help things. I mean, I'd never experienced that because my father wasn't making mistakes. No, he did everything with calculated purpose. However, there was something about Code that I'd learned, and it made me empathize with her. She was being pulled by strings. She had no choice in anything she did. Her life was never hers until she met the Eraserheads, so why could they not understand that?

"You talk out loud when you're mad," sounded behind me and startled me so much that I almost dropped my book bag.

Auto was in the hallway. I was so focused on my annoyance with him that I hadn't heard him following me.

"Code still had choices. She chose not to trust her real family and got some of us killed, so you can try to rationalize it all you want, but nah," he said. His hands were in his pockets. He had a nonchalant look to him but still a hurtful glare in his eyes.

"Whatever. I'm just a peon then. My word ain't shit."

Auto closed the gap between us. I expected a fight from him. I was prepared for it, but when he kissed me, I forgot all about anything I'd just said. Trickles of water from Auto's cap and hair stuck to my cheek as my breath flowed with his. *Oh, shit,* ran across my mind. Damn, he could kiss. He slashed my shock away before he pulled away to stare at me.

"You talk too much when you get into your feelings. Your word means a lot to me, Nia. I'm learning that. I don't need Code, but I need you right now, so shut the fuck up about her and kiss me again," he muttered low against my lips.

There were some things I hated to feel when I was up on a dude I was attracted to. It made me nervous. Had me doubly questioning myself about whether I was doing the right thing. Auto had me feeling so different, in a way I liked, and that he owned all on his own. It made me nervous.

"I don't know if I can though. I think you're tripping big time," I whispered, looking at his lips then up at him.

Auto laughed low, more like chuckled in a way that always annoyed me, because it was arrogant. It had my nipples tightening along with a thumping heaviness in my snatch.

"Oh, yeah? I'm tripping?" he said, pushing back my hoodie. He reached for my braids and began twisting them between his fingers. "Since the moment you felt like you needed to talk to me about her, you've been tripping, so I'm chill on that."

Superiority. That's what was coming from him, and it was pissing me off. It had me ready to look like those ratty, chicken-headed girls on my block who always were putting their hands in their dude's face, sucking their lips, and rolling their eyes while going off. I never thought I would step in a space like that, but I was ready to until he kissed me again.

This time it was hard. This time it was him flicking his tongue to trace my lower lip. This time it was him guiding my mouth open to smoothly guide it inside and dance it around in a way that made me tremble. It felt good to have him pull me to him and feel the heat of his body. It had me picturing all those times he'd walk through his place in a towel and no top.

It had me reaching up to pull off his cap and glide my hand through his hair. It was a thick silk. I enjoyed it because once the tip of my nails lightly scraped his scalp in a massaging way, I swore he trembled, and it gave me that familiar sense of power. I broke away for a moment, and my eyes rolled once he kissed my neck and reached around my waist to palm my ass. I never had a huge ass. I had a small donk, and it pleased me how he palmed it and how it fit his large hands but slightly spilled over.

Standing on my toes, I didn't expect to have him pick me up and sit me around his waist. I didn't expect him to walk me to one of the empty rooms, close the door with his foot, and then lock it once he turned my back to the door. I didn't expect this dude to press me against it and work on my overalls just to skim his hands under my cropped top to cup both of my simple, plump melons. But here he was, and damn, there was his mouth as he sucked my titty through the black bra I had on, snaking his tongue to tease at my pierced nipple.

A moan spilled from my lips, indicating how much I was enjoying his touch. It also had him pressing me hard against the door again at that same moment. Questions flooded me. I wondered if he could eat the cake well. I wondered if he could play with the kitty in a way that felt like playing the piano. When I felt Auto hold my back and drop to a knee to lay us on the floor, I knew I wasn't going to tell Auto that I still had my V-card, because I wanted an answer to those questions, and sometimes niggas could be so damn stingy once they learned a chick was a virgin. Either they were the type who made it a fetish, or they were they type who was scared to fuck around with a virgin.

That's why I decided not to say a thing. Not that I ever had been in this place before in a long time. I sighed again when he yanked off my top then pulled off my bra. I watched him suck my nipple in his mouth again, letting his tongue flick it then slide it in a smooth manner against the steel bar there. I felt the blood rushing over my whole body at his mouth, at how I could tell he was studying each tattoo I had on my body, under my breasts.

And I got that confirmation when he said, "Damn, your ink is sexy, Nia."

I opened my mouth to respond, but that moment dissolved when he palmed the purring pussy. This dude purposely stared in my eyes when he did it, too, giving me a smirk while his hand pressed and massaged through my overalls. My hand reached up to hold his taut arm as he rubbed and palmed in an undulating motion. My hips rolled with it, my kicks squeaked against the floor, and my head moved back and forth at how good it felt.

Auto worked his stroking so well that I didn't realize his hand had moved to slide inside of my overalls, which were at my waist, until his fingers slipped over my dewy pearl.

I gasped in a heated pant the moment he slipped his fingers in me. I swore I didn't know how we got to this point, how it led to him tapping at my goods, to stripping me down and pressing his mouth to my kitty. But it did. My legs almost locked on his neck once he gave me the mouth game. Where he learned how to eat the cake the way he was right now, I didn't know. But nigga was on his A game and then some, blasting all my previous questions away. Like, my legs were jelly. I felt that quickening in me that had me arching and clawing at the floor. As I arched, the sound of a condom wrapper ripping didn't clue me in to what was next, but the feel of his body over me, his now-naked body, and the pressure of his large head at my gates did.

It took a moment, but once he breached that gate, and once I swallowed that discomfort, how he handled the kitty took me over the edge. No, I hadn't ever had sex before, but I was smart enough to figure shit out. My nails dug into his back. The way he groaned low only made my girl wetter and had me meeting each stroke he gave me. Rain drummed against the window, adding to our body's music.

Auto gripped my ass and shifted his body so he could look down at me. His face was so close to mine that each time he spoke, his lips brushed mine. "Why didn't you tell me?" he wanted to know.

"Because I didn't want to," was my reply. "Don't stop."

After that, he took it slow, had me singing out my moans until it was over and we lay sticky against each other. His hands touched all over me as my own returned the favor, tracing his chest. I didn't expect us to end up this way, but I wasn't mad about it. I wanted more, and by how he was looking at me, I could tell that he did too. Eventually we would, and eventually, I'd figure out a way to open him up about Code.

Chapter 13

Code

"He's not coming," I told Boots as we sat in Colleen's Diner.

It had been one of the places Auto would meet other members of the team when he wanted to pass along information. It was small and quaint. The color scheme was a mixture of brown, green, and cream colors. Kind of made me feel as if I had stepped back to the time of bell bottoms and afros. The smell of the place told me that soul food was being cooked. Fried chicken, collard greens, the sweet smell of yams, and the spices from the baked turkey wings serenaded the senses. The place was empty today minus me, Boots, and his people. Not that Colleen's was ever really that busy anyway, but it normally had a sprinkling of customers coming in and out.

Boots looked up from his plate as he chewed his food. His plate had greens, turkey wings, and corn bread on it. In two small bowls on his right sat corn and string beans. It was the first time I'd seen him eat such food. I honestly didn't think he knew what soul food was, being that all I'd seen was him eat was as healthy and organic as he could get.

"I kind of figured that out," he said to me.

"He didn't show up yesterday, and I'm pretty sure he isn't going to show today. So why are we still sitting here?" I asked.

"Because I'm eating."

"Can't you get it to go?"

He didn't answer me. Boots looked back down at his plate as he ate. I had to admit there was a bit of attitude in my voice. I'd wanted to see Auto and Smiley. I'd wanted to hug all my old friends and see if there was ever a chance they would forgive me. Boots didn't seem to care one way or the other. Since he'd had to move from his old hiding spot and came into the new spot looking as if he had been in a fight after meeting with Papa, I kind of figured he wouldn't be in the best of moods. And after sitting there well after he'd eaten his food, I wasn't in the best of moods either.

"Auto isn't coming," I told Boots, frustratingly so. "He did the same thing yesterday. He isn't coming. He's never going to give you those bullets back. Damn."

Boots didn't seem moved by my lashing out. He calmly wiped his mouth with his napkin and laid it down next to his plate. "Are you done with your temper tantrum now, Maria Rosa?"

I frowned and jerked my head back. The tone he had taken with me should have pissed me off. Instead, it made me squirm around in my seat. Even though he was being patronizing, his tone made me feel everything in me that was attracted to him. I guessed I was used to men quickly giving in or getting the hell out of my way when I was this annoyed. Not to mention, when Lelo was alive, he and Stitch had spoiled me like I was the sister they never had. I was used to getting my way.

Maybe I was annoyed by Boots' presence, too, only because I was starting to know what it felt like to care for someone outside of my family. I was trying to figure out how to get a handle on it. The last thing I needed to do was get all emotionally attached to a man like him.

Still, I caught my emotions behind everything and calmed down. "Yeah, I'm done."

"Good," he said while looking at his watch. "We can go now."

After Boots left more than enough money on the table, we headed out to his ride. Shango held the back door open to a new-model Expedition. Boots placed his hand on the small of my back and helped me up first. He told Shango to head toward downtown, and during the first few minutes, they talked about how they would go about continuing to shake up crazy.

"What happened to your back?" he asked me after we had pulled out onto Southlake Parkway and headed toward the light leading to the expressway.

Shango was driving while Alize was in the passenger seat. They all had been solemn since Oya had parted with Freddie. I too was sad to see Freddie go, but I knew he had to do what he had to do. My peace came with knowing that he and his daughter, Acindina, would be safe. She would be able to grow up and have a semblance of normalcy.

"Code, I asked you a question. What happened to your back?" he asked again.

I squirmed around uncomfortably. Boots and I had shared a bed again, and I was sure that, just as I watched him when he left the bed, he watched me as well. I could hide a lot of things, but the scars on my back wasn't one of them. I didn't know why Boots hadn't asked me when he first saw them on my back. Maybe he needed time to get his thoughts together. To see my back would give anyone pause. I'd told only Auto about how Papa doled out punishments when I deftly defied him.

"Papa, my grandfather, happened to my back," I said.

I ran a hand through my mess of hair and sighed. I closed my eyes and remembered being tied by my wrists,

forced on my knees as Papa put lashes across my back
while those he held in high esteem within the family
watched on. He'd sent me to kill an entire family. I'd done
what he asked of me minus one. I couldn't kill the little
girl. As she sobbed over her parents' bodies, I couldn't
bring myself to take her life away from her because her
parents had chosen to cross a man like my grandfather.

*"Be careful who you kill, Maria Rosa, but be even
more mindful of who you leave alive," he'd fussed at me.
"Little kids who see the trauma, like that little girl you left
alive, grow up to seek vengeance," he bellowed out.*

*I had always been defiant, but that was what he'd
taught me to be, so I spoke out of turn, "Is that what
happened to you, Papa?"*

*A swift backhand across the face silenced me. "Where
is she?" he demanded.*

*The pain in my face was so strong that my world was
vibrating. My brain seemed to be reverberating around
my skull. "I . . . I don't know."*

*"Liar," he called out, then struck the other side of my
face.*

*This time I could taste the blood that trickled down
my nose onto my lip. I cast a glance up at my mother,
hoping she would do or say something. But the woman
sat stoically. The only emotion that was even remotely
shown was the disappointment of me in her eyes.*

"I don't know where she is, Papa."

*"You're blind to the reality in front of you. That blind-
ness will get you killed, Maria Rosa."*

*I tried to look up at him as he circled me. His expen-
sive carnelian-colored shoes made a distinct noise as he
moved on the stained concrete floor. The sharp clacking
noise made my headache strengthen.*

*"She was only four, Papa," I whispered, trying to
defend my actions. I was only 14. I still had bits and
pieces of my heart.*

"How old were you when you held your first gun?" he asked me.

"Se . . . seven."

"Wrong," he intoned.

I didn't understand his answer because I distinctly remembered holding that gun between my shaky hands as I shot at many of the snakes in the room around me. Papa stood before me dressed in all white, minus the color of his shoes. When my mother stood to hand him a leather strap that had been cut into many shreds at the end, my heart slammed into my ribcage. Small seashells had been attached to each and every leather strand.

"You were four," he said, then walked behind me.

The lash I felt across my back, it was indescribable, but if I had to say what it felt like, I'd say it felt as if electricity had attacked my body. My screams rent the air, and even to my ears they sounded shrill. And once the electricity left me, the shock of the pain forced my screams to get stuck in my throat.

"At four years old, Maria Rosa, a gun in your hand killed a man who had crossed me," he hissed, then struck my bare back again.

Even if I'd wanted to, I couldn't stop crying, yelling out in pain, and squirming to try to get away. I fell face-first to the floor then balled into a fetal position, hoping my cries would stop the beating, but they didn't. I got beaten until he got tired, and with each lash, he told me the story of how I'd killed a man named Jin Su when I was 4. Papa told me how he'd brought me to the meeting and had me sit on his knee while he talked to the man. He told me whoever Jin Su was never even saw it coming. With my 4-year-old hands playing with a gun, and with the guidance of my papa, I'd pulled the trigger. I never even knew who he was or why I'd killed him.

Anytime I told the story of how I became Papa's assassin, I always left that part out. It had been too traumatic to relive. I'd lain in a crumpled, bloody mess at the feet of my papa. I never left anyone alive he'd sent me to kill since then.

By the time I finished telling Boots the story, I looked up to see we were heading toward Turner Field.

"Your grandfather is a sick son of a bitch," Boots dared to say to me.

I didn't respond. At this point, it seemed foolish of me to defend Papa after telling Boots that story.

"You have keloids, small ones, and then you have those obvious scars from lashings. Where did the small ones come from?" Boots asked me as we merged onto exit 248, heading toward Martin Luther King Drive, the state capitol, and Turner Field.

"Blade torture."

Boots frowned hard. "What the fuck? You telling me this dude used a blade to put all those cuts on you?"

I shook my head. "No, my mother did."

His frown left and was replaced by a blank stare. I could tell he didn't know what to say, and I didn't want to keep talking about it. So his silence was welcomed.

"Where to?" Shango asked once we got to the light.

"Head to the apartment. I need to pick up a few things. Then call Shredder and tell him we're moving out so we can go see Auto ourselves."

"He's moved them by now. No way he's in the same—"

Before I could finish my thought process, as Shango turned to head toward the baseball park, a police car—a black Charger—T-boned us from the left side. My neck snapped left then jerked backward. Shards of glass flew in my face. My hands went up defensively by instinct, and my head knocked into Boots' head because of the impact. For a moment, it felt as if I were floating outside my body.

I heard horns and yells from the people who had witnessed what they thought was a traffic accident. I moaned out as my world spun out of control.

"Shit," I heard Boots curse as he tried to unsnap my seat belt. "We have to get out of here."

I already knew there were just too many people around for us to have a shootout, especially on the heels of another one that had just happened days before. Boots' arm was clamped around my waist as he got out of the truck and pulled me out after him. When I heard more sirens in the distance and saw more rushing in behind the Charger, I knew we were fucked. There was no way it was just a coincidence that we were T-boned by a police car.

"Papa has people in the APD," I stammered, trying to catch my breath through the pain. My ankle felt as if it had been injured. The impact of the collision had turned my insides to mush. I knew Shango and Alize were strapped just as Boots and I were, and if any of us made the wrong move, they would shoot us down in cold blood. Papa had hands everywhere.

A crowd gathered wondering what had happened. Disarray was all around, and nobody knew exactly who the cops were yelling at. Another loud, clanging boom forced us to look up. A civilian car had slammed into the police car that had hit us.

"Get the fuck out of here, Boots," I heard Shango yell.

The left side of his face was bloodied, and I could see he was trying to get out of his seat belt but couldn't. Alize lay unconscious on the passenger side, bleeding from her mouth.

"You know what to do if you have to take a trip to the inside," Boots said in response as he took hold of my arm.

"I got it. Go on," Shango shouted as police closed in on the scene.

"Come on," Boots growled out.

We ran in the opposite direction. Neither of us cared that people were staring. The all-white pantsuit I had on was decorated in splashes of my blood. That didn't stop us though. We kept running, my ankle screaming and burning in pain. Boots probably could have run faster if he wasn't trying to make sure I kept up with him.

"Hey," someone shouted behind us.

We kept going.

"Stop or I shoot, Maria Rosa," he said again.

I knew that voice. A shot rang out in the air. I stopped running and turned and looked into the face of my cousin, Fuego. My hand went to the small of my back only to find my gun gone. I could only guess it had fallen out with the impact of the accident.

Fuego stood all of six feet two inches tall, with an athletic build and light eyes. His shoulder-length locs were braided back into six braids. He stood regally in a stance that deemed him an Orlando. The police uniform he had on would make citizens think he was the saint and only Boots and I were the criminals. Boots had stopped as well. I couldn't see what he was doing as he stood behind me, but I knew his silence meant he was paying attention to his surroundings.

"Fuego, don't do this. Just let us go," I asked of him.

He shrugged. "I can't do that, Rosa."

"You can."

"I can't. With you turning on the fam, Papa's out for blood. Not to mention he has all this other shit going on. I can't just let you walk away. Mos def can't let the nigga with you go. Papa wants him dead or alive."

There had always been a few of us who rebelled against Papa in our own way. Me, Freddie, and Fuego used to sneak out all the time to party and drink on the weekends. Anything to get away from Papa's strong hand. It all stopped when Fuego had to go away to join the Army and then the police academy because Papa wanted eyes and ears on the inside in all levels of the government. Fuego could be an assassin if he wanted to be as well. His specialty? Fire. Papa taught him how to kill with fire because he was afraid of fire.

It was my turn to shrug. "I can't just give up, Fuego. You know that, right? And I can't let you take him either."

He nodded once. "I do. I expected nothing less, which is why I didn't come alone. I'm sorry, Rosa, charge it to my . . ." he started, then stopped like he was thinking. "I got a pregnant wife," he said.

"I understand," I said quietly as Boots placed the handle of his gun into my hand.

Before Fuego could blink again, I brought my hand around, gun cocked and aimed. I lit up the sidewalk around him. He moved hurriedly, and it looked as if he were doing the Chicago-style Jookin as he tried to get away. I was sure he knew that if I'd wanted him dead, I could have killed him, but thoughts of his pregnant wife wouldn't allow me to end him. I walked forward as I shot at Fuego. People screamed and scurried past me. I heard shots being fired behind me. I turned to look and found that Boots was in his own firefight.

Cops were shooting at him left and right. It was hard to determine who was really a cop and who was just dressed the part. Obviously, that didn't matter to Boots, because he kept shooting. My momentary distraction cost me. Fuego rushed me, tackling me to the ground. He'd been one of the only males in my family who could either best me in a fight or give me a run for my money while training. This was no different. My gun fell between two parked cars as we wrestled on the sidewalk. He grunted, then sent his elbow into my face.

I returned the favor with a knee to his nuts then a punch that made him fall backward. I scurried back on my elbows. I noticed one of my heels had come off as I scampered to my feet. While Fuego was still kneeling and holding his nuts, I rushed in and kneed him in the face. His head fell back against a car door. I grabbed the collar of his uniform and kept kneeing him until his head lolled to the side. He was out of it.

I turned to rush for Boots, who was surrounded, but Fuego's hand restrained my injured ankle. I fell face-first to the ground. My cousin punched me in the back of the head. I grunted out when my forehead scraped the concrete. Fuego grabbed a handful of my hair, pulled me backward until I was no longer facedown, and then wrapped his legs around my waist as he placed me in an MMA chokehold while his back was on the ground.

"Just stop fighting," he grunted through clenched teeth.

As I fought to breathe, I saw Boots fighting for his life. His hat had been crumpled to the ground. From where I was, I saw that something had been stabbed into his left arm. His jaw had a nice black and red bruise to go with the one on under his right eye. When I had looked before, Boots had been surrounded by six men. Now there was only four. Two lay dead on the ground. Boots dodged the fist of one officer, then shoved a knife into the back of his neck. As the cop fell, Boots snatched his gun from his waist and shot another between the eyes before the other two cops bear-hugged him around the waist and sent him crashing in the window of the restaurant behind him.

I gritted my teeth and sent my right elbow into Fuego's side with as much force as I could muster. I was winded. My eyes had started to burn. It was hard to get any good hits with the position I was in. I knew it, and Fuego did too. So instead of continuing to elbow him, I frantically searched for his fingers. I finally got a good grasp on the left pinky finger and bent it back as far as I could. Sometimes the simplest of shit could be a lifesaver. I didn't stop bending even as he roared out, until I felt the digit snap. He released his hold on me quickly.

I dry heaved. My throat was on fire as I slowly made my way onto my stomach. As much as I wanted to lie there and catch my breath, I had to get up. I sluggishly made my way to my feet. Before Fuego could get to his, I kicked him in the head with the foot that still had a shoe on. His head hit the front of the car, and he fell back, unconscious. I quickly picked up a gun, not knowing if it was the one Boots had given me or if it was Fuego's, and limped down the sidewalk toward the fight between Boots and the two officers. As Boots kicked one officer back out of the hole where the window had once been, I aimed and shot him through his right temple.

Boots climbed back out the window, and the other officer could be seen lying across a table with a fork in his throat. There was no doubt that we had been seen, so we needed to get out of sight quickly.

"You okay?" he asked me after he looked down to where Fuego lay.

I simply looked at him. "Sure, Boots. I'm limping, my cousin just damn near killed me, I think a piece of glass is embedded in my nipple, and I was just in a car accident where a car rammed the side of the truck I was sitting on, but yeah, nigga, I'm fine," I replied sarcastically.

He looked worse for wear himself. "Shut up," he told me. "Come on. We need to disappear."

He didn't have to tell me twice. We walked as quickly as we could to the inside of a nearby parking deck. Boots grabbed his cell from the inside of his jacket pocket. He dialed a number, put the phone to his ear, but didn't say anything. I watched as he pressed a number then ended the call. He guided me to a corner near an elevator, and we sat there. The wails of police sirens were everywhere. I didn't know how we were going to get out of there.

I wanted to know, "What about Shango and Alize? You think they're okay?"

Boots thumbed his nose as he looked at the broken-off blade of a knife stuck in his arm. "They'll be fine. They know what to do."

"You sure?"

He nodded once. I let my head lie back against the concrete wall behind me. Every time a tire screeched or a car passed by, I was on edge.

"We're not amateurs, Code. They'll be fine," he snapped.

No matter what he said, I could clearly see the frustration in his features. I was about to say something else until sirens in the deck scared me to my feet. I quickly checked the magazine in the gun I held. Boots backed us farther into the corner by the elevator as he peeped around the corner. An ambulance sped past us, then came to a screeching halt. The driver-side door opened, and Shredder jumped out. A white woman I'd never seen before stepped out of the passenger side. Both were dressed as EMTs. The woman nodded at Boots, then made her way around to the driver's side while Shredder opened the back of the ambulance. Boots took my hand, and we rushed ahead and hopped in the back.

"One of you get on the stretcher," Shredder told us while looking us over. His eyes settled on me. "You look worse, so you get on. Play as dead as you can just in case."

I didn't have it in me to argue. I did as I was told. Boots watched me while Shredder strapped me down.

"Get us the fuck out of here, Dolly," he said to the white woman driving.

Come to think of it, she did look like a younger version of Dolly Parton. Pain tap-danced around my body. All I wanted to do was sit in a hot bath of Epsom salts or something that would take the pain away. I lay still, just as I was told to do, while Boots and Shredder talked. When Shredder actually started to clean the scrapes and bruises on my face, I gazed curiously up at him.

"You know what you're doing?" I asked.

He nodded before answering, "I have to ha . . . have a backup oc . . . occupation," he stuttered. "We all do. Helps to blend in better."

I was quiet as he worked on my face. The sterile smell of the closed space was comforting until we were stopped by cops. However, when they saw Dolly driving, they let her through the roadblock with no problem. We made it back to the new place where Boots had been hiding without incident. I finally took that one damn heel off and tossed it when we walked into the house.

"Sentries are set up all around the perimeter. Guards are on the street at all entrances and exits. Shango and Alize are in police custody," Dolly informed Boots as he moved around the front room. "My husband is handling it. I'll get to making sure your face or hers"—she pointed at me—"never shows on any media outlet. Is there anything else you need from me?" she asked.

"No," Boots curtly replied.

Shredder came from the back room with a duffle bag and tossed it to Boots. Boots looked inside and pulled out stacks of money.

"Your payment for the rescue. You'll get the rest when Shango and Alize are back with me. Tell Salazar his work is appreciated as always. Thank you," he said, then walked to open the door for her.

"No thanks needed. Salazar will have them out and back to you within the hour," she said, then disappeared as quickly as she had appeared.

I looked from the door back to Boots. "What was that?" I asked him.

He answered, "Me using my white privilege." He turned to Shredder. "Come get this shit out my arm," he ordered.

"You don't think something is definitely fucking crazy about all this?" I asked Boots hours later. The TV in the front room was on CNN, the one in his bedroom on Fox 5. He'd been stitched up and all his other wounds taken care of. My ankle had been wrapped. I had a big white bandage in the center of my forehead and 1,000 milligrams of hydrocodone in my system.

Boots looked over at me from the window. He was dressed in Levi's that fit his physique perfectly. A fresh pair of shit kickers, as he called them, were on his feet. A red, white, and black checkered shirt covered the muscles in his chest and arms.

"Which part? The one where your grandfather is trying to kill me or you, his granddaughter?"

"No, the part where we're both still in our youth and have been trained to be willing to die for any of this. I can't help but wonder what the other part of life looks like. A part that doesn't involve training, fighting, shooting, killing, and fighting a war that I'm not even sure is worth fighting. I saw you and your team out there. Shango was willing to die for you if need be, and I'm sure Alize would too. My cousin, Fuego, is willing to die to please Papa all so his family won't get backlash if he fucks up. I've been willing to die for so long, I often wonder what it is to live. And you, you . . . I don't know what to say about you, Boots. But something tells me I'm missing something. I can't quite put my finger on it, but I feel like there is more to this fight with you than meets the eye."

"What's your point?"

"Why are we so young and yet so willing to die for whatever it is we're fighting for? Why have we taken up someone else's agenda?"

"I have no idea what you're talking about, Code. I'm a businessman, a simple businessman whom your grand-father fucked over. My agenda is to show him not to fuck with me, my money, or my merchandise like this ever again. See? Simple."

Although Boots was looking me square in the eyes as he spoke to me, I couldn't help but think he was holding something back. I'd always been a smart woman. Boots was too thorough in his dealings. He was always guarded, always seemed to be one step ahead of everything. He was so well put together at a young age that I often wondered who was backing him. I had an inkling that this was deeper than bullets, but I knew I would probably never find out. That also told me that no matter what I had started to feel for him, I needed to let it go. Once his business was done here, he would move on. I would be just another notch on his belt while he was in the A on business. I decided to let him hold on to his secrets. If he wanted to remain incognito, then so be it.

Chapter 14

Boots

There was going to be no way to effectively get to a man who had caused my people, my family, so much destruction. There was just no fucking way to clear this shit up. Destruction had gone down, which was good, which was what I wanted, but at the same time, I needed that shit to flow in a way that I controlled and manipulated to get into Caltrone's inner circle. There was no clear way to get that, to hide in plain sight to work though the chaos while in the background as Mr. Sunjeta.

Pain had me clenching my jaw tight. My arm was fucked right now. My people scattered. I had no core team at this point but Shredder, and I had to draw on a link thanks to my family's allies—Dolly and her husband, Salazar, who were so deep in political power that they could request a lunch with President Obama and get it—that I really did not want to use at this moment. Shit happens though, doesn't it?

Now I was standing in my room with Code behind me while I was deep in thought. In my spirit, I knew that Alize or Shango could very well not be okay. I had seen that blood that Alize had spit out. I had seen the pain in my brother's eyes at knowing that she seriously hurt. So, though they might be locked up, I knew in my heart and mind that only one was coming back, and it pained me. It gave me that familiar fire in my heart that I felt the day I learned the story about my brother's and his wife's murders and about my nephew being lost in the streets and how I felt about the overall beef between the families that took place.

There was a logical choice that I had to make here. I just needed to chill and calm down. I found myself in my bathroom taking a razor blade to my beard and lining myself up while in thought.

"You have questions, and you have concerns, I get that. In every battle, a leader goes through periods of shit that has to be figured out. Right now, this is my test, okay?" Code was in the doorway watching me. I had felt her follow me before she even got up from the bed. It kinda got to me. She was getting to me.

"It's whatever, just don't get us killed," I heard her say, which grated my nerves.

"The only one who is aiming to kill is your old man. Clear that up," I snapped.

Everything had me shook, and I knew that Caltrone had exacted a code straight from *The Art of War*. But the thing about me was, shake me if you want, a nigga wasn't about to take my kingdom. Best believe that. As I thought, a smile formed on my face and I dropped my razor, then held out my hand to indicate for Code to move. Once she did, I walked out of the room.

"Give me a few. There's about to be a lot of changes going to happen, so ride with me on it," I said, glancing her way.

Even battered, Code was downright sexy as fuck. Her usually naturally plump lips were swollen, with a cut on them, bruises and cuts peppered her skin, but it was the fire in her that got me and that had me giving her a reassuring nod.

"Okay."

That was all I needed.

Going to my office, I pulled out my phone and sat down, looking at my locked door. Several rings sounded, and then I heard a click, one more click, and a ring. "What up!" an African accent riddled with French greeted me, and I chuckled.

"It's time for a business trip."

"Already?" Sweetness asked.

"Everything I planned to cause a distraction in Atlanta is going down. It's now time for a quick trip and layover. Handle that," I calmly stated.

"How many?" he questioned as I heard French hip-hop playing in the background.

"I'll text you that and the date. Just handle it, and I'll talk with you later," I said, hanging up.

Once that was in motion, I moved to the next phase.

"So you want to fuck with me, and then I'll fuck with you," I muttered under my breath. Glancing at my cell, I hit dial.

See, after my father's meeting in London, several things began to line up in the stars, and one of them was finally coming face-to-face with Phenom. I was able to finally speak to the man I had been sent to look after. Though brief, it was deep and something that had to stay private for both parties because of the raw emotions behind it.

Our meeting was overdue, and it took place under strict caution and deception. I was able to touch the hand of a man I idolized from all the stories I'd heard about him. I had to tell him why I was really in the A. Fate was a strange creature. Who would have thought that I would end up in the crosshairs of one of my nephew's good friends? I never saw that coming. My intent was to come to Atlanta and get in good with Caltrone, but only as a supplier of bullets.

I needed to get in close to the man who had gone almost twenty years thinking a lie was the truth. My pops had spent years speaking to people, tracking down others because he just couldn't figure out how two best friends ended up mortal enemies. In the end, he'd found the missing link, put two and two together, and grieved the loss of two best friends and family. I had to tell Phenom all that shit. Had to watch as he swallowed his pride and realized that he too had been tricked, had the wool pulled over his eyes. It sucked when you thought, felt deep in your heart, that you were due your vengeance, only to find out two families had been played against the middle.

But that was another story for a different time. My plans had started to come unraveled.

I dialed my father up and waited for him to answer. "Son."

Sitting up in my chair, I exhaled deeply. "Pops. Everything is a rat race. The streets are blazing, and the distraction is going down."

"Good. Were you able to get close to him?" I was asked.

"For a brief moment yes, as I reported. Now things have changed," I responded.

"Explain . . . break that knowledge down. Was it the bullets, my son?" my father questioned.

"That and I have his granddaughter." I paused to get my words right, then went on, "He wants the bullets, and he wants his granddaughter dead, the one I spoke to you about."

"So you happen to have her." He gave a light laugh before going on. "Knowing him, he is a thorn in your side right now. Wants you dead. So this is a call to tell me that you are going on a business trip again?"

"For now. I have business with the Dragons. I believe by strengthening that, meeting up with you and the main family for another face-to-face with Phenom and Anika, we can come together for a plausible endgame. I have the traps down, and they are already detonating. The rest is for the other players to deal with while I continue to work in the back," I broke down.

"That sounds good. The point is to have him open to the knowledge of what really went on, and from the sound of it, now is not the time, so yes, come home and rest. What about the girl?" he asked in a slight break of his Texas drawl with that of his old roots in BK accent.

His question hit me hard. I wasn't 100 percent sure what to do with her, but one thing was to just initiate a true erasure and let her sleep with darkness. I was on the fence with it. Wondered if I could truly get her full loyalty in such a short time. Was unsure if I wanted to risk every-thing right now just to keep her near. We were on some Bonnie and Clyde shit right now without Caltrone even knowing it, and I didn't give a fuck about it on that end, but my father's end I had to respect.

"From the silence, I can't tell what you really want, son. Yet, we all know that born universal truth. I told you. Don't make my mantle yours because you feel I want that or need that. Build how you want, which you have, but now, secure a future with who you want," he said. "Sometimes the best forbidden fruit is surrounded by snakes, son, and it takes a warrior to accept being bitten just to bring home the fruit for dinner."

"She's scared of snakes but was raised to be one," I found myself saying in a chuckle.

"You were too. Was necessary to understand their and our mentality. Show and prove, son, you know it," my father added.

I sat in thought, knowing he was right. "Show and prove, Dad. I'll keep everything breezy. I'm in savage mode, but I know the teachings. This won't last for long."

"I know it won't. None of us OGs want it to anyway. We love you too much to let it continue," he said.

Those words I heard all my life and I knew he meant it. I remember seeing him when I was a kid, broken about his leg, broken about losing my brother, his grandson, King Kulu, the Kulu kids, and then my mom. Funny thing, I even saw the rare moments when he was broken about losing his old friend. So I knew what he said, what he meant was truth. Not just verbal affirmations, which because of how he raised me, I was able to ride with him and respect this whole mess. From how he raised, I even had respect for that crazy-ass nigga, Caltrone. I guessed that's also a small part of why his granddaughter got to me so well. I saw the man he was meant to be through her, and she made the true knowledge so appetizing.

"So . . ." I said, trailing off from my thoughts.

"So travel. Handle business as you do. Everything will fall into place, as it should. You're young, but above all, you are smarter then I was at that age." I heard him close something before pausing as if in thought.

"Your mother would always tell me that the camel keeps on marching while the dogs keep on barking!" he said in Eritrean. "You got the dogs to growl and tear at you. Now the rest will fall into place, son. We're not ass out, remember that, but they ain't eitha, dig? We'll meet, my son, because this battle cannot go on forever. My love to you, son, and I will see you soon," he said with a click.

My pops was right and had me grinning at his slick words. Sometimes it takes the counsel of a good man to get you back on perspective.

I said I had respect for that nigga Caltrone, just a small drop in a bucket of respect, but that was slowly being washed away with how he did my family and me. Tears ran down my stoic face. The only show of emotion was that of my tears. Each one dropping on the body of a woman I loved like my own sister, my own family, Alize. There were no words in the anger that I felt when Shango managed to get her body released to us. It was some shit he had to let pass only to get her brought back to us, and I wasn't happy about it. I wanted my revenge for it.

Like I said, I knew in my heart that only one of them would return, and I was right. I learned from Shango that because of the accident, Alize had been hurt badly, blood spewing from her mouth and nose, but that didn't stop the cops, paid cops by Caltrone, from manhandling her and breaking her down more. The bruises on her body showed that, and they weren't from the wreck. Around her small throat were rope marks. The cops said she had tried to hang herself, successfully, but we all knew that wasn't the case.

My hands shook with fury as I ran them over her, stopping to hold her icy hand. She had been battered, and from what Shango was telling me after he examined her thoroughly, the tears and bruises around her genitalia and rear indicated raped. My Alize had been taken from me and abused like an animal. Was no honor in that at all. Was no dignity. Nor was there any logic in treating my people this way when all I was, was a businessman with something you wanted.

"When are we leaving?" I heard Shango ask me from behind.

There was a broken sound to his voice. The man was lost. He had lost not only Oya to another, but he now lost the second woman he truly loved. That sharp agony was all through him. I could hear it in his voice, and I wasn't prepared to see it. We all knew what we were doing was dangerous and could get us killed, but it didn't mean we'd be able to swallow any loss easily.

Old man PT was there. The man was hurting. Alize was like blood to him too, almost like a daughter, but because he always shared raunchy jokes with her, it was like a different type of connection with her. His usually ageless face was wrinkled with emotion and constrained tears as he said a prayer of Alize's body before wrapping it up for us to cremate back in Africa.

"Soon," was all I was able to say.

Chapter 15

Auto

12:30 p.m.

My crew and I were strapping up. Bulletproof vests on. Combat boots and all-black military attire suited us. Automatic assault rifles, hand grenades, tear gas, and face masks were all around us as if we were going to war, and technically we were.

"We're moving out," Wolf said once he and his brothers were suited and booted.

I nodded. "Remember to stay on that back road until we get there. Put sentries in the trees by the abandoned railroad tracks just in case. Once Nicola's and Armando's men get there, signal them with three flashes from the flashlight. They should respond in kind."

"And what about Caltrone's men posted there?"

I shrugged nonchalantly. "I would suggest you see them before they see you. Take clear, precise shots. We only get one chance at this, and if any one of you fuck this up, I'll kill you myself."

"Auto," Reagan and Smiley called out to me at the same time.

I ignored their obvious disdain for my threat and continued speaking. "I mean it. Don't fuck this up," I told Wolf, staring him dead-on. "No more strikes."

He nodded and signaled his brothers to follow him. I turned to look at Smiley and Reagan. Jackknife sat silent, staring me down. Normally he would whistle or sign, but he was stoic.

"What?" I asked him with a sign. "You have a problem with what I'm doing too?"

He signed, "No. Just don't think you should be so hard on people."

I responded in rapid hand movements. "Can't afford mistakes, Jack. Everyone pulls their own weight, or I get rid of dead weight. Simple."

He frowned then stood. The redness in his eyes told me he was annoyed or angry. He walked up on me, then snatched my iPad from the table. His hand moved fast as he typed. Once he was done, he held the pad up.

Does that mean us too? it read, then he pointed at Reagan and Smiley before pointing to himself.

He shoved the pad into my chest, picked up his rifle and a duffle, then headed up the stairs so he could leave as well. I shook my head. I knew everyone was emotional, but they had to leave that shit behind. We had a job to do, and I didn't have time to baby anyone or tiptoe around their feelings.

"Come on. We're moving out," I said.

Reagan shook her head before heading out to the truck with Jackknife.

"Did you hear anything I said to you last night?" Smiley asked me.

"I did. I listened. Doesn't mean I have to change my plans. You don't believe in my plan, fine. Doesn't mean I don't."

I snatched up my rifle. Pulled the strap over my head and shoulder. Smiley was dressed like the rest of us. Anytime I looked at her I thought back to the night before. First time in a long time I had a woman in my bed. The sex was good of course, but it wouldn't sway my thought process. I was going after Caltrone Orlando. And it would be my way or no way at all.

"I never said I didn't believe in your plan, so don't put words in my mouth," she snapped. "Look, just don't fight emotionally. That'll get you killed, okay?"

I studied her for a moment. Although I knew she was right, her words still grated my nerves. That was probably more so because she'd gotten under a nigga's skin. She made me talk last night even when I didn't want to. Since I'd met her, she'd been making me do shit I didn't want to. She asked me about my mother. No chick I ever dealt with had ever asked me about my mother. I'd asked her if the fact I was Asian was a problem for her. She laughed at me. Told me I should have asked that before we fucked. I had to chuckle at it because she had a point. We studied different ethnicities in Asia, trying to see which people my features most represented. She thought my mother looked Taiwanese but couldn't be sure.

So as she studied my mother's pictures and searched the net, my hand ended up between her thighs again because, to me, there was something arousing about the fact that she was so into finding out who I was and where I'd come from. I didn't think she would care. Yet she'd proved me wrong. Because of that, I ended up between her thighs for most of the night.

"I'm emotional, but I'm not fighting emotionally," I told her as I walked up to her. "There may be madness to my method, but there is a method, nonetheless."

We didn't exchange any more words. We didn't have to. She knew no matter what she said, we were still going to rob Caltrone Orlando. As we walked up the steps that led us to the dark room that would take us up to the empty pool, Smiley hummed a tune I couldn't readily place. She climbed out of the secret entrance before me, then reached back down to take two of the duffle bags I had. Once we were all at the truck, Smiley kept looking at Reagan and back at me. At first, I thought they were doing that female shit again where women communicated without words.

Jackknife sat in the driver's seat of the truck. He was buckled up and ready to move out. Reagan had just put the last of the bags into the back of the truck. She was about to get inside when Smiley stopped her. Reagan looked just as confused as I did.

"What's going on?" she asked Smiley.

"You can't go," Smiley told her.

I frowned. Jackknife stuck his head out the window to see what was taking so long for us to get in the truck, I presumed. He may have been deaf, but with the way he read lips, you wouldn't know he was deaf unless you knew him personally.

"What?" Reagan asked.

"You can't go, and you know why."

"Don't tell me what I can't do," Reagan snapped.

"Well, you shouldn't go, Reagan. This is dangerous."

I jumped in. "Clearly I'm missing something here. One of you want to clue me in on what's going on?"

Jackknife whistled to get my attention then tapped his watch.

I signed, "I know. We're coming." I turned back to find Reagan and Smiley staring one another down.

"I don't think he would want you to go, Reagan."

"You didn't even know him to know what he would want. Don't do this, Smiley. I told you because I trusted you."

"Will somebody please tell me what the fuck is going on?" I demanded. "We don't have time for this. We have to go," I yelled.

"Reagan is pregnant, and I don't think she should go because this can be dangerous," Smiley answered. "I'm sorry, but I couldn't let you go out—"

"What? Pregnant? When? By who? When did this happen?" I spat out all at once.

Reagan sneered at Smiley as she shook her head in disbelief. When she turned to look at me, I could see the tears rimming her eyelids. I knew there had been something going on with Reagan. I could see it in the way she had been acting. I thought it had been the sadness behind losing Seymore, Lelo, Dunkin, and Code, but now I knew there was more.

"Just because I'm pregnant doesn't mean I have to sit around like an invalid. I can handle myself, pull my own weight," Reagan said. "I don't need you to baby me, and I don't need people blurting my business all out in the street," she said, then scowled at Smiley.

Smiley dropped her head for a second. I could tell she didn't want to put Reagan on blast, but I was glad she did. I had questions and not enough time to ask them, but Smiley was right. There was no way I was going to let Reagan go with us knowing she was pregnant.

Jackknife whistled again.

"You're not going," I told Reagan. "Go back inside."

She was livid. "Are you fucking kidding me right now, Auto?"

"Go back inside, Reagan."

"No. I have the right to go."

"You're pregnant. I can't let you—"

"I have the right to go after the people who took my child's father away from us," she leveled at me.

Her voice held sadness, but there was also determination. She wanted revenge. Angry tears rushed down her cheeks, but she slapped them away. I frowned because I didn't know which of those we'd lost she was talking about.

"They took him away from me before I could tell him he was going to be a father. I had to tell him as he lay dead in my arms. So please, Auto, don't take away my chance to avenge him."

Her voice cracked, and my eyes burned as I realized she was talking about Seymore. I remembered that day in the shop. She had cradled his head to her chest while she cried. It all made sense now. Before I just thought she had been distraught like the rest of us over the loss of family. But in hindsight, her tears had been the same as Stitch's as she held on to the man she loved.

Her words got to me. They cracked at what little of my soul I had left. That wall that I'd built around me threatened to break under the pressure of what I had to do. I couldn't risk losing her, and I wouldn't have been able to live with myself knowing that I'd possibly lose Seymore a second time. All I could think about was his mother and the look in her eyes when I told her Seymore had been killed. She deserved to know that she had a grandchild on the way, and I wouldn't take the only piece of Seymore she had left away from her.

"I'm sorry," I told Reagan. "Go back inside."

"Gotdamn it, Auto, no!"

"Go back inside, Reagan." This time I yelled louder and harsher than I'd intended to.

"Auto, please, I deserve the same vengeance you do," Reagan pleaded. The tears that rolled down her cheeks made me turn my head so that I wouldn't see the look of betrayal and pain in her eyes.

"Reagan, you're wasting time. Go on," I said while I walked around to get in the truck.

Something that sounded like a firecracker echoed behind me. I didn't have to turn around to know Reagan had slapped Smiley. I watched from the truck as Reagan rushed back down the stairs into the pool and disappeared inside. I pulled out my phone and locked the mansion back down behind her. Smiley slowly got into the back seat. Shame clung to her like a second skin.

"You did the right thing," Jackknife turned and signed to her.

"Damn sure doesn't feel like it," she verbally replied while signing back to him.

It took us about twenty minutes to get from Stockbridge to Caltrone's warehouse in Lovejoy. I had to put what had happened with Reagan in the back of my mind for now. Business was at hand. Jackknife parked the truck in the hidden brush on the back road. The wind was heavy. It blew the trees around violently. Made them dance and rock as if they were going to come uprooted.

"Is everybody in place?" I asked after I put my Bluetooth in my ear.

"In place," everyone answered all at once.

"But I got a problem," Wolf said.

I waited to answer him. Jackknife moved into position. Smiley was right behind him. The three of us were going in after the guards at the door were taken out. They were big but not burly. They had been taken down with the sniper shots from the building directly across the railroad tracks. Wolf had assessed the surrounding areas all week and had determined that he could kill the two guards from a great distance with a high-powered rifle. That would give us the stealth we needed to get them out of the way and then replace them with two of our own men without anyone noticing.

The three of us had to be in position to storm the inside of the warehouse ten minutes after the shift change. Every night since we had been casing the joint, we noticed it took the lead guard ten minutes to yell out orders and get in position. It would be tough to take down twenty men inside of that warehouse, especially with the workers inside. And now with Reagan left behind, it was going to be harder.

Once Jackknife, Smiley, and I hid just shy of the fence in the woods behind the warehouse, we took a few minutes to make sure we hadn't been seen or heard. The fence was supposed to be electric to keep the workers in and unwanted people out, but we'd found out they didn't work. We'd been tampering with it every night during the stakeouts. Every night during the shift changes, one guard stepped out back to case the perimeters of the fence to make sure all was clear.

"What's the problem, Wolf?" I asked once we were in position.

"The wind is too strong. I can't make the shot if the wind doesn't die down."

I took a deep breath, sighed, and looked around. The wind was still thrashing around the leaves and branches on the trees. "Are you sure the wind is a factor?"

"Yeah, boss. If I take the shot, there is a chance that it won't hit the target and we could possibly give our position away or alert them to our presence."

I looked at my watch. It was seven minutes to one. "Shit," I cursed.

"I can handle it," Smiley said quickly.

"Wait, what?" I grabbed her arm to stop her as she was about to climb the fence.

"Look, we don't have time for this. The shift is going to change in less than seven minutes now. We need to be in position to do something as soon as they're done changing over. We don't have time to waste."

"I'm not letting you go in there by yourself."

"I'm not an incompetent, Auto. I know what I'm doing. If my daddy wasn't good for anything else, he taught me weapons and how to be tactical. I got this. You worry about everything else," she said.

Before I could say another word to her, she was scaling the fence. Jackknife was smiling and shaking his head. He whistled, nodded her way then back my way, and rubbed his fingers together in a way that indicated money. Since Reagan told me they had been making bets on when Smiley and I would hook up, I already knew what that was about. I flicked him off and pulled the night-vision goggles down on my eyes. I watched Smiley until she stealthily disappeared behind the main building.

I watched the time closely. At exactly one o'clock, the first two men at the door switched places with another two.

"Wolf, make sure Bardou and Conall are ready," I said into my earpiece.

Bardou and Conall were two more of Wolf's brothers. They stood the tallest and most deadly of the crew of brothers as they had no regard for human life. Amoux was still recovering from the injury Boots had given him.

"They're good to go."

The exchange in shifts didn't take long at all. The men at the door posted up. Their faces were always covered. They were dressed in all black as we were. I wanted my two men to blend in perfectly just in case the lead came out to check on them at the post. I watched as Smiley moved in. Her movements were precise. She made a little noise by rapping her knuckles on the side of the building. The one on the left side of the door sent the other one to see what the noise was. As soon as he rounded the corner, I watched Smiley shoot him twice in the head. She gave him a double tap. The silencer on her gun never gave her away.

She moved back into the shadows and waited. After a while, when the other guard had not come back, the one left went to look for him and wound up getting the same fate. And just like that, we were ready to go. Bardou and Conall quickly rushed in to help Smiley hide the bodies in the thick brush near the other side of the fence before they rushed up to the door to stand guard before anything could be noticed.

Jackknife and I scaled the fence. Siberian followed close behind us. I hadn't come to bring a firefight, but I knew what would more than likely go down. I pointed to each place I wanted my team members to be.

"The window in the back near the wall safe is open," Smiley informed me. "They always leave it open because whatever it is they use to cut the drugs has a pungent odor."

"Nicola and Armando are going to love you for this shit, Auto. Fishscale, the purist shit there is. Remember what happened when word got out that nigga Dame had been robbed of his shit too?" a familiar asked in my ear.

I stopped my approach and touched my Bluetooth. "What the fuck? Stitch? Nigga, what the hell—"

Stitch chuckled and clicked his teeth. "You didn't think I was really going to leave and not get at the niggas who took Lelo from me, did you?"

I looked around, trying to determine where he could be. How he'd managed to stay in Atlanta was a mystery to me. One that had caught me completely off guard.

"I told you to get your family out the A," I whispered aggressively into the earpiece.

"And I did. Now I play."

"How did you even know where we were?"

"Been talking to Reagan. She called me again, pissed off and crying that you wouldn't let her come with you tonight. I told her not to worry. I'd kill enough for both of us."

I shook my head and chuckled. To be honest, it was all I could do at the moment. I had a team of fighters with me, and I should have known Stitch wouldn't leave quietly. So wherever he was, I would leave him be and let him do his thing.

A chorus of, "Whaddups," met Stitch. He chuckled and returned the greetings. I moved into position by the back window. Smiley waved at me from the shadows next to the power box.

"Hit the lights," I told her.

The warehouse went black twenty seconds later. I tossed tear gas into the window. Chaos could be heard inside of the building as women screamed and guards started shouting for them all to shut up and get down. I crouched low and moved swiftly to the front of the building. Bardou and Conall snatched the front doors to the warehouse open. I rushed in gun first. I took down the first three guards who rushed for the entrance. They couldn't see us as we swarmed the building. Bodies fell left and right. The shrill cries and screams of the women were starting to get to me, and I prayed that the Higher Being would forgive me if any innocent lives were lost.

"Behind you," I told Smiley as she rushed up the stairs shooting at the guards hidden behind the high stack of crates.

Because they couldn't see us, they shot around blindly, which was still dangerous for us, and judging by the falling bodies of the half-naked female workers, them too. We had to take them down quickly.

"Two rushed into the office by the wall safe," Siberian relayed.

He was breathing hard. Yelps and groans could be heard in the static of my Bluetooth.

"We have to hurry. They probably called in reinforcements. Wolf, tell Armando to send his men in. Quickly," I yelled rapidly while gunshots sang a cacophony of noise around me.

I heard Smiley yell out in pain, and I rushed up the stairs. Her goggles had fallen off her face. I followed her grunts and moans. Could see her cornered off fighting one of the guards. Her gun had been taken away from her, but she didn't let that stop her. As I tried to sneak behind her attacker, I watched as she took a backhand to the face. She stumbled and fell back over a crate that had been behind her. The guard tried to rush in to grab her and was rewarded with a boot to his groin. Smiley jumped up. Brass knuckles on her fingers, she threw a rapid succession of punches that would make Ali proud.

It was easy to see she'd caught her opponent off guard as he stumbled backward then tumbled over the railing. Using parkour, a style of holistic training used to over-come obstacles, Smiley took a running start, used the wall for leverage, and jumped over the stack of crates in front of her and over the railing behind him. She landed on the floor, did a tuck and roll so that she rolled over her shoulder instead of her head, then jumped up.

He swung. She ducked, then came up behind him. Knife in hand, she hopped on his back, one arm around his meaty neck, and slit his throat from ear to ear. *Impressive shit,* I thought. Shorty didn't need my help, so I rushed back down the stairs and headed to the back where the safe was. As soon as I bent the corner, bullets started to chase me. I ducked and ran to hide behind a barrel. I pulled a grenade from the pouch on my hip. Bit the pin to pull it out, then tossed it. The explosion rocked the small space. While smoke was still covering me, I rushed in and took the two men out.

I looked at the safe in the wall and wondered what was on the inside. I knew there would be no way we could crack it and get out in time, so I opted to leave it. I kicked the door down to the office since the blast had split it down the middle. I could hear the laughter of my crew behind me, which let me know we'd taken down the enemy without any causalities to us.

The office had blueprints laying out on the table. I doubted they were of any real importance. I didn't see Caltrone being a man who would leave that kind of shit lying about in random places. The money that lay strewn about made me smile, but it was what was in the safe that had been left open in the floor that left me speechless.

"Smiley and Jackknife, get up here. We just hit the jackpot," I yelled.

The hard patter of footfalls made me turn around. Smiley and Jackknife stood behind me.

"Holy shit," Smiley whispered breathlessly.

Jackknife's eyes were as wide as mine. As much as I would have loved to stand there and relish the beauty of the bounty we had found, we didn't have time. I tossed Smiley and Jackknife two of the black bags that had been lying on the floor, and we started quickly packing the bags with as many of the gold bars as we could.

"Auto, I can't carry this," Smiley said after she had finished stuffing her bag.

Jackknife whistled and pointed to a rolling cart in the corner. I grabbed it, tossed the three bags on it, and rolled it out. The warehouse was filled with commotion. Unmarked vans and trucks had Armando's men loading up drugs and money. I smiled to myself knowing this feeling of accomplishment wasn't something I was used to in the last couple of weeks. I'd been hit and hit hard. I had now returned the favor. I rolled the cart out of the warehouse. Smiley and I waited while Jackknife went to get our truck.

"How do we know these are even authentic?" Smiley asked me.

"Just by looking at them I can see a maker's mark, statement of weight, and fineness stamped directly onto the bar. But just to be sure, once shit dies down and we're on our way off U.S. soil, I'll get my jeweler and pawnbroker to do an acid test for it."

Smiley looked at me strangely. "On our way off U.S. soil? What are you talking about?"

"Auto, hurry up and get out of there. We got incoming. Lots of those motherfuckers," Wolf shouted in my ear.

"What's the ETA?" I asked.

"Nicola's men are set up trying to keep them at bay. Even with that, ten minutes, tops."

As Wolf talked in my earpiece, Jackknife backed the truck up. I snatched open the back door to the Suburban and started to help Smiley load the bags in. To be honest, I was thankful for the distraction. Although she was now a part of the team, I hadn't told her that after this was over, we were all getting the hell out of Dodge. One reason I didn't tell her was that I didn't want to deal with the way I would feel if she didn't care enough to leave with us.

"Or are you afraid she won't leave with you?" I remembered Trigga asking me once I told him of my plan.

Then I denied it was because I was afraid of her rejecting me, but the more I stayed around her, the more I came to grips with that being the case. I could feel Smiley still watching me as we loaded the truck. Once done, I slammed the doors shut and told her to get in. I knew she wanted to ask more questions and get more answers, but the gunfire in the distance quelled all that. We had to go. Armando's men were filing out. Vehicle after vehicle sped off. My team ran for the woods and took cover. Jackknife floored the gas and got us the hell out of dodge.

The plan was for Armando and Nicola to have their men take on the firefight once Caltrone's people caught wind of what was happening, and then to split the bounty among themselves. But of course shit didn't always go as planned. As we sped out onto the side street, three black Hummers blocked the exit.

"Shit," Smiley said.

Jackknife hit the brakes hard. We still had guns, but not enough to take on three Hummers full of armed men.

Jackknife turned and signed, "What you want me to do?"

His brows were furrowed and face etched in agitation. I was about to say fuck it and tell him to put his foot on the gas. We'd mow as many of those motherfuckers down as we could, but I didn't have to. Just as I was getting ready to speak, a blast to one of the Hummers sent it sideways into the air. Fire boomed and blazed. A few of the men had been sent flying because of the blast.

I yelled, "Yeah! Fuck yeah, Stitch!"

I knew my boy's work anywhere. The nigga loved rocket launchers and was fascinated with explosives. Another blast took out another Hummer, and the men started to scatter.

"Get us the fuck out of here," I told Jackknife. He barreled through the chaos full speed ahead.

I smiled as Jackknife finally made it onto Tara Boulevard. My heart was beating fast, chest heavy as shit, but as each member of my team checked in, a feeling of contentment washed over me. I imagined that old man losing his damn mind about all the drugs and money he'd lost. Yeah, that nigga was going to respect me or kill me. And since I was still alive, respect was in order.

Chapter 16

Smiley

Exhaustion had me breathing mad hard. I glanced left and right, then dipped into a back alleyway heading to my mom's house. Since linking up with the Eraserheads, everything had changed for me. I was no longer running the streets for survival. Now I was pulling my weight, doing cons professionally and making big bank from it, all while helping them settle beef with their enemy, a dude I learned was my grandfather. Last night, I aided in all of that.

We'd successfully lifted off some crazy drugs and money from Caltrone, but it was a hit I knew would have consequences. Something in my spirit still told me that it would piss him off on another level.

Although I had since emptied out my mom's house and moved to my own secret spot, I wanted to come back and get the last few items I'd left behind. Yup, you would think I'd learned my lesson with being snatched out of my mom's place by the police and being found by the Eraserheads. But no. I wasn't thinking clearly. My mom's home was a piece of me, but I knew that I had to let it go. After the hit, we all got together to discuss what to do.

Auto wouldn't explain to me about what he had said with leaving the States. It made me nervous because all I knew was my environment. I was having a hard time imagining going to a new state, let alone out of the

country. Every time I asked, I was either ignored or interrupted. I hated that shit. It always put it in perspective
that I truly wasn't a part of the crew like they said I was.
But yeah, part of the interruption was with Reagan, who
still was ticked off at me.

There's no love when a person has to snitch. I never
really rolled with that code unless it made absolute
sense and protected the person in a logical means. With
Reagan, I had to snitch, had to stop her from risking her
life and that of her baby. I was scared and was holding
up my promise with her, but now the girl wasn't talking
to me at all. It was why I never kept any female friends.
Chicks could be so attitudinal and extra sometimes.
Shit bothered me when usually I could brush shit off. I
guessed that meant I opened myself up too much then.

Anyway, after being ignored, I hung back, took my cut,
and when nobody was watching, I dipped out. There was
a special package that I was waiting for, and I had just
gotten a text that it was waiting for me. This baby was
a strict priority package and dangerous. I had it sent to
multiple locations, rewrapped by some of my own allies
out of state, and then sent to my mom's home as a means
of not being traced back to me.

Heading my way was something that I knew would
help Boots out and bring a smile back to his face. Word
from Shredder had told me that he had lost a member
after some drama with Caltrone's men. When I got that
information, my heart broke. Alize was a dope chick. The
times we spoke, I always liked her vibe, but to hear she
had died put a different scope on this battle with Caltrone.

But back to my baby, $1,200 was the auction starting
price for what I purchased, ending with me winning
this hot market steal for two Gs. Searching the black
market for parts for my trackers, my apps, and the
3-D machines for Boots was my thing. One day, while

searching for parts, I came across an auction for a new type of 3-D machine, specifically one that crafted guns called a Ghost Gunner. Shaped to look like an Xbox cube, this baby was a computer-controlled processing machine designed to let anyone make the aluminum body of an AR-15 rifle at home.

What I liked about it was that everyday people could use it. Like, there was no regulation on it, and it printed guns without serial numbers, which was why the guns made from it were called ghost guns. It also had the capability of automatically carving different types of materials to craft my Glocks, such as polymer, wood, and metal. Shit was sick!

Not only was this crap legal, but I could hook it up with what I was designing with Boots and make it where the piece was a ghost product for real. That's why I was heading to my home. I was geeked and briskly walk-ing, keeping aware of my surroundings. With a purple cropped Batgirl hoodie, tiny shorts, striped leggings with black kicks, and my twisted braids fishtail braided into two ponytails, I kept my appearance on the low, no makeup this time. Everyone in the neighborhood knew each other, so I knew that I'd have no issue, but since I hadn't been home in some time, I figured that eyes would be watching and being nosy like usual.

With my book bag on, and eating chips, I slipped in the back of my mom's home and looked for the package. A huge smile spread across my face once I saw it hidden under a chair. Excited, I quickly pulled the small box out, flipped it in my hands, then stuffed it in my backpack. Pulling out my keys, I got ready to unlock the padlock on the back door of my mom's house when I froze.

Casual steps my way, with the top of silky black waves with slight salt in the mix came into sight. A sudden nervousness hit me at the same time as a light cologne.

Out in the backyard were several men in suits and shades. In the small drive in the back connected to the alleyway was a blacked-out silver Mercedes. I had a knife hidden against my inner ankle, a Glock strapped to the inside of my cropped hoodie, a bladed chain around my bare waist camouflaged as a belly chain, and that was about it. Each one of those things would take a minute to get to, and by the time I made even a scratch against the man coming my way, I knew that I'd have a bullet in my skull.

There was nowhere to run. I was screwed. "What do you want?"

"Is this how you greet your grandfather, *bella?* I can honestly say this is not how I imagined a second reunion between us would go," a crooning accented voice said my way.

Before me was the man who had caused hell to all the Eraserheads and a man I had been trying to avoid since learning he even existed, Caltrone Orlando. A white-hot fear traveled up my spine and made me back up. The anger that I grew up having thanks to my own father kept me from showing that fear. I stared up at the old man, studied him, from the shine on his black Italian shoes on up to the well-tailored suit he wore and the smile upon his caramel face. The man was handsome, and I saw my father in his features along with the memory of my mother's pain reflecting in his dark coal eyes.

There was evil in that darkness, evil that enjoyed inflicting pain, and it bothered me. It put knots in my stomach as my hands trembled while gripping my book bag. *Granddaughter?* This man had to be playing with my mind, because last I checked, and from what Code told me, my father was his nephew, not his son.

"I don't have a grandfather," I quietly said, pacing myself and quickly locking my emotions away to stare back up at him with the same soulless dark eyes.

Deep laughter came from Caltrone. He walked up to me and sized me up. "You intrigue me, granddaughter, but you are wrong. You are my granddaughter, and Demetri Lorenzo Orlando was my son. But to your mother and you, and those I chose not to tell, he was Lorenzo. My blood runs strong in you, and no one knew that he was my actual son, for safety purposes for his new identity. But now you know, my little one."

"Bullshit," I calmly said.

There was no way that I would give him any idea that he had just effectively shaken me to my core. Everything I had found out about my dad in the past, I knew as a lie, but this mess, this added shit. Yeah, that took the cake. No damn way this was true.

"No, granddaughter, there are many things that I am, but a liar? No. Since meeting you when you took that bold step to introduce yourself while you robbed me with my enemy, I've been trying to determine exactly what type of Orlando are you. Are you truly of me or are you weak?"

"I'm not of you at all, so label me as weak. I'm good with that." I had backed away as far as I could on the back deck of the house, and in my peripheral vision, I could see that my whole home was surrounded. I wasn't sure what to do, but I knew I couldn't run, and I was furious at myself. How could I have been so stupid as to come back to this place? What in hell made me think that after all had gone down, it would be safe to come back here?

Eyes never leaving Caltrone's face, I watched him as he moved back and forth, his hands folded in front of him as if praying. He glanced around me again, then at the house, and the way his face contorted when seeing how there was paint peeling on the railings, and how there was red clay dirt on the deck, bothered me deeply because I knew that he was judging my life and how I had to grow up. *Fuck him.*

"I've decided that you are of me. Already from how you speak, I know you are of me. You remind me of another one of mine who I have found, and this makes me proud. Though . . ." Reaching out, he grabbed me by the chin and pushed my hoodie back. A warm, appraising smile then spread across his face. He gave a nod and licked his lips, "We'll be changing you into something more subtle for an Orlando, *reina*."

"Who said that I want to be a *reina*? I don't know you, nor do I want to," I carefully said while trying to lean back from his watching gaze.

Still turning my face from side to side, he chuckled at my words. "What a beautiful jawline, how exquisite, and what lovely shade of nutmeg. No, more like a mixture of caramel and chocolate. You are a unique beauty. Your father might have thought that I would not want you, but he was wrong in that thought process. You are of my bold bloodline. Of course I would want you. I said I had no use for you, but I was wrong. Like a diamond in the rough, you need guidance and craftsmanship. Then you will be perfect for *mi familia*."

A shiver went through me at his words, and panic rose up, causing me to pull away while dropping my book bag on the low and pushing it under the chair.

I shimmied past him and moved to stand away from him as best as I could. The book bag I prayed that one of the Eraserheads would find. What was in it was of value. I hoped that if they noticed my bag left on the porch, they'd know that something foul had gone down and that I needed help.

"I don't want to breed for your fucking family," I spat out in defense.

"Nia, let us not be so"—watching me move past him, a look of disdain flashed across his handsome features as he sighed—"dramatic. I like the strength in you. I don't particularly care for this weak side. Now walk with me. I would like to spend the day with what was lost to me and discuss some things."

Like I said, there was nothing that I could do. If I fought, it would only piss him off and shorten my life even more, so all that I was able to do was reluctantly comply. Head bowed, I slipped a hand in my pocket and sent out a coded text to the two most important people in my life right now, Code and Auto. For backup, I even sent a message to Boots. For the second time recently, I had been snatched up at my mom's place. It was definitely time to let it go. As I sat in the back of a car with a man I knew in my soul my mom did not want me around, I said a mental goodbye to the place where I grew up and the spirit of my mother.

Smooth jazz played while Caltrone sat casually with one leg crossed. A lit cigar was in his hand while he read a file. From my angle, I made out a picture. It was the football player I had looked up with a little kid, who seemed to be his twin. A frown formed on my face in thought. If Caltrone was checking him out, then he too was up a creek and about to deal with some shit, unless he'd already met him.

Various hoods passed us. I saw that we were heading away from south Atlanta and going elsewhere. Panic hit me, but I knew if Auto had gotten my text, he'd know to track me. So I put my faith in that and watched the highway.

"You have the look of my mother. Your perfectly shaped lips and slope of your nose. The way your brown eyes lighten to the color of honey. She even had the same small dimple near the side of her lip when she smiled," I heard Caltrone say as he closed his folder. "Except for that flaming skull on your hand, you have her looks. Why would you tarnish your beautiful flesh like that?"

"It kept unwanted eyes off of me." Talking to this dude was not something I wanted to do. However, he was trying to play nice, so I had no choice but to cater to his madness. I looked like his mother? How fucked up was that? Frankly, I felt that he was being condescending and an asshole, trying to pull me in by any means, because I knew without a doubt that I carried my mother's looks as well. The height was my father's, and maybe the jawline and the way my eyes flipped when I was angry, as well as his temper, but I refused to accept anything else.

"You are an Orlando. There is nothing in the world that you can do to hide your beauty, Nia. Nothing. You are already a uniquely bred woman. Those tattoos, the piercings, that awful black lip color that I've seen you wear, they do nothing but enhance you. It pulls in those you think would stay away. You should know that by now," he explained.

"What I know is that it helped me keep those I did not want to touch me out of my face. If you have a problem with it, then I'm sorry, boo boo, that's your fault," I said with an annoyed shrug.

I didn't have the patience for this bullshit. He saw in me what he wanted to see, another female he could barter or use for his own power play. I wasn't stupid. Everything he said was exactly what my father had told me when I turned sixteen. I no longer was a sexless-looking child he could teach how to hunt. No, as soon as I started to bleed, and curves came, I became a beauty worth treasuring. It made me sick.

"You're angry." A low laugh flowed through the back of that car, chilling me. "I see it in your eyes, and I find it alluring. Yes, Nia, keep surprising me. I enjoy it. Now tell me what you know of your father, my dear son Lorenzo."

I shifted in my seat and closed my eyes in thought. "Nothing. He was crap. He drank too much, smoked too much. Loved to swing his gun around and loved to inflict pain on my mother. That is all. He was some type of vet? That's all I know."

"That is only half of the truth. Explain to me how you found your way to the old barrio and met my grand-daughter Maria Rosa." A second file appeared in his hand. He pulled out pictures of both me and Code back in New York, and it chilled me in my soul when I also saw a picture of myself at my father's home.

"That right there is one of my favorite images," he said, tapping his finger on the picture of my father's dead body slumped in his living room chair, motionless. "There was a certain finesse and wildness in how you pulled that off, my dear granddaughter. That allowed me to know that you have potential. That you are of me and not inflicted by the mutt mentality. To kill your own father? *Dios,* what finesse! But excuse me, back to my first question."

A heavy lump collected in my throat. That tingling fear crept in my spine as my thoughts sparked on one hundred. "I really don't know what you're talking about with that. But me meeting . . . Maria Rosa was strictly by accident."

"Accident you say? Now I find that to be another lie. Please do not lie to me. I do not take liars well. I have a bad habit of cutting their tongues out and feeding them to my dogs." As he adjusted the knot of his tie, his eyes bore into me again. "No, I believe you are better than this, so let us try that again, *sí?*"

It was so intense inside that car, his voice so potent with venom, that it had me swallowing hard before responding, "*Sí.*"

"Ah, beautiful, you speak the language of the family?" he interrupted in joy.

"I . . . No. Maria taught a little, and I knew only a little from my dad," I squeaked out.

Caltrone gave a low growl and waved his hand, glancing at me in disgust for a second. "Go on, explain."

"I wanted to know where my father was, and when I did that, I found out that he had family. Th . . . that's when I ran into Maria Rosa," I muttered.

"Aw, now that aligns with my research. Afterward, she inducted you into the little fleas she calls Eraserheads?" he questioned.

Plumes of smoke filled up the car, making my eyes water in the process. The back of the car felt like hell, like I was sitting in a box specifically created for the devil himself, and all I wanted to do was ball myself up into a ball and cry.

"Yes," I quietly said.

"Tell me why you killed my son," he sharply asked. "I specifically trained him into blending in as a solider, and later as an officer in the Atlanta police. My next move was to put him in NYPD, and then you killed him? Tell me what your reasoning was."

In my mind, I knew the reason, ran over the reasons millions of times. I did it because I hated him. Hated what he did to my mother and me, what he tried to do in the end, the branding on my body. But with what Caltrone had just told me, things I never knew, everything changed for me. In front of Caltrone, I shocked even myself with the next words that came out of my mouth.

"He disrespected me as his child. I hated him. There's no simple reason except that he outlived his purpose and he had to die. He was weak," I said, heated. "I mean, he told me nothing of you," I found myself adding once I saw the amused glint in his eyes.

"Keep it where you had it. The rest is null. Some of my children have a habit of being unorganized and not disciplined. Lorenzo was my bright one until he became an addict. He still worked well for me but not in what

I needed. You were right in your assessment and right in ending him, because eventually, I would have done it myself," he said, then tapped on the roof and pointed. "Welcome to the family compound. Get out."

The passenger side door opened up, and a hand reached in and dragged me out and up. Orlando's eyes stared down at me, and I recognized the man in front of me as Mark, Code's cousin. Nervousness hit me, and I stepped back from him. I had heard her say that he was an aggressive type, the kind who enjoyed putting fear in others and hurting them in the process. He was someone I did not want to cross, but if I had the right tool in my hand, there was no doubt that I'd make it count and kill the nigga in front of me.

"Mark, tell Santana to ready Maria Rosa's room," Caltrone ordered. "It's time that she met another lost Orlando."

"Santana" rang in my mind. Code had told me of the woman who birthed her. The name linked to the woman who had helped in marking her back was Santana. Fucking hell, I was in deep.

"Don't you want to talk more?" I quickly asked, trying to put a chill in my voice.

"Yes, I do. Here is what I'd like you to do first: send a message to my Maria Rosa. Explain to her how much I miss her and wish that she were here to attend this lovely family reunion. There is so much we all need to speak about soon. Also, add in there that I intend to leave you in the delicate hands of her mother. I believe that you two will get along great and that you will begin to grasp the ways of a proper Orlando woman," he crooned. "I know you have the means to communicate with her, do you not? You know what? I'm a hands-on man. I'll do it."

I knew this motherfucker didn't really want me as he was saying. *This is all a game to get Code,* I thought until

I looked in his eyes. There was a coldness reflecting there that worried me. Maybe I started out as a pawn, but now it was something more: interest.

He snatched me by the arm, twisted it, then found my cell in my pocket. I watched him swipe then signal for me to pull up Code's information. I had her listed as Lady Death Rose, which I could tell Caltrone thought was amusing. He started typing, then dropped my cell and stomped on it, smashing it into pieces.

"As my son's only child, you are important to me. No seed of mine disrespects me or leaves me unless I allow it. In that, you are kindred, my dear, and it is why I won't kill you. However, you worked with my enemy and have helped in keeping my Maria Rosa from me, as well as stole from me . . . your blood." He paused then fisted his hands.

"My *gold!*" he barked out, his face flashing into that of a monster. "That, my dear grandchild, is *not* something I will tolerate. For that and your repulsive work with my enemies, you will be punished. It's time that you became instructed in the Orlando ways, or you can die." Caltrone leaned down and kissed the top of my head.

"I'd rather you not die. I see potential in you, my diamond in the rough." He glanced me over again, then flashed his teeth in an adoring smile and said, "So much of my mother in you. Welcome home, granddaughter." Then he walked away.

I stood there shocked, but then it flipped to fury. This "knee-grow" got me all fucked up, but of course I was going to comply. One thing I knew about myself was I was a survivor. If I had to die, and then so be it. However, there was no way that I could allow another death to occur by this monster's hand. So with that, I walked inside the massive mansion.

I was taken to Code's old room by a model-type woman who, I found out, was Code's mother. Once in there, she looked me over with disgust on her face. I watched her walk out with not even a hello, and then she slammed the door. Of course, I gave not one shit.

Clothes were laid out for me to change into. I ignored them all and sat on the edge of the bed. Maybe Auto's idea of running away with the Eraserheads was a good idea. I kind of wished I had stayed back at his place instead of going to my mom's, because I was definitely in a fucked-up situation. Sighing, I reached in my shoe to pull out my backup cell that had only Boots' and Auto's info, and I clicked codes to block out any tracking. *Welcome to hell,* I thought. I prayed that I played this part of the game well, because I did not want to die.

Chapter 17

Code

I had to get away from Boots. Why? Because some people brought out the worst in you. Some people brought out the best in you. And some people—rare individuals they were— some brought out everything. Boots brought out the best of the best in me, and then he would go and bring out the worst of the worst. The nigga was addictive. I wasn't sure if he even knew that he gave me a high that went unmatched. He took me on a high so natural that I would probably follow him into hell just to get another hit, to keep getting that fix that only he could give me.

My mother may not have had that many of those talks with me about the things between men and women, but Papa had. One of the few times when Papa seemed like a normal, everyday man was when he talked about the person who could make a man or woman forget all that mattered because they had a certain power that overrode all your logical sense. He told me it would be inevitable I found a man like that because I had the kind of spirit that attracted certain kinds of men. It was one of the reasons he put the fear of God in most of the boys who'd tried to date me back in Cuba and threatened the lives of most of the men once I came of age.

Papa said, "I won't be around to protect you always. So as soon as you find the man who you know without a doubt will make you question even your own good sense, you run. Because if you don't, it's like a hit to the vein of the most potent heroin. Once you get a hit, you're addicted, and that is the beginning of your end."

Boots was behind me. A fistful of my wild hair in one hand and the other hand had a death lock on my waist. There was something that always happened between us. We'd fight. He'd make me angry enough to kill him. Then he would look at me a certain way or say something that would take the fight right out of me. I was puzzled by how he was able to do that in such a short time. I couldn't explain it. I hated how he seemed to control that part of me, the part that made me . . . human. It made me hate that I lost all my control around him.

Sweat dripped on my back from his body. Heat had cocooned us. Not just the temperature, but the heat between the man in the boots and the woman who I didn't know lived inside of me. The heat between man and woman that made lust so strong it overrode common sense at times. Moments before, he'd berated me because, in his mind, I was somewhat at fault for Alize's death. He'd cursed me to hell. I yelled for him to join me. He wanted the location of Papa's hideout, but I wouldn't give it to him. Only because there were some of my family there that I knew had no choice but to do Papa's bidding or the consequences would be dire.

"I mean, just how fucking long will you be a pawn, Maria? Every time I think you may have some common sense left, you prove to me that common sense ain't so common when it comes to the likes of you," he'd ridiculed me with that gotdamn Texas drawl that made my womb quiver.

I truly hated this nigga. At least that was what I told myself.

"You need to thank my common sense that isn't so common, because if you run up on Papa on his turf, you're as good as fucked. And I'm not being a pawn. I'm looking out for those family members who I know still have some good in them."

"You mean like your cousin, the super cop? The one who was willing to take you back to the old man for the sake of saving himself?"

At this point, I was tired of explaining myself. Tired of trying to get him to step into my shoes and see where I was coming from. I'd come to realize that no matter what I said or how I tried to explain it, he would never see things from my point of view. That angered me, annoyed me to the point of wanting to strangle him.

But I couldn't strangle him. Even as he looked at me with a mixture of pity and rage, I couldn't bring myself to harm him as my mind screamed for me to do. The fact that he was shirtless and the sinewy muscles in his back rolled and coiled like steel cables could have been one of those reasons too. Those evenly placed dimples on his cheeks. Amber-colored eyes. The long beard on his chiseled chin. The wavy fade and that smooth brown skin that reminded me of peanut butter. All of it was my undoing.

Boots had something that no other man—other than Papa—had over me: control. Boots had control of me. Only his kind of control wasn't smothering. His kind of control didn't make me feel as if my soul was on its way to hell. Boots' kind of control made me question my values, the core principles I'd been raised by.

Boots' control made me forget I was mad at the condescending way he would look at me when I would speak of Papa in reverence, when I spoke of all the good he'd done to outweigh the bad. Boots' control only sought to make me think outside of the box I'd grown up in. It was a scary thing to question all you've known and to go against the grain.

"You've thought a snake was a stick, and then it bit you. Yet you still won't acknowledge the venom," he spat out.

Everything I thought I once knew, everything I'd lived by, was coming undone. It frightened me. What would I do without Papa's guidance? What would I do without someone to kill? What would I do without his money and his resources? What would I do without Papa's love? All of those questions had been attacking me since the night I left the auto shop after he'd sent a hit squad after my friends.

I was livid, past the point of anger. I was on the verge of a nervous breakdown. So I lashed out at the man who I'd thought was the cause of it: Boots. But he had my number. The man had been the remedy to my poison, the antivenom to my bite.

I swung at him. He caught my wrist and twisted it behind my back, then shoved me face-first onto the bed. I tried to get back up, but he was quicker than I was. He crawled over the back of my thighs and held me down by the back of my neck.

"You got a real problem with your hands always trying to connect to my face," he aggressively whispered in my ear. "Where is she? Where is the spitfire of a woman I met before? Just because all you've ever known is crashing down around you doesn't mean that you have to lose who you are. Don't let your loyalty become slavery, Maria."

I screamed out. Tried to use my strength to push him off of me. I hated to admit that since Papa had been after me, I felt weak. I put up a good front, but I felt the walls caving in on me. It was too much, the pressure of knowing that I was as good as dead to the man I'd once thought the world of, the only man I'd known as a father because my own had disappeared before I could remember his name. Boots was right. I was losing myself.

Not to mention I didn't want to admit that I liked the way he felt pressed up against me. The way the hold he had on the back of my neck made my spine quiver. That was how I ended up on my knees, perfect arch in my back while his dick penetrated the very fabric of my being. The sex was so good I felt like he was knocking on the door of my soul.

"Tell me what I want to know," he asked again.

But this time his voice wasn't laced in malice. This time his voice was coated in seduction. Could probably talk a nun out of her underpants. I could feel him swelling inside of me. The condom he had on didn't take away from the feeling he was giving me. His sex was so potent I would have given him the secrets to life.

So I did.

I told him what he wanted to know. My reward was the hard rock of his hips against the softness of my ass. He snatched me up by my hair, sat back on his haunches, snaked one strong arm around my waist, and made me reverse cowgirl him while he was on his knees until we both released all that pent-up sexual tension. Yes, I knew he used sex to get what he wanted out of me. Was I ashamed of it? A little. Did I care? Not really.

Twenty minutes later his phone started to light up and dance with vibrations across his dresser. He'd just stepped out of the shower when the first call came through. His phone ringing made me remember that mine had died a few hours before and was still on the charger.

Boots dropped the towel that had been around his waist. His thick dick slapped against his thigh when he reached for his black boxer briefs to pull them on.

He grabbed his cell, pressed the touch screen, then tossed it in the wingback red leather chair behind him. "Speak," he said.

There was a seriousness across his handsome features.
I sat on the bed and listened. I'd showered with the man,
and neither one of us said a word while washing away
the traces of our lust. I'd dressed in my signature white
suit. White six-inch stiletto boots adorned my feet. Had
pinned my hair into a bun with two Chinese hairpins
holding it in place.

"We got a problem over in Copper Hills, boss," a voice
came through.

"What kind of problem?" Boots asked with authority in
his tone.

"You're going to have to see it to believe it. You need to
get here, stat."

"Be there in twenty."

"Think you can make it in ten?"

Boots didn't respond. He finished pulling on his Levi's,
then picked up the phone to end the call. I watched as
he texted someone and looked over at me. He tossed me
a black holster and pointed to the top drawer where he
kept a case of guns.

"Grab two and follow me," he ordered.

He snatched his purple button-down shirt off the back
of the chair and slid his arms through the sleeves as he
walked out the door. I kept it simple, grabbed two 9 mm
Sig Sauers, and marched behind him. The condo we
were in was clearly one that had been suited to fit Boots.
Everyone in the building was a part of Boot's organization in some way. So as he grabbed his gray Stetson, after
stepping into the cowboy boots by the door, and made
his way out the front door, men and women opened
doors to follow him out.

Shango was the first face we saw. Boots had tried to get
him to take some time off, but he wasn't hearing it. He'd
gone from joke-cracking Shango to this indifferent shell
of a man. He stayed locked away in his place and barely

spoke a word unless Boots spoke directly to him. As usual, he was dressed in all black, but this time there were splashes of red and purple that could be seen throughout his outfit. Alize was gone. Oya was gone. Shango had come undone.

Boots stepped on the elevator, then jerked his head to the side for me to follow. Shango stepped in next, followed by two new men and women I'd never seen before. Two other guards stood outside the elevator as it closed. I could see others heading toward the stairs. I gazed at Boots. I had come to have much more respect for him than I did initially. At first, I thought him to be some showoff who wanted to make a name in the game, but he was proving to be so much more than that.

He had his shit together, and again, it made me wonder just how a man as young as he had so many resources at his disposal. Someone was backing him. They had to be. He always got on my ass about secrets and blind loyalty, yet he had his own secrets. For some reason, it didn't bother me as it once did. I felt heavy as we rode down the electric contraption to the first floor. My mood became sullen, and I felt the weight of the world on my shoulders. I remained silent as we exited the elevator. More guards stood there waiting for us. They flanked Boots like he was a dignitary.

They were poised and stoic like soldiers. No expression adorned their faces. I watched as they searched the silver Escalade before Boots was allowed to get anywhere near it. The weather was cool, but not cold. The wind blew softly, and the sun kept playing peekaboo with the clouds. People milled about on the promenade in Buckhead but watched on curiously, wondering who the man was who had all the guards. Traffic on the street was at a standstill. The people in the cars stared on just as the people walking by had. I could smell food from the different eateries around the area. Grilled steak, fried fish, and greens were just some of the smells. There was something sweet in the air as well.

Once the truck had been cleared, Boots took my hand and allowed me to get in first. Always the gentleman no matter what was going on around him. After Boots was in the truck, Shango took the wheel and pulled out into traffic. We sat silently at first, Boots tapping away on his phone and me in my own world. We didn't act like two people who'd just engaged in the act of coitus.

"You need to figure out what you're going to do after all of this is said and done," Boots said to me once we'd gotten out of traffic.

Shango had veered off and was about to merge onto the expressway.

To be honest, I hadn't wanted to think about what would happen when this was over. I had no idea where I was going or how I was going to get there. Auto had wiped me clean. I had no money to save my life. If by chance I did survive this reckoning, I was penniless and homeless. Homeless because for so long any place I'd laid my head was where Papa had placed me. I still had my old apartment, but I knew that if Papa didn't get to me, there would be no way I could go back there, especially since it was tied to the Eraserheads.

"I don't know what I'm going to do. I haven't thought that far ahead," I finally answered.

He glanced at me like he wanted to say something else but stopped himself.

I wanted to know. "Why do you ask?"

"Because I won't be here."

"Where are you going?"

"Away to mind my business. Got things that need to be handled behind the scene and I need to go off the grid," he said.

"I take it this is your way of telling me that I'm going to be on my own from here on out?" I asked.

Boots look over at me. He licked his lips and folded his muscular arms across his broad chest. "Take it how you want it, mama."

I didn't feel like getting into a war of words with him. It always ended one of two ways: I'd end up on my back, or he'd end up trying to break my wrist for swinging on him. So I kept my mouth shut.

As we exited off 75 and made a right down Upper Riverdale Road, I let my mind wonder. It was time I stopped hiding and running. It wasn't the way of the Orlandos. If Papa wanted me, he would have to come get me. I wouldn't just lay down and die. I had to admit, before I'd thought about just letting the old man kill me and getting it over with, but the longer I stayed around Boots, the more I realized it was a stupid idea. It could have been because Boots was always telling me how stupid of an idea it was, to be honest. I'd let Papa come find me, and once he did, I'd cross that bridge.

As we turned down Garden Walk Boulevard, I frowned because of the scene coming into view. The closer we got to Copper Hills, the more that frown deepened. Red, white, yellow, and black roses lined the entry way all the way to the old apartment Boots used to be holed up in. White carnations filled the front of the door.

Shango stopped the truck as we pulled inside, more like hit the brakes hard and jerked us forward. He quickly exited the truck with Boots right behind him. A few more of Boots' men walked out of the apartments. The place was quiet, a vast contrast to the buzzing hive of activity there used to be.

"He just walked right in and ordered his people to start placing the flowers out here. We could have started a gunfight, but it would have been stupid being that he was guarded like he was fucking Fort Knox. Instead, we chilled out and waited after we called you," one of the men said to Boots. "He left the flowers. Nigga even kneeled and said a prayer like he knew Alize. Then he was ghost."

I remembered the young man who was talking. He was the same young boy with locs and his jeans hanging off his ass the first time I'd come here searching for Boots. Now he stood in a suit that had been tailored to fit him. His locs no longer looked like insects lived inside of them. They had been freshly twisted, and they swung around his slender shoulders as he spoke.

Papa had sent flowers for Alize. She was a warrior after all. I knew he was a lot of things. People called him a monster, a killer, drug dealer, menace to society. But I knew a side of the man the world didn't. He believed in doing things with style and class. So even if he did wipe out half of your whole family, if he had respect for you, he would show it some kind of way.

This was his way of showing respect to Boots and to his fallen comrade. I had a good mind to tell him that, but judging by the way Shango had started to kick the beautifully styled bouquets over, I'd say it wouldn't matter. There were so many roses and white carnations, it looked as if we were standing in a field of them. I could barely see the parking lot.

Shango's angry grunts could be heard as he walked through, kicking the flowers. He picked a few up and slung them around while Boots stood there with a disturbed look on his face. I knew he probably thought Papa was up to another mind fuck, and he could have been, but I knew now wasn't the moment to say anything. One wrong move or saying the wrong thing would make me an enemy of the state again.

I stood by the truck and watched as Shango fell to his knees. I hadn't seen the man cry. Wasn't sure if he was crying then since his back was turned to me. But I could assume by the way his back expanded, the way his fists were pounding into the concrete ground, that he'd finally let go and started to grieve out in the open.

Boots walked over to Shango. "Just give me a minute, family," he said, holding his hand out to stop Boots from coming any closer.

Boots said something to him, but I couldn't hear it. I remembered I needed to turn my phone on, and I pulled it from my pocket. It didn't ring much these days unless Smiley was texting or calling me. As if on cue, as soon as it powered on, a few seconds later, Smiley's number popped up. I smiled a bit. Hadn't heard from her since we talked about Auto's plan to rob Papa. Word on the wire was that Auto and the team had successfully taken down the warehouse in Lovejoy. It didn't take long for word to get out on the streets about a coup as big as that.

Everybody wanted to know who had been crazy enough to do such a thing. They didn't know Auto the way I did. Yeah, he seemed meek, cool, calm, and collected, but I knew there was another side to him. Could see the madness just beneath the surface, and I knew that no matter how I tried to get Smiley to warn him, talk him out of it, he wouldn't hear of it. I used my thumb to slide open the lock on the touchscreen.

Come quick. The old man is here. Came to my mom's to get something. He was waiting for me. He said he misses you. If you don't come, he said he's going to leave me with your mother. Hurry, the text read.

My eyes started to water. *Shit!* Why would she be out there by herself like that knowing they had just robbed the man? Why didn't Auto make her stay put? How had he let her slip away when I was sure there was a bounty on their fucking heads? I quickly glanced at Boots to see him still talking to Shango as he checked his phone. The truck still had the keys in the ignition. I didn't think about what I was doing. I had to get to Smiley. I couldn't let my mother introduce her to the ways of the Orlandos. Smiley was tough, but my mother was tougher, and I knew she would break her down to her bare minimum in the name of Papa.

I hopped in the truck, closed the door, put the truck in reverse, and sped out. I could hear Boots calling my name, but I was already speeding away.

Made it to Smiley's old neighborhood in record time. For a Saturday it was eerily quiet. I parked Shango's truck on the street, pulled my guns from the holsters, and headed toward the front door.

"Smiley," I called out once I saw her front door ajar. I got no answer. I called out to her again. "Smiley, if you're in there make some noise."

I glanced around the neighborhood again and wondered where all the children were who used to be running up and down the street. Had Papa locked the hood down so tightly that people had run off already? I used my foot to kick the already-ajar door open. The place was quiet. Nothing seemed out of the ordinary. It was a bit cool on the inside. It had the smell of a place that had been empty for a while. Not a mold or mildew smell, but just an empty smell in a clean dwelling.

"I was wondering how long it would take you to show up."

His voice chilled me. My stomach took a somersault, and goose bumps took over my flesh. My spine stiffened as I turned around to face Papa. There he stood, legs apart, feet planted firmly on the ground, arms folded behind him. It was a signature dominant stance that told me he had no intentions of leaving until he'd accomplished what he came to do. He was dressed in all black, which told me he hadn't really come to talk. Anytime Papa dressed in all black, it signaled his intent to kill. Muscles bulged in his chest and arms. His handsome face showed no emotion. But it was the way his eyes held no regard for me that let me know I'd come to the end of my rope.

"Where is she?" I asked him. I thought my voice would have come out with a tremor. I surprised myself with how stern it sounded.

"She's getting better acquainted with her roots," he answered nonchalantly. "But I didn't come to discuss her as I'm sure you know."

As he said this, I saw four of my male cousins enter from a back room and surround me. He'd brought the best of the best. They too were all dressed in black. Papa had brought my own special hit squad. I found myself chuckling a bit.

"Couldn't kill me yourself, could you? Had to bring in the lesser ones to do what you can't, as always," I taunted my old man, playing on his emotional attachment to me.

He didn't seem impressed. I expected him to say something snide, but all he did was gaze at me with an unreadable expression on his face. He then looked at my cousins. "If you want to have a chance in hell of beating her, I suggest you find a way to disarm her," he told them.

Before the words could leave his mouth fully, I turned to my left, took aim, and shot one cousin between the eyes. Turned to the right to send a kill shot to another's heart. His body dropped to the floor like a sack of potatoes. However, before I could get to the other two cousins, prongs to my back from a Taser took me down to my knees. Migo rushed in to kick the gun from my hand. Then he snatched the other gun from the holster I had on.

I knew they could have easily killed me then, but Papa had probably wanted to make me suffer, so a beating was in order. When my teeth got finished chattering and I regained control over my body, Anton gave me a swift kick in the side that sent me sliding into the left wall.

The blood from one of the cousins I had killed soaked my side. The kick hurt, I wouldn't lie. Felt like my ribs had caved in. I pulled myself up slowly, then snatched my suit jacket off.

Migo rushed in for me. He was tall and lanky, so he loved to use his legs and long arms to his advantage. The nigga was like an octopus, and if you weren't careful, he could wrap you in those long arms and legs and take you out. That was all well and good, but I also knew that the closer I stayed to him, the less damage he could do. When his foot came for my stomach, I grabbed his leg then kicked him in his dick with my booted foot. He crouched over to grab his injured jewels, and I grabbed one of the Chinese hairpins holding my bun up and shoved it into his left eye.

I didn't have time to relish that small victory. Anton still had that damn Taser. I sidestepped the prongs coming toward me again, then took a running leap. With a Superman punch to the jaw, I backed him up off me.

Anton was stockier than his brother. He was also a wrestler, a ground-and-pound kind of dude. He got off on the way he could overpower women. The punch only took him off his game for a second. He launched at me. Lifted me from the floor like he'd been trained in the WWE, then slammed me against the empty bookcase. I went down with a hard thud. Looked up just in time to see his big foot coming toward my face. I rolled over quickly, yanked the hairpin from Migo's eye, then hopped up. I used the wall for leverage. Leaned back on it then launched myself forward. I stabbed him. Quick and precise little stabs that he wouldn't feel right away but would slowly take a toll on him.

Stabbed in his upper arms, chest, and abdomen. His grunts and groans matched my yells and screams. The stabs to the neck pissed him off, but not more than the fact I was too fast for him to wrap me in his famous bear hug. With the base of the Chinese hairpin balled in my hand, I struck his nose repeatedly with my fist. Anton's nose was the most painful place to hit him on his body. The hits angered him. Made him come after me like an agitated bull. I hit him with body shots with one hand and continued to stab him with the hairpin using the other hand.

Anton was winded. The stabs with the hairpin and the body shots were taking a toll. I was just getting started. There was a reason I was the old man's favorite. I was his replica. Anton was fighting to win. I fought to live. Papa had always told me not to worry about winning, but to worry about coming out alive.

Anton's meaty fist caught my jaw and sent me reeling. Another one to my eye took me off my game. I stumbled and fell back on my ass. He was on me like stank on shit. Lifted me up from the floor by my neck and shook me while he strangled me. The hit to the face had made me drop the hairpin, so I tried clawing his hands away from my neck. It didn't work. Unlike his brother Migo, his arms weren't so long, and I tried to claw his eyes out.

His yells and groans fed me. Made me want to go harder. I lashed out at him like I was a wild jungle cat. My claws kept sinking into his eyes, tearing at the skin on his face. By any means necessary I would survive. Blood had started to pool around my fingers. I expected him to drop me to the floor, but instead, he threw me against the wall. I was disoriented, crawling on my knees as I coughed up mucus and tried to get my breathing together. One of the

guns that Migo had taken from me was within my reach.
I rushed for it, turned on my side, and took out Anton's
knees. I couldn't really see as the tears had my vision
blurry, but I needed to do enough to keep him off me.

I could still see Papa standing there. Like a commander
watching his soldiers go to war, he stood silently. I made
my way to my feet. Limped over to Anton and placed a
bullet through his eye. Migo was still moaning out on the
other side of the room. As I walked past him, I placed a
bullet in his heart.

I wiped the blood from my mouth with the back of my
hand, then looked at Papa. "You're going to have to do
better than that," I whispered through a snarl, then sent
bullets after him.

Papa was quick to be as old as he was. He ducked my
shots. Did a tuck and roll then grabbed his gun from his
holster. A bullet to the shoulder almost made me drop my
gun. I turned around quickly, but he was agile. I made
the mistake of letting him get behind me. He put me in a
sleeper hold, lifted me from the floor, then slammed me
down so hard it felt like he threw me to hell.

Papa was a strong man, and age hadn't slowed him
down. He landed punch after punch to my stomach.
Snatched me up from the floor and then backhanded me
across the room. Before I even hit the floor again, he was
on me. His big hands latched on to my throat as he lifted
me above his head and tossed me back across to the other
side of the small front room. I left a hole in the wall this
time.

"You don't betray family, Maria Rosa. That was lesson
number one. Loyalty is the most important thing in this
family, girl," he said as he slowly trekked across the floor
to where I'd fallen.

He grabbed a handful of my hair and slowly dragged
me across the room behind him. My body was weak. One

of my eyes swollen shut. My lips were heavy, and all I could think about was Smiley. I prayed she was okay. I thought about Auto and all the friends I'd lost because of the mess I'd gotten myself into. Papa pulled me behind him until he came to a chair in the room that I hadn't seen before. He sat down and snatched my head up to look at him.

"I need to know one more thing before you die. Where's Frederick?" he asked

There would be no way I would ever tell him what Freddie had done. I couldn't tell him where he was anyway, since I didn't know. Boots had wanted it that way. It wasn't so much to protect Freddie, but to protect Oya, who was with him.

I didn't answer my old man. I spit in his face. My blood, mucus, and saliva painted his nose and upper lip. Papa hated to be touched by another's bodily fluids. I often wondered how he enjoyed sex when his OCD was so prevalent.

"Ugh," he spat, then slammed my face into the floor.

I couldn't even scream out as the hit to the head rattled me.

"Santana," he called out.

Mother? She was here? If she was here now, then how long had they had Smiley? What had they done to her? I moaned out because pain wouldn't allow me to be quiet. I could barely turn my head, but I knew the sound of my mother's heels. She slowly trekked in and then kneeled before me. She hummed as she smoothed her hand across my forehead.

"Maria Rosa, my dear precious daughter. You disappoint me and Father, sí?" she crooned in her sing-song voice. "I brought you into this world, my little warrior, and now I have to take you out."

Papa took a seat. He crossed his legs into a figure four and watched on sternly. My mother kept petting me like I was some kind of exotic animal instead of her child.

"Get up, Maria. Die with honor instead of on your belly like a coward," she taunted as she stood and backed away.

It was at that moment I realized I hated my mother. She'd never done anything motherly for me. The only time we had interactions was when she wanted to do something to impress Papa. I was more his child than I was hers. As I slowly made my way to my feet, I wondered if she ever knew how much I'd craved her affection as a child. I wondered if she knew I wanted it to be her who took me to buy my first feminine moon cup instead of Papa. I wondered if she knew my favorite colors, my favorite foods, the time that boy broke my heart so Papa broke his foot.

When I swiftly picked up a piece of wood from the broken bookcase and threw it at her head, I wondered if she even saw me as her child. Or was I just another way for her to get in good with Papa?

She dodged the piece of wood and laughed maniacally. Her hair was slicked back into a sleek ponytail. A black leather cat suit adorned her body, showcasing all the luscious curves she owned. She closed the gap between us and gave me a scissor kick that I was sure knocked a few teeth loose. My head jerked back, and blood spewed from my mouth. Pain sliced through my body as she sent the blade of the knife in her hand into my left side. Mother was doing her father proud. My legs almost gave from underneath me, but I wouldn't fall, not again. I regained my balance. I yelled out as she closed in on me, then I sent a head butt into her chin. An elbow strike to her nose then an uppercut caught her off guard.

My mother's eyes were her best line of defense, because she seemed to carry a pair in the back of her head.

She could be looking straight ahead but tell you what's going on around her. I raked my nails across them then punched her dead center in the throat. This would have thrown most people off their game, but not Santana Orlando. It fueled her fire. She came back at me hard. Shin kicks to the side of my face threw my equilibrium off. Another slice to my abdomen then a stab to the chest gave me pain I'd never imagined. A leg sweep took me off my feet. My mother straddled me, and with closed fists, knife still in hand, she backhanded me over and over like a wild banshee.

As she yelled and tried to bash my skull in, I reached for another piece of wood. I mustered all the strength I had left and hit my mother so hard she went flying off me. The knife she'd had in her hand went one way, and she went another. I turned and crawled toward the Chinese hairpin I'd dropped earlier. I could feel my mother closing in on me as I crawled. When she tried to stand over me and snatch me up by my hair, I turned over and jammed the hairpin through her eye. I yanked it out then jabbed it back in again.

Her shrill cries of pain satisfied me as I snatched the hairpin out again. She went stumbling back as both her hands cupped her face. I stood and sent a kick to her midsection that knocked her over the fallen debris of the broken bookcase. She was still once she hit the floor.

That kick took the wind out of me. It seemed that was last bit of fight I had left in me as sobs racked my shoulders. I cried so loudly and so hard that I was sure I sounded like a wounded animal. My legs were weak. I could barely stand. I was bloodied, and adrenaline mixed with fear gave me tremors that I couldn't quell. I turned to stare Papa down. Nobody, no one he'd brought in, could kill me.

I was what he trained me to be after all. I was afraid of snakes, so I was trained to be one. I fought with ruthless aggression that he'd instilled in me. If he wanted me dead, I would make him do it himself. I was in so much pain that when I let out a roaring yell that scared even me, I wasn't sure if it was because my body had been beaten and battered or if it was because I'd come out on top. The taste of coppery blood, sweat, tears, and saliva coated my mouth as I yelled.

Papa, Caltrone Orlando, sat unmoving, but his lips were turned down. He stared me down just as I did him. If I didn't know any better, I would say water lined his eyes.

"I never believed you were Satan until now," I stammered out.

"I often ask myself how is it that you disappoint me then give me pride all at once, Maria Rosa," he solemnly said. "Do you know how much I love you? Doted on you? Why would you betray me, my heart? Why? I've never denied I was that which you claim. You just refused to acknowledge it. So say that I am Satan as many would call me? Hmm? *Hierba mala nunca muere.*"

"The devil looks after his own," was what he'd said to me.

"*A cada puerco le llega su sabado,*" I spat out at him, telling him that every dog had its day.

His comeuppance was inevitable.

"*Sí*, that is correct. But today isn't my time."

His arrogance and smugness annoyed me, but the pain I felt inside at losing my grandfather hurt more than anything I'd ever felt before. The betrayal behind his actions made me realize that he would take down anyone who didn't follow his rule, even me, his favorite. I truly had nothing, and nobody left. Tears blinded me as I came to the realization that I would die alone with no friends and no family. I never got a chance to see Auto again. Never got a chance to laugh with Reagan, Stitch, and Jackknife again. I'd never get the chance to know my cousin, Nia, the way I wanted to. Papa stole the only sense of normalcy I ever had.

At that moment, all the love I had for him turned to hate. As the tears rolled down my face and I charged at the man who'd taught me everything I knew, I felt my end before I even saw it coming. Three bullets from his gun took residence in my chest. Stopped me in my tracks and made me fall to my knees. I never even heard my mother sneak up behind me. But I felt the stabs to the kidney and my lower spine that she gave me. Each one sealing my fate, my marriage to death.

My life flashed before my eyes, and I wondered if anybody would remember me. Wondered if I'd put enough good in the world to atone for all the evil I'd done in the name of Papa. When my mother's blade sliced my throat, after my body hit the floor, and while my blood soaked the hardwood floor of Smiley's home, I thought about Boots. Would he remember me? Or would I be just another crazy Orlando who'd met a violent end like so many before me? Who would he remember me as? Code or Maria Rosa? I saw Boots's face as my eyes fluttered closed.

As life slowly exited my body, I made my peace with God. I would never know that after Papa had killed me, later that night, in his private chambers where nobody could see or hear him, he would mourn my death like he'd only done once before. Not since he'd killed his best friend, Moses Ekejindu, had he mourned death like he would mine.

Chapter 18

Boots

"*Ana sabr heliko ask sabr abieni,*" was what I told Shango as he sat on his knees in pain. When I was a child, my pops would tell me this saying as a reminder of my mother. She'd tell him the same every time he headed out into the barrios of NYC doing work for the Kings. In Eritrean, it means, "I'm still patient until patience gets tired of me."

I was now using it as a means of encouragement for my boy. My circle had been effectively broken, leaving me vulnerable for attack if I were a lesser or weaker businessman. Let me break it down: if Caltrone was truly watching me, and wishing to take me down, then this would be the time he could effectively do so. As a professional killer, trained to be an assassin myself, I would use this moment of weakness to attack the head of the cobra, if the shoe were on the other foot.

"Code left, boss," was said behind me.

"I'm very aware of that, but what are you doing about it?" I calmly stated, still resting a hand on my brother's shoulder. Who was speaking to me was one of my younger members. I wasn't trying to be curt with the little dude, but it was what it was.

"Trailing her," he nervously said.

"Keep your distance with her. We're not her keeper. Report back to me on it later." I thumbed my nose and looked around at the flowers. "And clear this shit up. Put it in the park, tell the older women to plant them if they can, and that's that."

"Okay, boss," the kid said, disappearing.

Caltrone was a motherfucker. He was a royal motherfucker, but I got what was going on. He was a man about respect and true OG fighters, and I was raised on the same principles. In his gesture, I could see he still had something redeemable in him. However, how my feelings were made up right now, a brotha wasn't giving a fuck. I had the mentality of Vito Corleone and the anger of Tony Montana. He owed me, and he owed me on a major level.

However, after my boys did their homework in finding out who exactly were the ones who laid hands on Alize and Shango, and who gave that killing blow, I planned upon cashing that check and collecting the receipts later, while taking those motherfuckers' heads off. I mean, how could a brother not dictate payment in full? You don't touch the merchandise in the store, scratch it or break it, and think that you're not going to pay for that shit. That's just not how that works.

After giving my boy his time, standing by his side, I sat in my cleared-out office. Going off the grid was what I told Code that I was doing, but that wasn't entirely true. Being run out of a place wasn't my MO. I always made sure that when I left, it was on my terms, and that my crew could effectively run things without me. There was business that I needed to handle, and with my team being broken up, I had to move around fluidly in order to keep up my business and the real reason that I was in Atlanta.

Several phone calls were made. Plane tickets sent out to my people, my weapons packed up and gone. Now all I had left to do was to tie up some loose ends. This was the end of my run in Atlanta, and I intended to show just how much power and pull I had here. Word got back to me that the Asian Dragons were having a meeting with several of the bosses in Atlanta. Money and district zoning was about to go down, so I knew that if anyone needed to be at this meeting, Mr. Sunjeta was that man.

Gathering our things, Shango and I headed toward Sandy Springs several hours later. The people I'd had on Code had lost her, and that bothered me. Hopping on the highway, I chilled back, keeping my mind on the task ahead. All emotions were out of the gate, and thinking about those I lost, or the woman who had crept into my mental with her difficult ass, was not going to distract me from my overall purpose. I lost family, but I had a bigger pot to protect, as well as a foundation to shake.

Getting to Sandy Springs took a minute, and as we drove in silence, I hit the partition and studied.

"Once this meeting is over, you're on the next plane to Trinidad. After that, I better get word that you're in Paris, or we're going to have a problem, brother," I said.

Shango sat in a gloomy rigidity, his pupils were dilated, and there was a sinister anger to him that had me taking mental notes.

"I'm good. I vowed to protect you always, Boots, and that ain't changing no matter how I'm feeling," he said, fisting his hands on his thighs.

"You still have blood under your nails. You're still on some high shit, blacked out mentally. How can I know once we stand in front of the enemy that you'll be here one hundred percent, my dude?" I asked just to appease myself.

There was nothing but trust between us, but I needed to check his mental before allowing him to watch my back. Why? Because letting him loose hours before didn't look like it even helped shit. My boy seemed to be breathing hard, his shirt constricting with the tension in his body. Homie was still on some hulk shit. I should have left him behind.

"You taught us that Eritreans kneel on only two occasions: when they pray and when they shoot. Since you took us in as family, that motto has been ours. I'm your gun. A brother won't ever be trigger-happy unless you give the word," Shango explained. "Besides, we're all doing this for a bigger endgame. I need to honor Alize's work and I will, Raheem."

What he said was enough for me. "Honor her we will, Marcus. I promise you that, fam."

Clasping hands, we gave our familiar handshake, then sat back and discussed some plans. Once we made it to the high-rise where the meeting was set to go down, we were prepared and ready to go. It felt strange not to have Oya with us. The information that I retrieved from her was that she had managed to get Freddy's daughter out of Cuba. I knew from checking my itemization of weapons that some were sent her way, which meant that it was not an easy recon. But I was hearing good things. A brother was good and just hoped that once the rest of us made it to Paris, she'd be there. It was where we had Alize's body lying in state for Oya to say her goodbye.

"Boss?" pulled me out of my thoughts, and I glanced at the black double doors.

My hands smoothed down my suit, and I slid my hands behind my back. "I'm ready."

Loud voices were already shouting about zone restrictions and districting. Several bosses sat at a long table. The Asian Dragons, the Italian Cartel, Latino Kings, Jamaican Kings and Queens, as well as two reps for the African Queens all were there. Most importantly, Caltrone was there with two of his men. Mentally I smiled wide. All eyes were on me, which I enjoyed. I gave a respectful bow to the ones who invited me, who were the Asian Dragons, then I moved to stand at the head of the table.

"My apologies for the late entry. Please, continue," I said as a statuesque woman with warm, almond-shaped eyes, a sultry smile, and silky black hair dressed in accordance with her culture pulled me out a chair for me to sit in.

I allowed her to pour me some rum, and I thanked her.

"Sung Ji will attend to your needs as my guest here, Mr. Sunjeta," the North American leader of the Asian Dragons stated. "Let us welcome our guest, Mr. Sunjeta. Many of us have already made our acquaintances due to business procured by him, which is why he was invited to our unique meeting."

Hand on my glass, I swirled the rum around, took a sip, and smiled.

"Such a young man, yet he walks in here as if he owns the world. I'm curious about that, are you not?" one of the bosses asked, more specifically one of the Italian bosses.

Several nods were seen. I glanced at the Asian Dragons leader, who gave me a nod.

Pushing back from my seating, I grinned and said, "The introduction that I was waiting for. Gentlemen, as was explained, I have done business with many of you and been spared by some."

I glanced at Caltrone, who watched me in a cool and casual manner.

"I do not find that an insult at all. Of course, you attack what you don't know or deem as a threat, but let me be clear. Young that I am, I'm still a businessman."

At that, Shango signaled to my men, who handed out laptops. On each one was a homepage with my information and business.

"Before you is my resume. At twenty-two years old, I am the youngest man to be employed in the special operations division of BKP Defense. As their representative, it was my duty to visit the lovely city of Atlanta and meet with prospective buyers. Some of you already do business with our shipping and manufacturing division—the ones who help transport your various cargos around the nation. It's our trucks, cars, and people you buy off to keep silent about their loads," I explained.

A smile then spread across my face as I locked eyes with Caltrone. I could see the wheels moving in his mind. Based on the facts that my father had given me about Caltrone, I knew he was starting to connect the dots about who I could be or what bloodline I was potentially a part of. I had a lot of power for a 22-year-old man, and that alone gave a lot of the people in the room pause.

Talking with my hands, I moved back and forth in front of the table, a projector also highlighting my information. "Sadly, my welcome here hasn't always been pleasant, and there are minor losses that have been procured in my time here through no fault of mine, but due to a misunderstanding. One that I am sure will be corrected in the near future. As you beautiful people understand, I do not just deal in armory. I deal behind the scenes of many of your businesses, and I would hate to break that relationship anytime soon. I have a company to report to and money to be made here."

The representative of the African Queens asked, "Is that all you want from us, or is there something more?" The woman was quite fine with her naturally long lashes and the way she'd tilt her head as she addressed me in a flirting manner. A brother was not about to go there with her though. For all I knew, we could be family. But back to what I was about.

I gave an amused chuckle, then laid on my accent. "There's always more to business, honey. I want receipts. I want the right to nestle on down here without any issue from any of you . . . anymore, I should add. And just continue the contracts we've all agreed to. Is that so hard? I mean, when I have pinjas trailing me down, going after my coworkers and effectively taking them out, I find that very hard not to put in a grievance."

At that second, Shango thumbed his nose, moved around the table with one of our people following him, and then turning to reach out for a duffle bag. Dropping it next to Caltrone, he flashed his teeth in a slight snarl, then walked back to me, handing gifts to the other people at the table, except the Asian Dragons leaders.

The bosses opened their gifts, except Caltrone. He waved a hand and had his people take the bag away from him as he folded his hands in front of him and watched on while grumbles could be heard around.

Watching the expressions around me gave me joy. For some, there were pictures of missing loved ones, a few had body parts, others a card with a figure showing my thanks for their loyalty. "I may be young, but understand, I'm ready for any threat that may come my way."

"But you are a businessman in the street as well?" Caltrone asked.

Nodding and slipping my hands behind my back again, I made sure to address my audience. "Yes, I am. Like we all do, I have to understand the people I'm hoping to represent, as well as the city and its people. I don't come into zones and do things on some backward shit."

"As we sit and break bread and discuss district territories, all I ask is the respect and privilege to be recognized in those contributions. I am no threat to any of you. I have no need for holding down blocks or collecting blocks. I have one area that is mine, as you all know. It will not encumber on any of you outside of what we all contract with each other. I am the man who brings in what you all need." As I spoke, Shango leaned down to whisper in my ear and show me a message on my cell from the African Queens.

I quietly read it, thumbed my nose as my eye twitched, then glanced at Caltrone.

Voice dripping low in constrained anger, I flashed a smile and tapped my temple. "I don't need to know the rest of your private affairs with each other. If you all will excuse me, I have business to attend to. I am a busy man, crafting the best weaponry out there, and in order to make all of you people happy, I have to keep that going. Good day, gentlemen and ladies. I tip my hat to you all and hope to do business soon."

Standing, one of the Latino Kings spoke up. "So we don't get to ask you questions, homes?"

"No," was all I said as I walked out.

The sound of a voice being cleared, then the zipping of a bag as my name was called had me stopping. "Senor Sunjeta. I believe you will be stopping to answer my question above all. First, I do enjoy the gift you gave. I'm impressed with your chagrin, because if my house were rudely desecrated, I would do the same."

My gaze turned to Shango, and we turned slowly to lock eyes on Caltrone. "You know the old saying: to be an ideal guest, stay at home."

Caltrone gave an amused chuckle then shifted back in his chair. Many of the bosses around him were deathly silent, including the Latino Kings. It showed me who had the true power in the room, though the OGs who ran the Asian Dragons International weren't punks either.

"For a young man, your mind intrigues me, because I feel the same way. You see, my home was violated, and I have a very low tolerance for inhospitality. Especially since I am a gracious man. I brought protection and abundance of wealth to my guests, only to have them piss in my house? No *bueno*," Caltrone smoothly detailed.

I understood exactly what he was referencing, and it made me chuckle. He assumed that I knew about or had something to do with him being robbed. A sense of power settled into my spine as I never let my gaze fall away from Caltrone's. Two leaders were speaking right now. Everyone else in the room was of no consequence.

"Ah yes, sir, I understand that clearly as well. I can relate. I find it interesting that a businessman as myself, who came into this community to only do business, has been dealing with that same type of difficulty. See, my house was rudely plagued with roaches." I moved around the room in a calm manner, my hands slipping into my slacks as I looked around the table before me.

"See, I fed my guest, and even extended a hand to those around my guest who support him, only to have those people leave my house nasty and disgusting, for more roaches to grow in. When a man has an infestation in his home, he has no choice but to bomb it, even though he had no desire to deal with such difficulties prior."

Caltrone said nothing. He sat back in a cool manner as well and lit up a cigar before speaking up. "There's only one thing that can be done with such infestations and unruly guests. Clean your house, young man, and hand your guest their leftovers as they leave. In the old days, this is how it was done to show hospitality and future invites into homes. You return what was taken, and I want all of what was taken from me."

I stopped my pacing to move to the door. Shango widened his stance, and he rested a hand on the handle of the door.

My conversation with Caltrone was clear: as my main guest, he was telling me to get my affairs in order and handle my shit. He wanted the Eraserheads dead, mainly Auto, and he wanted his body as proof of my loyalty. If I was to show my power here, to show not only my pull but my sincerity in doing business with these kings at the table, then I had to get my hands dirty. I had no problem with that. It only furthered my agenda in the process.

"In order for there to be continued invites at my house's table, I need all the gentlemen here to understand me when I say I want my respect. I gave it by introducing myself to you all, and many of you believed me insufficient. That's not my fault, but yours for your arrogance, and I mean that in all respect," I said while still watching Caltrone.

My hand slid up to my jaw to rub my beard as my mind ticked off in thought. "I've noticed too many of your houses all breaking down to feudal wars shit among each other. Even the great Dragons beef it up just to eat pretty at Caltrone's table. Gentlemen, I want nothing of that. I'm here to be a dealer, nothing more. My zone is my own so that I can bring only quality to the men and women here. If you treat me good, I treat you good. Caltrone, as a means to set things even, your request will be handled with a pretty bow on top as well," I said with ease.

Caltrone looked me up and down, smirked, and let a plume of smoke part from his lips. "You've been educated very well then. Give me what I want, and I'll welcome you to my table. This is my world and my rules. Remember your place."

I gave my own sarcastic laugh, then walked out once I signaled to Shango to open the door. "I never forgot it, amigo."

Anger rode my spirit. If I hadn't left, I would have sent bullets through everyone in there and ended them all, allies and enemies. I wouldn't have given a damn. Not with how I was feeling right now. The disrespect was killing me. I was losing too many people in this pursuit to wake up one nigga who didn't give a fuck about a damn thing but himself. Yet he felt he was about honor. I had to get my mind right in this. Had to think this through clearly without reacting like the young dude I was.

As I told them, I was young, and I was fucking ready to pump iron in a majority of them. However, it would not serve my other purpose: to be a major player in the true business of this armory and drug game. Putting myself where the real hands were, the ones who helped drop the drugs or guns into the street dealer's hands, was where I was aiming to be. There was a reason behind that as well. If I positioned myself high, then it would be harder for Caltrone to take me out, because at that level I wouldn't be some street kid. I was a certified businessman with stocks just like the white-collar bastards.

Walking silently down the hall, I could feel the hairs on my arms rising as I thought. Shango was at my side, jaw clenching as well in his anger. We had a lot to deal with at this moment, and just to keep up with my word, we had to ride out of Atlanta. Back in my ride, I sat thinking, and I pulled off my jacket.

There was no reason for me to kick off a war right away. Everything I needed was going down as we spoke. From what I learned with watching the man I was after, I found out that he was occupied with going after ATL's hottest athlete. Because this same athlete was also ducking and diving, growing through his shit, I knew that it would be distracting Caltrone from his game. Yeah, the man was still making mad dough, and still running his family with a fist, but behind the scenes, I was hearing something else. New blood was introduced in the family via the athlete, which was now making my role more important than ever. If everything played out right on my end with the bait and hook, then I'd officially be closer than ever to my goal.

For now, though, I was still pissed about two things and about to handle one of them.

"How are we going to handle this, Boots?" Shango asked as we stepped out of our black truck.

We'd made it back to our side of town. I was in all black, from my shit kickers to the long black hooded coat I wore. I stood in front of an old colonial-style house with a wraparound porch. The home of Smiley. While I was in the meeting, a text had come through alerting me to something that needed my immediate attention. I wasn't sure what it was. It just pissed me off that she had texted me. But when she showed me the reason why, I knew we had to come through the block.

"They get the book bag on the back of the house?" I asked, still standing in the front yard of the house, eyes cast upward.

"Yes, sir, the notebook is still in there, and the Queens didn't touch a thing," Shango said.

I knew they wouldn't due to us all being in the same family. The reason they were able to contact me and knew to call me was that Smiley had my number on the front page of her blueprints in the notebook.

"Good. Do we know for a fact where Smiley is?" I quietly asked, still staring in place.

Shango moved by my side, staring up. "No, but we all know this verifies it, boss."

For some reason, it felt as if I were on some high. My hands kept flexing, my palms itching. I had a taste for blood. Ready to put bullets in to the ones who took more of my people. But I had to remind myself, all things in due time. Karma is a motherfucker, and the war will handle those who need to be handled. That's all I could do, because I was ready to scream.

I felt like I was looking at Alize all over again, and it was killing me. "Take her down."

Shango gave a nod and quietly muttered, "A'ight."

"Wrap her in the black cloth," I added, then ran my hands over my face.

Posted up, spread eagle, naked with bruises, cuts, and too many bullet wounds to count was Maria Rosa. She stood stuck to a cross. Her head was slumped forward with her hair cascading down in a veil. Carved into her once delicate flesh over her stomach was the word "Traitor."

Scarlet red ran down her body as if a paint can had spilled over. Baby girl's wounds were so chaotic that it was as if someone had decided to hack at a brick of ice with a pick. The sight was fucked up, deeply. Had this not been African Queen zone, it would have been a while before anyone reported the body.

I knew from the act that Caltrone had left a message, that he would not tolerate anyone in his family disobeying him and turning on him. It made me worry for Smiley, and it made me worry for Caltrone's new target, Enzo and his family. Air escaped my lips as I blew off steam and dropped to one knee over Code.

There was no excuse for this. Family was family, no matter how they turned on you. That was my motto. Kill them if you had to, but don't do some shit like this. My fingers brushed back her hair. Then I closed my eyes at her battered face. It had me glancing at her hands, had me noting that they were torn up.

"You fought until your last breath, huh?" I muttered, watching her. "You were mine for a minute, *mami,* so for that, I'll give you the same burial as we are giving Alize. One fit for an African Queen."

I gave one last touch of her hand then stood up, still watching her. "Wrap her up gently in a swaddle. Keep her face clear and lay her in the back of the ride. We need to go. I have one more thing to handle before we leave Atlanta."

Smiley's backpack was on my arm. I felt something heavy in it and glanced inside to see a box that I almost thought was an Xbox. I figured it had something to do with those blueprints Shango relayed. It felt crazy how this house, once the home of a loving mother and daughter who were in private going through hell due to the mother's husband and the girl's father, was now a place of death.

But I guessed that's the way of things in war. Machiavelli said it well, that a leader should have no other goal or thought or take up any other cause but that of studying war, its organization, and its discipline. Because at the end of the day, the art of war was a necessity to learn for one to command in war. I wasn't here to lead the war. I was here to be a vessel and a general in the battle, and that's what I did in leaving my footprint in this story.

On some hood shit, if you give pussy good dick and then you walk away, you know you got her if she was begging for more. Every bastard who called themselves a street king, or cartel, or king, like the ones in the meeting were pussy. Some were smart like Caltrone, and some were not so smart. That wasn't my problem, because I for damn sure knew that I was hitting them with that ooh wee just to get them to come for more of my bullets, weapons, and then some.

While I sat in the back of my truck, staring at a woman who had me feeling like she was my Bonnie and I was her Clyde, I knew immediately that everything I did would be for my family, and now for her: Maria Rosa, aka Code. I respected her survival, and I aimed to honor it. So I kicked back, watched the city, and thought of my next plan, because I for sure was going to be back for the next player in the game.

Chapter 19

Auto

Forty-eight Hours Later

Images of Code's naked crucified body were all over the place. Anybody who was anybody and even those who were nobodies had seen the way her body had been displayed in front of Smiley's old home. It had been forty-eight hours. Forty-eight hours since Smiley had been abducted in broad daylight and Code murdered. I called it an abduction because there was no way she would have gone with that man willingly.

I could tell Smiley had been feeling some type of way about the fact that I wouldn't let her in on the plans I had about taking the rest of my team and hightailing it out of the U.S. She kept asking questions that I refused to answer, but only because I didn't know how far she was willing to go for us. Yeah, she had been with us when we took down Caltrone's warehouse, but that didn't necessarily mean she was ready to say fuck all she knew back here in the A and dip out with us. She slipped out on me while I was sleeping. Had I known her plans, I would have never let her out of my sight.

For as bad as I wanted to rush in to save her, guns blazing, I couldn't. I had to wait for intel, and the longer I waited, the more my soul broke into pieces over what could have happened to Smiley. I hadn't slept since she sent me the text that she had been taken.

God knew that if anything happened to her while she was in that motherfucker's hands, I'd kill that nigga myself. I should have just ended him the day we rolled up on him as he was leaving with his financial attorney. I didn't know why I just didn't kill that nigga then. Yeah, I did. I was lying. Caltrone was intimidating. I didn't feel like I was pussy for admitting that. The man had a presence, an aura about him that gave you pause. It made you want to kill him but made you curious as to how one man could have all that power in the same breath.

For the first time since meeting Smiley, I thanked God that she had the wherewithal to track her every move. Before the tracker lost signal, I was able to pinpoint her location. For that reason, and that reason alone, I had to call in for backup. I needed Pascal, Amina, Jaahlive, and their whole crew for what I was about to pull off. Pascal was the leader of one of our brother crews in Vegas. If ever I needed something blown up, they were who I called.

Chaos was popping off all around the A. Shootouts, murders, and disappearances. Half the shit was being swept under the rug as just gang violence, and the other half had the hood in a death lock. Three nights ago, I'd robbed Caltrone of guns, drugs, and money. I'd abandoned my shop, my car lot, and my home, and so had the rest of the team. I kept Reagan and Jackknife close to me because we were all we had. We had no family where we could run and hide. We were our only family. I paid out Wolf and his brothers then told them to get on a private jet to Trinidad where they originated from. No more of my team would die because of me.

Reagan sat in the front room of our compound. Her head hung low as Jackknife held her hand. They hadn't taken the news of Code's death too well. Something in me wanted to let go of the little sanity I had left. I wanted to just have a mental breakdown and say fuck the rest. Wondered if I could just live inside my head and call it a day. Gotdamn, how much havoc could one man wreak on one group of people? If Caltrone could do that to his favorite, then I knew that what he could be doing to Smiley was ten times worse.

"Just hang in there," I mumbled under my breath, hoping Smiley could feel that I was on my way to get her.

"Think we were too hard on Code?" Reagan asked me while tears rolled down her cheeks.

"I . . . I don't know," I answered honestly. Part of me stood by my decision to exile her from the group. The other half of me felt as if maybe, just maybe, if we'd given her a chance to redeem herself, she would still be alive. We—no, I—left her out there alone.

I didn't know why, but for some reason I expected her to be able to fend for herself. Code had always been a strong woman to me, so I expected her to be able to fend off the old man and make it out of this thing alive. I guessed I had no idea just how much of a psychological hold her grandfather had on her. I never expected to see her strung up on a crucifix with blood crying from the letters that had been carved into her stomach.

I could piece two and two together, and I knew that she could have only been at Smiley's place because she'd gotten wind of her being taken too.

"Look, I did what I thought was best for the team as a whole. I couldn't afford to do otherwise," I said. My hands shook as I pulled out my ringing cell and saw Pascal calling. "Yeah," I answered.

"Just touched down. They're locked down tight. We're not going to be able to pull that landscaping shit here. We pulled up and pretended we were there to do some

landscaping. Almost got shot. Amina had to pretend we
had the wrong address, and that still almost didn't work.
We're going to have to do something else," he informed
me.

Normally Pascal and the crew could pretend they
were a part of some kind of landscaping or cleaning
crew to gain access to a home. None of the rich, snobby
motherfuckers ever questioned people of color doing
their yard work. It was like second nature. But I guessed,
like everything else, Caltrone wasn't having any new
faces around him. It was safe to assume that because of
the financial loss he'd suffered, his trust was low and his
guard was high.

I didn't want to ask Armando and Nicola for any more
help, although I was sure if I called, they would answer.
Stitch was still around the A, but he refused to tell me
where he was holed up because he knew I'd try to force
him to get the hell on. I didn't want to be the reason his
children lost another father.

"So you're saying you're going to be of no help to me?" I
asked Pascal.

"Now I can never not be of service to you, Auto. We
couldn't get in through the front door. Doesn't mean we
can't sneak in through the back. I'll find a way to do what
you need done. Get to the location within the next hour,
and I'll be ready to rock. Trust me, I got it under control,"
he assured me.

I ended the call, then looked at the last two people left
with me. "Are you two sure you want to do this?" I asked
them.

Jackknife nodded then signed, "I'm ready. But once
this is done, I want us to get off the grid. I'm tired. Body
is weary."

I looked at Reagan, who said, "And I want to have my
baby in peace. I owe it to Seymore to see that our child
never knows what it is to grow up the way we did."

I owed him the same. I owed his mother as well, and I intended to be sure she saw her grandchild grow up. Dressed in all black once again, I picked up the duffle bag full of guns and headed out.

Took me all of thirty minutes to get to Lithonia. Not because of traffic, but because I took back roads so I wouldn't be seen coming. Caltrone was a smart man, and I was sure he had people set up where he would see me coming from a mile away. Or he could have very well been arrogant enough to assume I wouldn't show my face after the coup I'd pulled. He'd surely be a fool if he did.

Dusk had fallen upon us. That was the only way I would attempt to tackle something as audacious as attacking Caltrone on his home turf. Just from remembering what Code had told me about some of the security at his Spanish-like estate, I knew the trees had eyes. There was no way we could be stealth about our approach, and I really didn't want to be.

I parked the van about two miles or so down the road. It was painted to look like someone from AT&T was in the neighborhood. The van advertised AT&T U-verse on the side and blended in well enough for people not to pay too much attention to us. Reagan got out first and headed to her vantage point. AT&T uniform on, with a tool belt on her waist, she wasn't given a second look. Next Jackknife did the same, and I was left to sit with the ghosts of my demons.

A moment of nostalgia hit me hard though. I wanted Lelo to be in my earpiece arguing with Stitch. I wanted Seymore to be laughing while they argued. I needed to know Dunkin was back at the shop, preparing for when we all came back.

I missed my family, and I couldn't help that. I missed them all like hell, and if I had any of this shit to do over again, I probably would have said fuck it, taken my losses, and moved shop. I missed Code. I missed the way she busted her guns. I missed her sassy attitude. I missed her smile. I missed her contagious happiness. I never wanted to see her go out the way her old man had taken her out. There was no way I could get back those who I'd lost. But no matter how much sadness was riding me, I had to let go of their ghosts, even though it hurt me to do so.

"Auto," I heard Stitch's voice in my earpiece.

It was good to hear him. Made me chuckle a bit. "You're trailing me?"

"You know it," he replied. "I saw what happened to Code," he said.

"Yeah," was the only reply I could give.

"It's fucked up that I felt no remorse when I heard she'd been killed. Felt like my family got some kind of justice. But then I saw the pictures of her body. Shit fucked with me."

"I know. I felt the same way. I didn't expect to ever see her taken out like that."

"Her old man is crazy as fuck. Like a rabid dog, nigga need to be put down," Stitch said.

I agreed with him wholeheartedly, but before we could continue our conversation, Reagan's voice kicked in.

"I knew he would be here," I heard her say. "Yo, Stitch, Jackknife says he if he could, he would argue with you just for a sense of normalcy."

Stitch chuckled and so did I. My crew and I were trying to hold on to any little bit of hope we had left. Even though we were laughing, the pain was there. The overwhelming sense of death and loss was stifling. The four of us joked around a bit more with Reagan relaying what Jackknife was signing. Felt like old times, but seeing Caltrone's guards take an interest in the van I was sitting in sobered me up.

"Looks like it's action time," Stitch said in my ear.

I knew he was right, but I wanted to wait for Pascal to show himself. He knew we were here. Had sent me a confirmation text as soon as we pulled into the neighborhood.

"Not yet. We have to wait for Pascal and the crew," I said.

I sat up in the van. Kept my head low so it looked as if I was tapping away at my iPad. About four of Caltrone's guards started walking toward the van. Even though I was parked at what I thought was a safe distance, apparently that didn't matter to them.

Stitch barked in my ear, "Well, he's going to have to do something fast. If they get any closer, I'm letting loose."

"Where the hell are you anyway, and how did you get there without being seen?"

"Four houses to your right. I'm on the roof. Long-distance assault rifle cocked, aimed, and ready to go."

I glanced in the general direction of where he said he was but didn't want to take my eyes off the guards. They were getting closer. Too close for comfort. I was pretty sure if they got close enough to even think I was Asian, they would let loose a barrage of bullets. There weren't too many Asians around the way, well, not too many who'd been crazy enough to rob Caltrone. That alone would be enough for them to react violently. I was sure the bounty on my head was worth it.

A loud bang and a cloud of smoke shook the area and forced the guards to turn their attention away from me. I chuckled. Pascal was always right on time. I stepped out of the van. Mac-11 in hand, I let a spray of bullets take down two of the guards from behind. A few seconds later, an unseen assailant took down the other two.

"Kill shots," Stitch bragged in the earpiece. "Watch your back, bro," he warned. "They're scattering out like roaches."

More explosions sounded off. If one didn't know better, they'd think there was a fireworks show going on. I had no idea how Pascal and his crew were able to pull it off, but I was glad I kept them on retainer for jobs such as these. I pulled my gas mask over my face. The bullets in the Mac-11 belonged to Boots. I didn't plan on giving the man his bullets back, to be honest. If I said it once, I'd say it again: I didn't think it would be a good business move to return someone else's merchandise and not recoup any of my losses.

They worked like magic. Any bulletproof vests they had on wouldn't do the guards any good. I still had to be careful though. I wasn't familiar with the grounds and didn't know if the sentries in the trees had been taken care of. I ran like I was trying to get through a maze, and I kept wishing, hoping, and praying Smiley was still alive. I caught Amina and Jaahlive out the corner of my eye. Both still dressed like they were a part of the landscaping crew. Rocket launchers in hand, they stood across the street on another lawn and lit up the front of Caltrone's home.

I took that as my cue and made a run for the back of the house. The first blast I'd heard had taken care of the guards in the trees. Their bodies lay strewn about the back lawn. Body parts scattered around like lawn jockeys. If it hadn't been for the gas mask I had on, I was sure I wouldn't have been able to function in the smoke and fumes that were floating around. The glass in the back patio door had been shattered. It crunched underneath my feet as I rushed in.

About five men rushed into the room as chaos reigned around me. I used my gun like it was an extension of me. Pumped bullets into bodies without a second thought because I knew the same thing would have been done to me without question. I was prepared to fight until the death of me, but after the five men I took down in the kitchen, I expected to see more come rushing in. When they didn't, the hairs on the back of my neck started to stand up.

I moved around the disheveled den. Even in the clutter and debris, I could tell it had been decorated to feed a king. Gold cutlery lay strewn about. Wineglasses and napkin holders that looked to be worth more than my whole condo decorated the Italian marble flooring. Chairs were turned over. China cabinets were tilted to the side. The chandelier was barely still hanging in the ceiling. There was a thick door that I thought led to the kitchen, but when I tried to run the knob, I found it locked.

"Smiley," I yelled out, hoping she was still in the house.

If Caltrone had moved her, I'd be fucked, because I wouldn't know where else to look for her. I moved around the room again, but my gut kept drawing me to the locked door. I shot the knob and then kicked the door open. I expected darkness to greet me, but that wasn't the case. Light illuminated the room and there, bound to a chair by her arms and legs, was Smiley. She was naked, blood leaking from the different cuts on her body. They were small cuts like someone had sliced her with a razor, or they could have been paper cuts. Either way, the sight made my stomach coil into knots. Her caramel rich skin was festered with the nicks. Her head drooped forward like she was too tired to hold it up any longer.

I took the gas mask off as I walked down the stairs. Gun still ready to let loose if need be, I called out to her. "Smiley."

Her head slowly came up.

"Oh, shit," I choked out.

One of her eyes had some kind of Chinese hairpin sticking out of it.

"Oh, shit, baby. Who did this to you?" I asked as I rushed in to her.

She started to shake her head. The uninjured eye widened as she shook her head faster. It was only then that I saw her mouth was taped. Her eye darted to one of the darkened corners in the room. I could see a feminine outline ease out of the shadows. Before it could register that I'd walked into a trap, a sharp pain to the back of my head took me to my knees. The hit disoriented me, made slobber fall from my lips. The gun fell to the floor, and a boot to the face put me down beside it.

"That's enough, Marco," I heard Caltrone say. "Stand him up," he then ordered.

The woman I'd seen and the man who'd kicked me yanked me up from the cold concrete floor.

"Let me kill him and get it over with, Father," I heard to my right.

"Shut up, Santana. I'm very disappointed that you took your aggression with Maria Rosa out on Nia this way," he snapped in a cool voice.

"Little bitch thought me wearing an eye patch was funny, so I returned the favor. Now she'll sport one just the same."

I was barely able to stand because the hit to the head had almost knocked me out. But I stood as best I could. Wouldn't let that nigga Caltrone put me down like he wanted to.

"I'm disgusted with your lack of restraint. Don't act like your brothers, Santana. You see how their end came about," Caltrone said coolly. "Don't become like the mutts."

Even though his face carried no readable expression, the tone in his voice said he meant business. The woman who had a strong resemblance to Code, even though she was the richest shade of chocolate I'd ever seen, looked as if she was offended.

She huffed, dropped my arm, and then frowned. "Papa, how dare you say such a thing to me," she declared, voice clearly showing she was offended.

"Lower your motherfucking voice when you address me, Santana. I don't have time to deal with your fragile ego because your daughter got the best of you. I told you to break Nia in, not damage her face and body."

Since I'd been dealing with the old bastard, I'd never heard him use such profanity. Santana swallowed hard. The red leather patch over her eye did little to take away from her beauty, but the pout on her face made her appear like a petulant child and not a grown woman.

Caltrone turned his attention back to me. He walked to the corner and brought out a brown folding chair. "Sit him down," he ordered Marco.

Marco shoved me down in the metal contraption. I felt blood trickling down the back of my neck. My jaw felt as if it had come unhinged because of the kick. I kept my eyes on Caltrone as Santana placed a chair behind him. Dressed in all black, he adjusted his slacks and then took a seat in front of me.

"Well, this was easy," he stated calmly. "All I had to do was take her and you came running. Same with Maria Rosa. Nia has led you both to death."

I glanced at Smiley. Her eye asked me if Code was really gone. I didn't answer her. Turned back around to stare the devil in the face. I could still hear faint gunshots upstairs.

"You've surprised me, Auto. Your tenacity and courageousness intrigue me. If I didn't have to kill you, I'd make you a part of the team."

"Then it would be best you kill me. I don't do well with fuck niggas on the same team as me," I countered.

Caltrone grunted. He wasn't amused. "You're so young and full of anger. Grew up in the gutter too long. Your language is befitting of a hood urchin when you could be so much more. You're nowhere near as polished as your father was."

My eye twitched when Caltrone stood and moved the chair he'd been sitting in.

"You don't get to be a man such as myself without knowing about everything and everyone around you. There is not an enemy who has attacked me who I didn't do my homework on. But I didn't have to look far for you. You have the lips of your mother but the eyes of your father."

As Caltrone spoke to me, he rolled up the sleeves of his shirt. I couldn't front like I wasn't interested in hearing all he was willing to give about my mother and father. I guessed that was the little kid in me who craved to know where and who I'd come from.

"Jin-Su was a good man who got too greedy in his last days. He aligned himself with the wrong people, and in the end, it cost him dearly. Isn't it funny how life works, young man? That whole six degrees of separation thing is real, did you know? I had no idea that years later my granddaughter and Jin-Su's son would become fast friends. That's the funny thing about life and fate."

"You're talking in riddles and shit, and it's starting to annoy me. If you're going to kill me, just do it and get it over with," I snapped.

"Killing you would be too easy, Devin," Caltrone crooned. "Killing you wouldn't hurt you. Killing your team, however, would end you."

He walked over to Smiley as he pulled a gun from underneath his shirt. I knew he was going to kill her because of the determination in his stride.

"No," I yelled, then tried to stand only to have Santana give me a back kick that almost caved my chest in.

I fell back into the chair and it almost toppled, but Marco stilled it. I expected to see Smiley's brains splattered across the room, but all I got was the click of the gun and Smiley's shivering body. Tears rolled down her face, and it pissed me off. It angered me like I'd never been angered before. Caltrone never intended to shoot her. He was fucking with her, breaking down the core of the young woman I knew her to be. Smiley was scared to the point that she was visibly shaken, and I'd never seen her that way before.

"Ah, just as I suspected. Your weakness is your love for those around you."

"Just let her go. I'll stay. Just let her go," I pleaded.

"Now why would I do that? You took one granddaughter from me, and I need another to replace her."

I yelled out, "I didn't take her away, nigga. You pushed her away! You did this!"

Marco's fist to my jaw caused me to see red. The pain was so intense that I felt as if my jaw had split in half. I'd never been one to take an ass kicking lying down. I jumped up from the chair and charged that nigga. Scooped him up in the air then slammed him down. The surprise that registered in his eyes just before I started to pummel his face with a closed fist fed that beast within me. Because I'd caught him off guard, his defenses were down. I wasn't going to let up. I made that nigga's face beat my hands until a sharp kick to the back of the head knocked me off him.

I rolled over then stood back up. I was sick of that bitch Santana and her damn kicking feet.

"I ain't ever been a fan of hitting women, but you, bitch, you're not a woman. You're a gotdamned jungle cat in heels," I snarled at her.

She smirked, then gave me a full-out smile. The woman was beautiful, no doubt. And her smile had seduction laced all through it, but I'd known Code well enough to know that her mother was anything but a woman to underestimate. Code often called her the black widow. Not many men who went up against her came out alive.

Santana charged at me. She aimed high, and I ducked low. Caught her with a jab to the stomach that sent her stumbling. She caught her footing, then came at me with aggression like I'd never seen from a woman. A butterfly twist kick almost leveled me. She stood in a boxer's stance and gave me two quick jabs to the face then a spinning crescent kick that took me down to one knee.

She was no slouch. I had to give her that. And obviously, she had been trained in martial arts. Santana laughed as I got back to my feet. I already knew coming in that I shouldn't limit myself to one kind of weapon. I knew Caltrone was no fool kind of nigga. I thought outside the box, knowing that there was a possibility that I could be caught. I had to think about what I would do if I found myself in this type of situation. That was why I didn't come with only one weapon on me.

As Santana ran in to give me an axe kick—that would have surely split my skull because of the platform six-inch stiletto boots she had on—I reached behind me and pulled out a can of pepper spray. The one good eye she had, I put out of commission. She yelled and screamed. Shit sounded like a cat on a hot tin roof. As I said, I wasn't a fan of knocking the shit out of women, but Santana was more than a woman. She was a trained assassin and a skilled fighter. I punched that bitch in the eye she had the patch covering. She went flying back into a wall.

Marco tried to get up, but I was quicker than he was. With a punt kick to the head, I put him back on his ass, snatched up his gun, and turned it on Caltrone. I would have shot that nigga dead, but he was standing behind Smiley.

"Two things can happen here, Devin," he started. "I can kill you, or we can work something out."

I would have told him to kill me. But Smiley's battered face stopped me. I couldn't read what her eye was telling me. All I knew was that she was in pain. I could tell by the way her jaw kept flinching and the way her breathing was labored. They'd worked baby girl over.

"I really don't want to negotiate shit with a nigga like you," I spat.

"Understandable. Still, if you want to see Nia here again, your best bet would be to negotiate."

For a long while, I just stared at him.

"Make up your mind, Devin. I can assure you the rest of your team has been apprehended. All I have to do is say the word and they're all going to be dead."

Just as he said that, a square hole opened up in the wall. Reagan, Jackknife, Pascal, Amina, and Jaahlive were shoved through.

"I'm a sensible man despite what you may perceive me to be. My pride nor vengeance rule me. I rule on logic. Black and white. There is no gray area. I realize that I approached you wrong, and I want a chance to do it all over again. All I want from you is my gold. Give me my gold back, and we can call shit even."

I didn't believe this nigga to save my own fucking life.

"You must think I'm the stupidest motherfucker alive if you think for one minute I believe that shit," I threw at him.

"Are you calling me a liar, Auto? Are you saying I'm not a man of my word? I can most assure you I am," he stated matter-of-factly.

He then trained the gun on Reagan. He didn't have any bullets in that gun when he'd pretended as if he was going to shoot Smiley, but when he pulled the trigger, a bullet to Reagan's shoulder told me he had bullets in there now.

"You see, I told you if you give me my gold, I'd let them live, but if you don't, I'm going to kill them one by one. And each death will be slow and painful. Could take days, weeks for each one of them to die."

Another man who I was sure belonged to Caltrone's crew walked in with a body over his arm. He dropped the body like a sack of potatoes. Stitch had been found. I prayed to God he wasn't dead.

"So, tell me, Devin, do you want to live the rest of your life knowing you're the reason your whole team met death by my hands?" Caltrone asked arrogantly.

He knew he had me over a barrel and there was nothing I could do about it. There would be no way I would allow my team to be killed.

"If I bring your gold, you'll let them all walk out of here?"

"In fact, I'll let all of them leave with you right now," he said, then smirked. "All except Nia of course."

"That's bullshit."

"No, my friend. That's smart. I need insurance to ensure you keep your end of the bargain."

Smiley was shaking her head. Reagan's cries worked my emotions. Jackknife's jaw was swollen. Stitch was still out on the floor, and the whole Vegas team hadn't signed up for any of this shit. There was a good chance that when I brought the gold back, Caltrone would kill me and take Smiley anyway. I could deal with dying, but the thought of Smiley being left in that man's hands didn't sit too well with me.

I walked over to her, and the air surrounding us seemed colder than it had been when I was standing on the other side of the room. I chalked it up to being near Caltrone. The nigga made my flesh crawl. I slowly removed the tape from Smiley's lips.

"Don't do it," she whispered to me. Her lips were dried, chapped, and bloodied.

"I have to. I got us into this mess, and I have to get you all out of it. Do you trust me?" I asked her while cupping her face.

She nodded. "I do, but it's a setup, Auto. He's going to kill you."

I laid my forehead against hers, knowing that there was a strong possibility this would be the last time I'd see her alive.

"Trust me, okay?"

Looking at her up close, I knew the longer she kept that pin in her eye, the slimmer her chances were of saving it.

"Get her some fucking medical attention," I snapped at Caltrone.

All he did was stare at me. The smug look on his face made me want to say fuck everything and put a bullet in his skull. But the nigga had me by the balls.

"Nia will be fine. She's a trooper, just as her mother was. You have one hour, Devin. After two hours, I will assume you've reneged on our deal, and I'll be forced to go to drastic measures to assure what was mine is returned," was all he said before turning and escorting Nia out of the room with him.

Chapter 20

Smiley

Every aspect of war, of battle, is based on how well one side can deceive the other. Before one can attack, one must seem unable or weak. Over and over I told myself that simple line, paraphrased from Sun Tzu's *The Art of War*. In my mind, I could hear Trigga telling me above all things that while in the streets, I needed to remember this in order to survive if ever in a fucked-up situation.

It was funny to me, because the same was said to me by Boots. Before I even had decided to become an Eraserhead and was still figuring out my place in this massive game, Boots had pulled me to the side and told me those exact same words while I was dropping off my plans for my guns. He said that it might come a time where I would have to figure out exactly how I was going to play my role if I was going to be allowed to be used. He then said if it ever came to a time where Caltrone got to me, then keep Sun Tzu's words in my mind and trust in him because there were things that he could do that Auto couldn't in the game of surviving Caltrone.

He let me know that he would send me a way to know that it was him if ever I got tripped up. Back then, I just laughed it off. I didn't know him, and I was still learning to trust him and Auto. Now, I wished I had listened more to what he had told me.

I honestly didn't like that idea that I could be a pawn, but when talking to Boots, we both agreed that I would be a pawn. No matter where I went, as long as Caltrone knew about me, I'd be his pawn. That wasn't something I wanted to accept, but now, held behind Orlando walls, I realized that both Trigga and Boots were right, and I was now at a point where I had to decide what I was going to do. I also was sitting thinking about what Boots meant by trust in him.

What could he do? Hell, what could I do?

There wasn't anything that I could truly do to get out of this situation. All I could do was survive and attempt to see if I could use this situation to my advantage. I didn't realize that it would be my last memory of my vision before losing my eye that would tip me over the edge and enact a side of me I never knew I had. Code's battered body was on display before my eyes. Santana was near me when Marco showed her the image. We all sat in Code's old room. I hadn't put on any of the clothes she laid out, and it pissed Santana off.

She kept talking to me about the way an Orlando woman should act. How an Orlando princess should act and how it pissed her off that I even existed to be considered as an Orlando princess by Caltrone. Basically, every angry word or slap she gave me, I ignored. I even laughed at her fucked-up eye patch because I was so pissed and upset at being held against my will that I figured that I'd dish out my own mental game of warfare on Caltrone's people. It was a mistake that I would take back because I didn't understand the context about it all until Santana was introduced to the dead body of her daughter, displayed like she was Jesus.

Once we all saw her mangled body and how Marco smiled and said he enjoyed slicing her, everything changed from bad to worse. Santana gave me one look, and it was over. She kicked my ass hard. Blamed me for being a part of a group that got her daughter killed. Tears ran down my face at the memory, because I was deeply in shock that Code had been killed by her own people, her mother included.

That reality was the start of my mind shutting down and going into survival mode. If these crazy mother-fuckers had no issue with killing their own, all this blood bond shit was nothing but lies then, and there was no way for me to negotiate a way out. Now because of her death, I was Santana's punching bag, and even though Caltrone was upset that she had ruined my beauty, I knew that Santana didn't give a fuck. It was evident once she walked me out of the room and dug her nails into my wounds.

My gaze, or what was left of it, locked on Auto as I was being taken out. A different type of agony was in me be-cause I knew that Auto was a dead man walking. Caltrone was setting him and the rest of the team up for something worse. Getting his gold back and the property was only another game of his. Yes, I could tell the old man wanted his things, but he also wanted blood for the disrespect dealt to him for being one step ahead of him.

I had heard his shouts about that. He was pissed that Auto had been able to mastermind a power play so smoothly that even he had been blindsided about it. At that time, I listened to everything around me in order to get an upper hand. I learned that there was another female in the house, one worse than Santana. One she was worried about because she was Caltrone's main female. Her soft monotone voice drifted through that conversation as she called Caltrone Papi.

It put a chill in my spine to hear the woman tell him in a cool voice that it only happened because he was focused on his lost heirs. She easily was able to calm him with those words, saying that they would make everything right. That they would carry on the power, lineage, and that Auto, along with his team, was nothing but bait for Caltrone's downtime.

That was when I leaned of the existence of a woman called Lilith. Caltrone's queen pin.

Blood and sweat dripped down my body into the lacerations embedded in my skin. I knew I looked like hell. I never was one about my looks, but it did piss me off that I had lost an eye. I wasn't sure how I would adjust to having my vision altered, because a good shooter needed her vision to be a good aim, and now that was taken from me.

Anger riled in me. I wanted to kill Santana. Not just for myself and what she put me through, but now having had my own understanding of what Code had gone through at the hands of her mother. I wanted her dead. As I slowly walked while in my thoughts, the pain in my eye gave me a headache that had tears falling down. I didn't want to cry, but I was against my will. I had to play weak as I tried to figure out a way out of this. Gun smoke and the scent of dead bodies had me coughing and dragging my feet.

"Shut up, bitch," was spat at me. Along with a stinging slap across my face and a punch to the stomach.

I hunkered over from the assault Santana was putting on me. "You got my daughter killed, and then your stupid fucking friends come in and mess everything up yet again? Just to save your disgusting life! You're not worthy. Where were they for Maria Rosa, huh? I hate you roaches."

Like that, Santana threw me onto the white marble floor of a grand bathroom. That bitch was crazy. I'd clearly heard her say she'd helped her father kill her daughter. But she blamed me and the Eraserheads? Though we were in a new home that was used as a setup for Auto and the crew, I guessed we were all going to stay here as a layover for whatever plan Caltrone had going for Auto.

"You signed her death warrant the moment you birthed her," I spat out while on my knees.

Kick to the ribs, Santana spat on me then kicked me in the head. "Bitch, you know nothing!"

Ringing began in my ears. It made me shut my eyes, including the one with the pin in it. This life was not something I had wanted. Not leaving and trusting in Auto had been the worst mistake of my life, I was slowly realizing, because had I run, I'd still be okay and safe.

Every aspect of war, of battle, is based on how well one side can deceive the other. Before one can attack, one must seem unable or weak, echoed in my mind again.

No, I won't let this madness make me turn on Auto. I lay on my side, then screamed once a hot scaling blast of water hit me. Santana had hit me with a hose of water from the shower. She stared at me with so much hate that it turned my stomach at the joy that she got from my pain. Though she was hurt herself from her fight, she didn't act like it. She stalked over me, squatted, then scrubbed me down with her nails and simple white bar of soap.

"Papi said not to remove the pin, but here I am law, and you need to learn what it takes to be an Orlando." Like that, she evilly gripped the pin.

I screamed, "No, no, no . . ."

But she wasn't hearing it. She pulled, and then yanked it, removing the pin. Pain ripped through me. Strangely, I could still see, but soon it disappeared with the trail of blood that spilled over from the gash. Cradling my eye, I heard her malicious laughter. Bitch was crazy as hell. All of this was crazy as hell.

As I rocked in agony, I could hear her moving around me. *Play weak, Nia,* I told myself through the pain. I had copped my surroundings. The bathroom was a tight room of all marble. Though Santana was some crazy martial artist ho and could take me without a thought, the bitch couldn't counter water and soap.

As I cried and rocked, I then made my body slide forward to ram her hard. The sound of her heels slipping from the impact had me using my one good eye to look up and see her flailing around. She stumbled back, and I rushed her again so that her head would make contact with the pedestal bathroom sink behind her.

Water was everywhere, and I used it to my advantage. She still held that pin in her hand, and once she hit the floor, I was on her. Naked and bloody, I didn't care. I snatched the pin from her and let it land into the side of her body. Over and over I slammed it, screaming for Code. Screaming for how she came at Auto, and screaming for me.

"Don't you ever touch me," I yelled out. "This is for Code!"

There was no escape for me, but there was this, murder and death. Once I stopped stabbing, I stared at the pin. Maybe it was my time to go out by my own means. For the first time in life, I seriously thought about killing myself, but the sound of feet approaching stopped me and had me realizing what my role could now be.

Turning, I stared at the face of a newcomer. I thought it was going to be Marco and I was ready for him to lay hands on me, but instead, it was a tall cat with a Cuban and American flag tatted on his neck. He walked in, glanced behind him in the room, then quickly closed the door.

"Damn, *mami*, all you had to do was wait a little bit," he said as he walked forward. "My man isn't going to be all that happy about this."

I watched the dude as best as I could in his all black move around then kneel near Santana. He checked her pulse then looked at me. "Now Lilith will be watching you because of this and, *mami,* that is going to be a hell you will need to prepare yourself for," he said.

"Back the fuck away from me," I shouted as he stared my way.

The brother with the locs on his head like a crown chuckled then held his hands up. "They call me Fuego. You can call me cousin. I won't hurt you, *mami.* Not all of us are certifiable psychopaths. I'm just crazy. It's a difference, I promise."

Confusion had me pushing backward to get to the door as I listened. "She kept attacking me. Caltrone told her not to take the pin out, but she did, and she was about to use it. I had to get her before she got me."

Fuego stood, nudged her with his black Tims again, then shrugged. "I never liked how she did things. Nor did I like how she handled Maria Rosa. But you ain't got to worry about that anymore. She's not dead, but you did fuck her up pretty righteous. You handled it like a true Orlando."

She wasn't dead? Son of a bitch! I guessed this eye really threw me off for sure. Pressing my palm against my eye, I gave a sigh as the man in the room pulled out a towel to press it against Santana's bleeding body.

Again, I stared at this enigma. Why was he being nice to me? There was no way that I could trust him.

"Every aspect of war, of battle, is based on how well one side can deceive the other. Before one can attack, one must seem unable or weak," was all he said as he moved to turn the water off then grab a towel.

Shock had me almost dropping my poker face as I watched him. This nigga just quoted the same paraphrased line from Sun Tzu. Why did he just quote something that only a few people knew? Who was this dude?

"You look cold. Take this," he said as he tossed me the towel.

Snatching it midair, I wrapped it around me and kept my back to the door. "Why did you just say that?"

Fugeo dropped down to pat Santana, then stopped. "Say what? Oh, this? Every aspect of war, of battle, is based on how well one side can deceive the other. Before one can attack, one must seem unable or weak. The homie is more keen to Machiavelli's *The Prince,* but he told me to say this instead to jar your memory."

Boots!

My mouth dropped. I quickly moved forward and almost shouted in praise, "I thought he was joking about having ways that even Auto don't know."

"Yeah, when he says things, you might want to listen," Fugeo said with a low chuckle. "He sent me as a visual beacon of hope. He's working on a way to get you out."

"But you're an Orlando?" I whispered while we kneeled over Santana's twitching dead body.

"And a cop," he coolly stated. "You're also an Orlando, *mami,* but as you see, not everything is as it seems. Papi Caltrone is the devil. I listen to his word. But I'm also my own man with my own family, and I know this life can't always be how it is."

"So you work for Boots?" I asked carefully.

A nod was all I got before he stood. "Kind of. Yeah. But more like I work for his father. Long story. He needed an inside man, and I'm that. He has a favor now."

Standing again, I followed Fugeo to the door, "From me?"

"Yup," he said, sliding his hands in his pocket.

I wasn't sure why Boots needed an inside man with Caltrone, but I didn't care. This was my way of survival, and I was going to take it by any means.

"What is it?" I asked.

"He, Boots I mean, needs you to be his in. He can't sit at the table with Papa until Papa feels he's worthy, but he's close to it. He needs us to be his ears on Papa's needs."

Shock hit me hard. Boots was playing a crazy game, and now he was asking me to be a part of it. Laugher hit me at the irony. "He told me to be aware that I was a pawn for Caltrone, and now he's making me his."

Fuego gave a shrug, then blew out a breath. "We all are pawns. It's just whose side do we want to be on? I'm trying to live. My loyalty is blood always though, so it makes it complicated. But my man has a plan outlined, one I'm now seeing unfold, where my loyalty can't be questioned."

"What does that mean?" I asked, walking with him out of the room as he helped me.

"It means that Papa can't be king forever. A new blood is rising. I met two of them, and now you came up too." Fuego laughed. "This war is about to be sick with it."

I was confused, but I was listening to everything being said. "I just want to live, and I want to save Auto and the crew."

Fuego glanced at me, then nodded. "Then be loyal to blood and pay attention to everything. You're an Orlando female. You just took out a bad bitch. Make Papa believe in your value and not just see it. Maria Rosa was special in that. She could make him believe and see her value."

"Okay, so how do I do that?" I wondered.

"First off, will you hold it down like I am?" Fuego said with the cock of his Glock. He pointed it my way, then smirked. "Because if you don't, I have every right to end you in order to protect my role in this while making it look as if this was retaliation for Santana."

Stepping back, I realized how dangerous this world was. I had to know my place. I had to know my role and make up my mind. This was never something I wanted to do, but now meeting my cousin Fuego and hearing him quickly explain to me how he was surviving as a spy for whatever plan Boots had going, I had hope that I could survive this long enough to get back to Auto and the crew. I was no damsel in distress, so I had to rely on me. Had to remember everything Code taught me, so I gave a nod and swallowed my fear.

"I'm down. Let him know that whatever he needs, I got it." I licked my lips then exhaled. "How do I show that I'm willing to be loyal to blood?"

Fuego gave me a smirk. He holstered his Glock, then began to break down what I needed to do to play the game. Fear shot through me because I wasn't sure if I'd be able to pull this off. But I was open and willing. I had survived a lot. Had managed to work though being locked up at one time and surviving this, so now I guessed I had to take all of that and apply it to living in an Orlando world.

Once Fuego finished, I stood in amazement.

My cousin dropped his voice, his movements and body language since the beginning of this all not revealing anything but his loyalty to Caltrone. "Trust in the new blood, because like you, they don't want this life, but they will do whatever they can to act like they do just to survive."

I understood that personally, because right now with everything, I was currently stuck in the same situation. "Okay, I can do that. I'm new blood, but who else?"

Fuego winked then moved to the door. "Trust in Enzo and Drew. I have a hunch that not everything is as it appears with him and his brother."

Enzo. That was my cousin, the superstar football player, the one I was meant to meet one day. I swallowed hard then stumbled back. "No way."

My cousin once again chuckled, then let out a low whistle. "You want to survive, do what I said. Marco is coming. Get to it."

Then like that, all nice warmth in Fuego's eyes disappeared as a mask of anger covered his face. "You want what?" he asked.

Fear shifted in me again. Then I swallowed it, getting with the program once the doors flew open. "I want her eye," I shouted, pointing. "You don't put your hands on me. Caltrone told her to teach me to be an Orlando, but bitch was on some next shit! So I want her eye!"

My hand covered the bleeding one. I turned my head left and right, then Marco rushed past me to go into the bathroom. The conversation with Fuego had really only lasted a few minutes, though to me it had felt like an hour. So Santana's body still lay twitching from my attack.

"*Dios!* This crazy trick killed Santana," Marco barked out.

He rushed from the bathroom, then landed a punch in my face, causing me to topple over. "Who the fuck do you think you are?"

Once again, I was being stomped. I pulled myself into a ball and then turned my head to look up at him with seriousness in my face and no fear. My old mask of subtle happiness was gone and replaced by a stone-faced stare.

My name was Smiley for a reason. I never smiled, and now she was back as I played my game and spat out in malice, "An Orlando, and I want her motherfucking eye."

Surprise had Marco pausing his stomping. He stepped back, then shook his head and smiled menacingly. "Take her to Lilith. Papa said she had to learn our ways, then it's time she learned them."

He walked past me then chuckled. "Get Santana's eye, too. See what Papi says about all of that."

"She didn't kill Santana, cousin. That crazy broad is still alive and needs to hit up our doctor," I heard Fuego say in a bored voice.

"Malta sea! Yeah? A'ight, never mind on that eye. Get her to the doctor and get our long-lost blood up outta here," Marco ordered.

Then like that, I was taken up and dragged out of the room. Fuego explained to me that in order to survive, I had to be loyal to blood. By being loyal to blood, I had to step into the role of being an Orlando princess. As fear danced in my stomach, I thought about Code. I would honor her and get my vengeance for her. Boots needed me to do this so I would do it, for my sake and for Auto.

"Oh, who is this? A new toy?" I heard spoken above me in that soft monotone voice I recalled speaking to Caltrone.

Fuego grabbed me by my hair, then tilted my face up. "Her name is Nia. Papa's granddaughter. Since she just tried to kill Santana, it's your right to take the reins."

The woman curled her face. She snatched me hard by the face, then forced my closed eye open. "He has to have her fixed. You know he only respects beauty, so look into that."

"I've already reported that to Papa," Marco explained. "She said she wanted Santana's eye, can you believe that?"

Heated laughter came from the chick who didn't seem that older than me. "I like that. Do you know who I am? Of course you don't," she said, getting nose-to-nose with me, then licking my lips with her tongue. "I am Lilith. Say my name."

Repulsion had my stomach clenching. There was something about this woman that made me want to spit in her face, but I held that back and played the game.

"Lilith," I muttered, still in pain.

Staring up into the face of a woman with dark hair and strawberry blond highlights, dressed in a suit, I allowed myself to drop into a place of mental security to get through this. Auto's face appeared in my mind, along with my mother's. My mother was my angel and would protect my mind and soul in this crazy-ass plan of mine.

Auto? Well, the time I had with him was something I found myself cherishing and needing. I needed him to fight and to stay alive because I needed him. I had promised him that I was an Erasherhead and I meant it. I would do anything to make sure he and the crew were safe, even if that meant erasing myself and becoming a demon in hell.

I never wanted this world. Never wanted to be an Orlando, but now everything had changed. There was no turning back, and if I was true to the ENGA code, that every nigga had an agenda, then my agenda was this: all warfare was based on deception, and I would be a soldier in the war against Caltrone Orlando.

Chapter 21

Boots

Shango was at my side, and Shredder waited in our ride, shining the high beams on.

Auto stood in front of me with his crew. His face was battered from his failed attempt to rescue Smiley. Which was a shame. In his eyes were the occasional flickers of defeat mixed with anger as he held his Glock at his side.

My crew and I had hit up all of Auto's spots, waiting him out. Caltrone wanted me to show my loyalty, and it resulted in me hunting this little nigga down. It really wasn't that hard to do. After catching a glimpse of their ride at their old warehouse, I trailed them until we ended at a huge abandoned warehouse near the airport. Now here we were facing off, and all I could do was think about how fucked up it was to end a life so promising.

I watched Auto drop his weapon on the floor at his feet. In front of him were my bullets and Caltrone's gold.

"Had to get your property as agreed upon. Was just waiting on you," he calmly said as he stared me in the eyes, chin up, and standing in a wide-legged stance.

"Sometimes you can't save everyone, my friend. Sometimes you have to let things fall as they might." I raised my gun and rolled my shoulders.

"True, but sometimes you can change the outcome if you just think ahead. Ain't that what you told me when we came to our agreement?" Auto thumbed his nose, then snarled in wait.

"No doubt. All you had to do was give me my shit, yet you didn't, and now Caltrone has us in a difficult place of business," I explained.

Auto gave a sour laugh then stepped forward. "Then handle it. There's not shit you can do about it."

I laughed and shrugged. "True on that shit, blood. But all you gotta do is be ready. Then the rest is on you. You should have played the game better."

"Fuck you, dude," was all Auto said. "Do you believe that this is going to continue to work?"

I put my gun away, walked up to Auto, then held my hand out, which he took. "All I can do is hope. Caltrone wants me to kill you, but my thing is this: he told you to bring him back his stuff, and he'll hand you Smiley over. Now think about this. Is he lying? Or is he playing another game?"

Auto took my hand, shook it, and we gave each other dap. "Damn. You called it when you came to me for your bullets. You said that no matter what we do, he'll twist it all to his favor. He thrives on being a step ahead on everyone."

A slick grin spread across my face, and I nodded. "And that's his weakness. Now we play this how he has it."

"A'ight, but wait. I see it like this: he can't touch me if I work for you," Auto said as he moved around the crates on the floor that our teams were moving to a large van. "If your company hires me, then he can't touch me due to his word of bringing you in and protecting your people."

"That might be true, but I don't want to test that off the bat, which is why we stick to our plan," I said.

"What about Smiley?"

"Don't worry about that. Trust me on this. I have two people on the inside who will hip her to what I have planned."

"I don't want her staying in there with him too long. As soon as some shit kicks off, I want her out of there and with me. I tried it, and it didn't work, so now I'm trusting you," he said with a level of deadly seriousness in his voice.

My head nodded in understanding. I didn't want her there either, but until we got her out safely, then we'd use the moment to our advantage. "Don't even worry about it, my man. We'll have our window to get her out. As we speak, Caltrone will be dealing with a shitload of new bull that has been gunning for his prize, Enzo. All we gotta do is sit back and watch it all unfold. From there, I guarantee a window will open where she can slip out without issue."

"I'm trusting you in this," Auto said while watching me.

"If that doesn't happen, there's always a plan B. I don't intend to have her die. I'm extending my loyalty with you on this. We both lost a lot on both sides of this." I moved around the big area to stand face-to-face with Auto. "When we both offed Mouse, we decided that this battle was bigger than the both of us. That Caltrone was using us because he was bored. After that, I chose to trust you with my utmost secret. You protect my nephew. I need you all around to continue that, so me fucking with Caltrone. Sheeeittt. This ain't nothing but a cakewalk. I'll protect Smiley in a way you can't. I got you."

Auto watched me without saying a word, probably thinking about the plan I had laid at his feet. Two days after the attack on Auto shop, both of us sat down for our conversation I had insisted we have. See, I was adamant about getting my bullets back. All the homework I did on Auto and his crew gave me the basics about them, but it was only after we worked together against Mouse that I decided that it was time to fill him in on who I really was.

We sat in privacy in his office, and I broke it down and informed him that Code had come to me asking for help.

I let him know that baby girl wanted me to protect them. Which Auto thought was funny at the time as he had asked me to protect her too. He didn't believe that she would come to me or be so desperate to seek out my help. But he agreed that her coming to me was the best plan, because no matter what Code did, Caltrone would always come after her and try to end her life. A full erasure would only come with her death.

But if she tried to run, then I'd have to wipe my hands of her because there would not be anything I could do about it, and we needed her to "die" in order to erase her. It was a fifty-fifty situation, a catch-22 situation. If Caltrone got to her, we hoped whatever he'd do to her she'd be able to survive. My time with her gave me that faith in her. Auto suggested that if we'd gamble and come out on the wrong end, then she was dead.

From there, Auto let me know that in return for my services, once he robbed Caltrone, he was to give me my share of the profits. It would make up the loss for the bullets I would never get back. The ones used in battle. But of course, I let him know that I didn't want money or drugs because I wasn't into that side of the game. That wasn't my place in this world, though I could gain money that way if I so wanted to. Nah, armory was my thing. I only wanted my bullets back.

So fair exchange was no robbery, feel me? How did one think that Auto was able to pull off a robbery of one of the biggest criminal masterminds in the game without having some kind of backup? It was all me. Auto was honest in his knowledge that there would be no way that he could pull off that heist and make it out of Atlanta alive without some kind of ace in the hole because the plan was so choppy.

I helped him best I could by supplying him with additional backup with my team. The Eraserheads got the gold. He and his crew fucked some shit up, and the rest was history.

Now that we were on our next game, I had to kill Auto.

The homie reached up and ran a hand down his face, then sighed. "I'd hoped that Caltrone wouldn't snatch her like we guessed. But damn, now she's in hell, man."

"I know, but we'll get her out, I promise you that," I said in reassurance.

Auto gave me a slight nod, his emotions in check as he looked away to glance at the time. "A'ight. Time is ticking by, man. We got to make moves, and we got to draw his attention."

I got ready to head to my ride. Oya had been on my hip calling me from Cuba where she was with Freddy, updating me on our plane itinerary, and Shredder was now signaling me to get going.

"What about Code's body?" Reagan stepped up, asking in concern.

Stopping in my tracks, I turned her way. "She'll go with me. I promise that she'll be treated with the utmost respect, and if all goes well, you'll see her soon."

Reagan's eyes widened, then she dropped her head, resting a hand on her belly. "Okay, thank you, Boots."

I watched her for a long time without saying a word. I could tell from the side of my eye that Shango was watching Reagan too. Reagan was hurt. In the fleeting second, on some real shit, we thought we were looking at Alize. The pain of it had me checking myself before signaling that we had to go.

Parting ways, we all ended up at a secure meeting spot where I had asked Caltrone to meet me.

Caltrone stood surrounded by his people with a look of satisfaction on his face. Auto in my ride, we both got out, and Shango walked him forward.

"I was getting your shit, man, when this nigga came and grabbed me. I still held up on my promise. Where's Smiley?" Auto shouted out.

"Mr. Sunjeta, you amuse me with your effectiveness," Caltrone shouted out.

I gave a nod and pressed my Glock to the back of Auto's head. "Hey, it's just business, right?"

"Sí, this is true," I listened to Caltrone say. Brotha leaned calmly against his door as if he had nothing to stress about. "Auto, you are correct. We had a bargain, but Nia found herself too hurt to make the travel to see you, so I will be keeping her with me."

My jaw ticked at his words. I knew that nigga was going to play us. It was written in the damn stars.

"You lying motherfucker," Auto shouted.

It was then that we went into action. My finger began to itch, and I let it handle its business. Drawing out the kill wasn't necessary. This had to be acted quickly and on point without suspicion. I acted cold and callous. Several rounds went into Auto. His body jerked with the impact of each one. Shouts behind me had me turning to allow the rest of the bullets from my gun to land into the rest of the Eraserheads. Blood covered the dirt under them and their shouts silenced.

Tension had my shoulders rolling, and I put my Glock away. I backed up and turned back to my car.

"Mr. Sunjeta. It's different watching you kill in person. You have a coldness to how you handle the gun. Interesting," I heard Caltrone say behind me. "You held up to your end of this. I give you thanks. We will be in touch then."

I turned to see his men inspecting each body before going back to their cars, leaving the Eraserheads where they were. All around us was nothing but forest. I figured the animals would have a good day feeding on their bodies without drawing attention to anyone due to how deep we were in the woods.

Tilting my hat, I brushed off my jacket and stood near the door of my ride. "There was no point in playing with them, Senor Orlando. We're now linked as businessmen, amigo, and the company will be eager to work with you. I will be calling soon to secure the future of our contract."

Caltrone gave a nod then slid in his ride, and that was the last I saw of him in person. As for the bodies of the Eraserheads, I left them where they were. Besides, Caltrone asked me to kill Auto, but he didn't tell me to handle the bodies. I left, and that was that. Everything in order with blood on my hands, or was it?

Epilogue

Boots

Many Months Later

The Ashanti say, "Do not let what you cannot do tear from your hands what you can."

Being the man behind the scenes hadn't been easy, but everything shown had started to kick off as planned. I turned to lean back against the railing of my boat.

As I said, you can kill someone all day, but what counts is what happens to the body after that death. When I picked up Code, I had wrongly assumed that she was dead, but she wasn't. Through the fucked-up torture and pain she went through, baby girl held on to life like a fighter. As we left Smiley's community, we were on the highway when I heard her faint coughs and gasps.

I didn't believe what I was hearing when I pulled the cover back from her body. I pressed a finger to her neck and felt the slight faint of her pulse. That's when the game changed even further. "You're alive," I said to her.

She was, but barely. I could tell mama was hanging on to her last breath. I could tell she was in pain, and it sickened me that Caltrone would do this to his own flesh and blood.

She spoke, barely above a whisper, "Tell Smiley and Auto to never give in."

The gasp she took pained me as she started to choke on her own blood. I watched in silence as her grip on my hand tightened for a brief moment then lessened. Mama was still so very beautiful, even with the scars and shadow of death looming over her.

Code had erased herself by using Caltrone.

Watching her fade, I promised that I would honor her last words. Her death was smooth at that moment and calm with the reassurance that I'd carry on her wishes. Once she died, I realized that she was free and had nothing to worry about in this war. It hurt holding her like that and being witness to a warrior like her dying by a man who supposedly loved her.

Baby girl and I hadn't been an item long, but she had left an impression on me that made me angry at how she had left this place. I wished that I had made it in time to her. Kissing her lips one last time, I wished for a lot of things to happen that didn't result in this death, but we don't always win them all. All I could do was honor what she was fighting in her last breath to do: protect the ones she had cared for and loved.

After carefully wrapping her back up and leaving Atlanta, we all moved as if we were operating on a burn notice. I hopped continents from Jamaica to Spain, and then I took her with me to Nigeria where we anointed her and Alize's bodies with oils and wrapped them like the queens they were. We then proceeded to light their bodies in flames and watch as their ashes flowed over the motherland as a way to honor them both.

My crew and I all grieved at the loss. We then took two weeks of silence, then flew on to the French Rivera at our large beachfront chateau as a means to regroup and plan.

It's all in the foundation and formation of a plan, they say, in winning a war. On some real shit, I had to agree that's what it is, but this war was just starting. I came in as a force, starting out as the man behind the curtain in being a hand of help to my long-lost nephew and my brother's best friend. So far, that was still working as it was supposed to. In that goal, I also had used that medium as my guidance with the next plan, and that was getting close to Caltrone.

That part of the plan was so easy. Not that I thought it would be, but I was young and impatient. I needed things to happen quickly yet effectively. I never showed it though. I kept my cool, as my father taught me, and used his teachings and method to keep things steady. If I didn't, I'd probably be dead by now due to my impatience in the matter. I wanted my in, and I wanted it as efficiently as possible because Caltrone needed to know the truth about some things, but he also needed to know that his current actions weren't going to work anymore.

But, again, not everything went as it was supposed to, and my method had slowed down to the point of marinating. All my well-laid plans were working out as I needed. The foundation was cracking. Caltrone was going after his enemy with a menacing calculation that had me watching from afar in awareness and respect. The man was a beast in the streets and in how he handled business. However, there was this quiet satisfaction in me that my pop's plan with my own added to it was able to slide in on a man who made it his all to know everything about everything.

See, the weakness in knowing all is that you become arrogant, and arrogance is a weakness that has taken down many dictators and soldiers in war. Caltrone's arrogance was what I always was counting on, and he never disappointed me in it. I lost a lot to his arrogance. It bothered me to think about it, and it was something that I'd never brush off, but I was a businessman. When working with criminals, you have to calculate that not everything is going to go your way, and you lose out on your stock investment in others.

I had that happen with the loss of Alize, but I tried to partially make up for it by creating new investments in having my own set of eyes and ears in his world now. No one could replace her, but I would honor her memory. I glanced down at the invitation that was in my hand. The Nightwings famed baller Shawn "Enzo" Banks was holding an introductory party for all of Atlanta to celebrate his moves on the field. But from my eyes and ears really it was a more of a takeover party, celebrating him stepping into the world as an official heir to Caltrone.

Tapping the invite on my hand, I chuckled to myself. When you have difficulty gaining an in with one boss, you step back and make moves with another boss. Enzo was that. To Caltrone it would be said that my company contacted the young player to improve his security with the necessary arms needed for protection. He contacted me from hearing about my bullets in the street. Of course, this was all a facade, and of course, I planned to be right there at Enzo's big party.

Me being the man in the shadows, the guardian angel of sorts, had me chuckling at the businessman I was. This whole thing would not have possibly been laid out as smoothly as it was had it not been for Auto. Glancing at the waves that sparkled like emerald jewels, slender arms wrapped around me from behind as I fell into my memories.

"What you thinking about? Jefe?" Shango asked by my side.

"Code, the Eraserheads, Smiley, and this," I told him, holding out an invitation.

Shango and I sat in my blacked-out white Bugatti, waiting to head to Dubai where a new set of customers awaited in the overall game of things. I was still about my weapons, dangerous as it was, but working in Dubai was now adding to the identity I had created. Real estate, and in memory of the crew that fell by Caltrone's hands, erasing identities was now on my rooster.

"Auto and Jack just made it to Taiwan. Then from there, they're going to Japan. Reagan is asleep in the house, and Stitch and his family sent thanks for their home in Sweden," he let me know. "Did you hear anything from Nia? Is that why you're thinking?"

See, I couldn't be held accountable with what happened to the bodies that fell in the woods the day I killed the Erasherheads. All I knew was that I left there with my own agenda on my mind. I mean, yeah, sometimes people found their way in the woods. What if those people happened to be a part of the elusive group called the Misfits who sat back watching in military fatigues? So what that I actually shot every last one of the Erasherheads, but I did it in a way that left clean exit wounds that could be medically taken care of?

All I had to think about was I held up my end of the bargain. I couldn't control what happened after.

Thoughtfully rubbing my jaw, I gave a nod, seeing Oya with Freddie sitting on the shoreline with his family. With Shango and me leaving, it was up to her to hold down the fort like I knew she could.

"Yes, my friend. She came out of her eye reconstruction surgery, and I'm going back to Atlanta to get her. You game for a little more gunplay and chess, man?" I asked.

Not for a real answer, but to lay out the blueprint of our bigger plan.

Always my loyal shadow and best friend, Shango gave me a slick smile while dropping his shades and leaning in the driver's seat. "Like you said when we first met, the war is only beginning, and the chips got to fall. I'm down until I'm no longer here on this earth, man. We have family to protect, so that's all I'll focus on."

He was right, and my boy knew the deal. There was no stopping everything that had been put in motion. From the very beginning, I'd been nothing but a soldier in a war that started long before any of the Misfits, and Eraserheads, or I had been born. My part of it had been to stay on an intellectual base, work as smartly as possible, and even in some cases, act purposely foolish.

It was now time for the next level. All that I needed to do was sit back, help from my place in the background, and enjoy the show because it was all going as planned. This was no fairy-tale happy ending. People died in this battle, and many of them were my soldiers. Blood was on my hands, and much more was coming, but for now, this was our calm before the storm.

Driving off, I nodded at Oya, who stood with her hands on her ample curves with her large afro flowing in the sunlight. She gave me a salute, then waved. Time to fly to Dubai.

I fucking enjoyed being the one behind the scenes. Businessman always, but a protector of family first. Which was why I proudly said, "*Ana sabr heliko ask sabr abieni.*"

"I'm still patient until patience gets tired of me."